MICHELLE ADAMS grew up in the ▨ where she works as a part-time scier ▨ King novel at the tender age of nine, and has been addicted to suspense fiction ever since. *Between the Lies* is her second novel.

To find out more follow Michelle on Twitter @MAdamswriter or visit her website www.michelleadams.co.uk.

Praise for Michelle Adams's debut novel, *My Sister*:

'A magnificent exploration of the toxic relationship between two sisters and the hold they exert on each other . . . chilling and tragic in equal measure'
Nuala Ellwood, author of *My Sister's Bones*

'Fantastic; twisty and exciting yet original and beautifully written'
Gillian McAllister, author of *Everything but the Truth*

'A ▨ ously chilling tale of two twisted sisters . . . grabs you by the ▨ it from first page to last'
Camilla Way, author of *Watching Edie*

'I love this dark and disturbing thriller. Tense and twisted, it glued ▨ to the sofa' C. J. Tudor, author of *The Chalk Man*

'In ▨ Michelle Adams has created a truly terrifying character who ▨ rts her power from the first page, drawing you in to the last ▨ cately plotted' Amanda Reynolds, author of *Close to Me*

'A first-rate schocker of a psychological thriller' *Irish Independent*

'An intimate tale of family secrets with a twisty plot and a unique voice. Suspenseful and shocking . . . guaranteed to chill you to the bone'
Dead Good Books

'A psychological thriller with a whole heap of heart . . . I was agog at every ▨ *Books*

By Michelle Adams

My Sister
Between the Lies

BETWEEN
THE
LIES

MICHELLE ADAMS

HEADLINE

First published as an Ebook in Great Britain in 2018 by
HEADLINE PUBLISHING GROUP

First published in paperback in Great Britain in 2019 by
HEADLINE PUBLISHING GROUP

1

Cataloguing in Publication Data is available from the British Library

ISBN 978 1 4722 3661 6

Typeset in Sabon by Palimpsest Book Production Limited,
Falkirk, Stirlingshire

Printed and bound in Great Britain by CPI Group (UK) Ltd,
Croydon CR0 4YY

Headline's policy is to use papers that are natural, renewable and recyclable
products and made from wood grown in sustainable forests. The logging and
manufacturing processes are expected to conform to the environmental
regulations of the country of origin.

HEADLINE PUBLISHING GROUP
An Hachette UK Company
Carmelite House
50 Victoria Embankment
London EC4Y 0DZ

www.headline.co.uk
www.hachette.co.uk

For you, Lelia, a dream that came true.
You are my miracle.

Drowning. That's what you said it felt like. Slipping beneath the surface, descending deeper until you started to choke. Your fingers trailed across my chest as we lay in that hot little room, lost somewhere unreachable together. 'It's like I'm being swallowed up,' you told me. 'Like I can't catch my breath when I'm with you.' You propped yourself up, your fingers sliding into your hair, and winked. I saw that little smile and I realised, at least on some level, that you knew you could do nothing to stop it.

But Chloe, I never thought of it as drowning. It was nothing like that for me. Because when we drown, we fight, we panic and kick out. We gasp for every desperate breath as we try to escape. Because when we drown, we die.

Maybe you don't remember, but you didn't fight. You allowed yourself to sink. You don't want a way out. You don't want to forget about me. You tell me you have changed, but to me you are still everything I ever wanted.

This isn't drowning, Chloe, I promise you that.

I don't want to die. I don't want you to die either.

That's not what love is about.

1

In those first few moments there is nothing. No pain, no fear. My eyes flicker open and in the grey light of a distant moon I see my surroundings, dark leather and the curved edge of a steering wheel. I see a shiny splatter of something oily, the deep burgundy of blood slick on my skin. What happened? How did I get here? Where am I?

I raise my head and look around. Is that rain falling, splashing cold against my face? I listen as my breath drifts in and out, glance towards the empty passenger seat just a few inches away. I try to look up, my neck agony, see the shattered remains of the windscreen. The edges of the broken glass are red as if punctured with fire. I fumble a shaky hand down towards my seat belt, fiddle at the button. I don't have the strength to press it. My eyes are glazing over and I can't see clearly. I slip forward against the strap, my weight dead, but I think, just probably, I'm still alive.

How much time passes, slumped like that on my own, fading in, fading out, travelling in some strange and lonely place? The cool chill of the rain wakes me, lashing against the window, driven by the power of the wind. A night of violence is descending here. An ice-blue light flashes in the distance, reflecting in the cracked glass. It winks at me through swaying trees. Eyes open, eyes closed, tossed between life and death like a piece of ratty seaweed caught in the swell of the waves.

A voice calls out as rain drums the rooftop. 'Can you hear me, love?' A hand slaps against the wet glass. I feel the pull of fingers as they grapple against my skin, my bare arms slippery, my hair stuck to my face in matted red clumps. I turn my head towards the figure at my side. A yellow jacket, and a black hat hiding the man's face. He shouts something into the night. Are there more people here? Water runs from his shoulders, the spray cold, sharp as it hits me. I hear the crunch of broken glass beneath me as I move.

'Just hang in there. Try not to move too much.' I think he opens the door. I can feel the heat of his body close to mine. 'Can you tell me your name?'

Can I?

Somebody slips a collar around my neck. It's colder now, quieter. I can't feel my hands. My eyes are getting tired. Then I hear somebody yell, and they drag me from the car, their movements desperate and rushed. Their voices carry on the wind. 'We're losing her!' they shout.

Eyes open, wide. It is not a subtle waking, no gentle lull between dream and reality. It's quick, the pull of a plaster, the sharp slice of a knife. I am out of breath and sweaty. Memories of the dream recede as I glance around the room, a conscious effort to remind myself of where I am. That I am safe. That I am alive.

I turn over, pulling my face from the pillow, and sit up in

bed, the only sound a gentle rain pattering against the window. I rub my eyes, listen as a door opens then closes. Footsteps on the stairs, the hush of voices as they chatter in the kitchen.

A family.

They tell me my name is Chloe. When I woke in the hospital, my voice scratchy and coarse, my throat almost too sore to speak, I didn't know who I was. I couldn't remember anything about my life. Who I was, what I did. How I lived. I asked one of the nurses, a plump woman called Helen, whose small-framed glasses balanced on the tip of her nose. She placed a chubby hand on her hip. 'Don't you remember?' she asked me.

I shook my head. It throbbed, felt swollen. I tried to think back, and I thought that maybe I had a vague memory of an accident, the same memory that I now dream of each night. But I wasn't certain. I looked out of the window, knew there was something familiar about the rain, the distant sound of waves crashing against the shore. But what?

'Your name is Chloe. You had an accident. You were in a coma for over a month,' she said. 'But you're doing well, so try not to worry.'

Helen went back to the business of making notes, recording various measurements: pulse rate, blood pressure, my temperature from the inside of my ear. I looked at the card balanced on the bedside table: *Get well soon, Chloe*, it read. *All our love, Mum, Dad, and Jess*. My family, apparently.

I couldn't remember them either.

Now I push the heavy embroidered blankets away and pick up a glass of water from the bedside table. My mouth is so dry and has been ever since I arrived here. It's the dust, the whole place full of it. My family's home is old and vast, some parts of it untouched for decades. I reach for the lamp, little dangly tassels hanging from the shade. I turn it on but it does little to brighten the room, the corners remaining dark, cast in permanent shadow.

I gaze about to remind myself of where I am. This place is home now, yet even after several weeks it feels unfamiliar. The walls are lined with a textured wallpaper, a heavy rose-print pattern in a sickly salmon-pink. The corners are peeling away in two separate places. The ceiling is white, but appears grey and dirty on account of the heavy fog outside. It hasn't lifted in days. The surround of the ceiling light is flaking too, everything falling apart. I take in the details each morning in the hope that it will help me to feel like I know this place. But nothing in this house is mine. I belong somewhere else. I belong to another life that I can't remember. A life that doesn't exist any more.

I stand up and move to the window, push aside the threadbare curtain. It is impossible to appreciate the vastness of my family's estate from the first-floor window of the old rectory where they tell me I grew up. Acres of wet farmland surround the house, the grounds stretching all the way to a rolling perimeter of forest. Somewhere in the distance there's a village. I would like to walk there, get out of this house, but my father says it's too soon. I am a grown woman, yet I'm kept inside like a small child who needs protection. They tell me they want the best for me. So I stay here as they ask. But it's hard to trust people when you're not even sure you know them.

The muted colours of the hallway press in on me as I

walk downstairs. The light outside is low, a winter's light, silvery and soft. It's a reminder of just how much time I've lost, the passing of a season I didn't witness. What is the last thing I remember? I'm not sure. I can't recall the life I had in the summer before the accident. So for now I have to make do with this place, these people. This version of myself.

Chloe. Whoever that is.

My father is already sitting at the table as I arrive in the kitchen, my mother busy at the worktop. Jess, my sister, pulls out a chair for me to sit. I watch as my mother takes anxious steps in my direction, a pot of tea in one hand, a plate of muffins in the other. She fusses about me as if it's still my first day here. She prompts me to take a chocolate one, then I watch as she sets the plate down on the long kitchen table.

'Would you like some toast?' she asks. 'We got some nice jam in.' I smile and nod. She looks to my father, who signals his approval. An atmosphere of expectation hangs in the air, has done ever since the day I arrived. It's desperation, I think, a need for me to feel at home. They want me to be comfortable, relaxed, for this situation to work.

'Chloe, I'm afraid I have to go into the hospital this morning,' my father says as I nibble the muffin, the edges dry and stale. 'I have a number of commitments that I'm afraid I simply can't put off. Your mother and sister are going out too.'

'OK,' I tell him. 'I'll be all right here on my own.'

He stands up and drains his coffee cup before kissing my mother's soft cheek. He moves towards Jess, attempts to ruffle her hair. She tuts, moves to avoid it just in time. Then he leans over and places a cold, dry kiss on my cheek. A shiver runs down my spine. 'I don't want you to worry about anything,' he says. 'Everything is going well. But I think it would be a good idea if we sat down together a little later on, eh? It's been a couple of days since we last had a session.'

A session. His part in helping me rebuild my life. These began when I first returned to this house. As a psychiatrist, my father appears to have taken on the responsibility of accelerating my recovery, determined to help me remember the past I have forgotten. But after several weeks, that past still eludes me. I would have expected my family to have told me more about my life by now. Where I used to live. Who my friends were. How I spent my time. But nobody seems to want to tell me anything, and I'm unable to remember for myself. All in good time, they say. I will help you, my father tells me. He wants me to remember. But it's only ever on his terms.

He picks up a copy of *The Times* and folds it under his arm. 'We will have you feeling back to normal soon, Chloe. We're making excellent progress. But please, while you're here on your own today, make sure you don't go outside. You're not quite ready for that. Oh, and I almost forgot.' He produces a small ceramic dish with three tablets inside. 'Make sure you take these.'

I place the tablets on my tongue, a concoction of analgesics and anti-seizure medication, washing them down with a sip of water. From the frosty window in my father's study I watch as he gets into his car; Jess climbs into my mother's, and they both, one after the other, drive away. To lives I know nothing about. My gaze follows the cars until their lights are swallowed up in the thick wall of fog. And as I stand there in clothes that are not really mine, in a household to which I don't belong, I think about his instruction not to go out. I have the same thought I have every day: if I did go out, somewhere other than here, where would I go? But I can't answer that question. Because beyond this house, and these three virtual strangers, I know nothing else about my life.

My father tells me that once we have finished the therapy sessions everything will be as it once was, nothing more than a faint, well-healed scar left behind to connect my past to my present. But no matter what he does, no matter how hard he tries, I'm not going to be able to slip back into my old life. The person I used to be is dead, taken away from us in the crash. And even though I'm confused about most things, there is one thing I do know: you can't bring the dead back to life. The old Chloe is gone, and I'm afraid I might never get her back.

But what scares me even more is that I think my family don't want me to.

2

In the moments after they leave, the silence is suffocating. Every day is the same: the quietness of a strange house, the emptiness I feel inside. In those first few moments alone I feel a deep-rooted sensation of panic, worrying about what I am going to do until they come back and provide me with a purpose, a place in the world. Because despite my fears, they're all I have. Until they come back it's just me, and I have no idea who that is.

They have told me a few things about my life, but it's like having a jigsaw with most of the pieces missing. The knowledge I have about myself is so limited and vague. I know that my name is Chloe and that I'm thirty-two years old. That before the accident I worked as a lawyer. I had a house of my own, not too far away from here. But I don't have any details that would give life and colour to these facts. I was happy, they tell me. My life was good. But it all feels flat and fake, like a sticking plaster over wounded skin. I need to pull it off, see what's beneath.

I sleep a lot, off and on, like a newborn baby. I can't manage for long without needing a rest. Watching television is a waste of time. I can't focus enough to follow the plotlines, and even things my sister tells me I've already seen hundreds of times seem complicated and obscure. Still, I try to watch the news each night after dinner, reminding myself of a life outside these walls, the idea of time passing by. I spend hours poring over old paperwork my father has produced: my birth certificate, school reports, and albums of photographs my mother put together. All these things that show I once had a life. That Chloe Daniels existed. Now in place of that life I have a scar across the left side of my scalp where Dr Gleeson excavated an epidural haematoma. It's sensitive to the slightest thing. I've taken to wearing a woolly hat at all times, but I'm not so detached from reality that I can't appreciate how ridiculous I must look to the people with whom I share this house.

At first I refused to come home with them. My parents. My family. It seemed odd, I thought, to go to a house with people I didn't know. When we were alone, I confessed to Dr Gleeson, the neurosurgeon who stopped the bleed in my brain, that I thought they might be imposters, that perhaps they were there to take advantage of my amnesia. They smelt funny to me, and still do; apparently a heightened sense of smell is a side effect of the surgery. A scalpel in the brain can really affect the senses. He just laughed, rested a slender hand on mine and told me not to worry. He said they were good people, that there were things we could do to help me remember. Like the photo albums my mother created as a gateway to my past.

Each morning, sitting at the kitchen table, I leaf through to see if anything comes back. Me feeding a goat when I was a child; riding in a shire-horse carriage on a day trip to Weymouth. Sometimes I recall a sensation rather than people or places: the smell of the sea, or the rush of saliva when my father talks of vinegary chips. It's as if my body seems to know things even if my mind does not.

I move to the fridge and glance at the list that my father made for me in the earliest days after leaving hospital. I was like a zombie then, narcotised and unused to the medication. I am still taking corticosteroids, antibiotics and antiepileptics: reduce the swelling, prevent infection, minimise the risk of seizures. But I can't concentrate long enough to work out my new regimen, so the list tells me the tasks I have to do daily.

Number one is a reminder to perform my exercises. They are simple enough: arm raises and leg movements designed to restore my muscles and strength. We also have a huge inflatable ball that I sit on and rock about. Apparently it's good for core strength. Next on the list is medication. Just like in the hospital, my tablets are laid out for me in a small pot on the side, but I know I'm not supposed to take the next set until my mother gets home. They like to make sure I'm getting it right. The third item is food. I open the fridge door, and find a plate of sandwiches wrapped tight under cling film.

I pull one out and take a bite, but despite my steroid medication, which is supposed to increase my appetite, I never really feel hungry. The only craving I have is to get out of the house, rediscover my own life. Stuck inside this place, with its high ceilings and draughty doorways, makes me feel like I am still in a coma. So after I finish my sandwich, I do what I do every day that I am alone: I slip my arms into the sleeves of one of my mother's overcoats, and slide my feet into her shoes. I take the keys and open the front door, and with the aid of the walking stick that the physiotherapist made me bring home I walk to the end of the driveway. It's tiring and difficult, and each time I do it I have to return to bed afterwards, to sleep for an hour. But I make myself do it, to feel the damp air cold against my skin, the wet atmosphere as it wraps around my body. I do it because it's all I have.

I've been walking up to the gate every day for a week now, ever since the day my father first refused to take me back to my own home. The one I used to live in in my previous life. I don't know where it is yet, or what it's like, but I'm sure just seeing it would help other details return to me. He told me I wasn't ready. He told me I was too ill. I asked him to show me a picture of it, to tell me something about it, but still he wouldn't talk. I looked at my mother, begged for her to relent. She stared down at the floor, quiet under his watchful eye.

'You're not ready yet, Chloe. I will let you know when you are. This is what I do for a living. I know best when it comes to these things.' That was all he said.

So I decided to leave, my mind made up. That was when I found the gate locked. That was when I realised I couldn't leave even if I wanted to. So here I am again at the edge of my parents' land, my hands gripping the damp wood of the gate. This is as far as I can go thanks to an unbroken perimeter fence. I glance up the road into the thick white air. I can't see anything, but I know there is a village out there; a hairdresser's, a garage, houses full of people and lives.

Surely there has to be. I rattle the gate, test it as I do each day. But it is locked with a code. Something else I don't know. Something else they won't tell me.

Standing here unable to leave, I feel as if they are trying to keep me prisoner.

3

My mother returns home just before lunch, sits with me at the table while I eat. She watches as I take my tablets, then makes me a cup of tea before helping me into bed. I notice her gaze passing over my body, mentally listing my injuries as she pulls the covers up to my chin.

'Once you've had a rest, how would you feel about getting dressed for dinner today?'

'I'm not sure,' I tell her. She often suggests this, as if the act alone has the power to make everything all right.

'Well you can't stay in your pyjamas for ever. And remember what your father said earlier. He wants us to sit down together tonight. I'm sure he'd appreciate the effort.'

I look to the cupboards. 'But they're not my clothes,' I tell her. 'All my clothes are still at my house. The house that none of you will tell me about.'

'Not all of them,' she says, indignant, ignoring my plea. 'We brought a few things with us, remember?' She reaches down, holds up a small bag. 'This is your home now, Chloe.'

* * *

My father is back early from the hospital: Mum's car has had to go to the garage and Jess needed collecting from some study seminar. Something about forensic toxicology at the local university so that she keeps busy during the Christmas break. But his work is far from finished and he summons one of the doctors from the hospital to discuss some cases that can't wait. I hear the other doctor arrive, his car cutting tracks through the gravel driveway. Dusk is already settling when I move to the window, see him approaching the house through the mist.

The strangest thing is that I recognise him. I'm not sure, but I would guess I must have seen him at the hospital. I listen at the edge of the door, watch him come inside, loop his jacket over the banister in a way I'm sure my father must hate. Still, he doesn't say anything.

It's another hour before I go downstairs. I can hear their voices from behind the half-open study door, a mumble at first, then much clearer. It sounds as if they are still discussing work.

'The thing is, Guy, what we have to accept is that her condition is much worse than we originally thought. We must ensure that our approach is tough, that it leaves no room for confusion.'

There is a heavy sigh as I approach the bottom of the stairs. 'I appreciate that, Dr Daniels, but I'm concerned.'

'About our chosen way forward?'

'About what will happen if it takes us too long to re-introduce her to the . . .'

He stops. I am just passing the half-open door.

'Chloe, is that you?' my father calls. I take a few steps

towards the study, push a hand against the rough wood. 'I thought you were sleeping.'

'I was, but I woke up a while ago.'

The man I vaguely recognise is sitting in a chair opposite my father. His fingers are pressed together, forming a steeple. Reminds me of school, when we used to play cat's cradle. He smiles at me and raises his hand to wave, which seems to merge into the offer of a handshake.

'Hello,' I say.

'Hi. I'm Guy. We've met before, at—'

'The hospital.' He seems surprised. 'I remember your face.'

'Dr Thurwell is one of my colleagues, Chloe. He saw you just after you came out of the coma.'

'It's great to see you doing so well.'

'Thanks,' I say, and after that there is a moment of silence, nobody sure of what to say next. 'I'll leave you to finish your work.'

My father gives me a nod. 'Thank you, Chloe. I'll see you at dinner.'

At seven p.m., we sit down for dinner. The sky is dark outside, the wind strong. We eat in silence, waiting on my father's command, as we do each evening. My father serves us as my mother pours him a glass of red wine. They talk as they normally do, without my input. Instead, I listen. I watch Jess, my younger sister, back from university, hanging on my father's every word. I wonder if I was ever like that, if I was a daddy's girl. Then as we finish eating and my mother and sister begin to clear up, he turns his attention to me. I feel my heartbeat quicken, as if from the detritus of my life I need to find an answer to whatever it is he asks.

'What did you do this morning? Did you spend time looking at the album?'

'Yes, but not much else. I felt pretty tired most of the day.'

He nods his head agreeably. 'It's to be expected. Slowly does it, Chloe.' And then he reaches across the table, touches my hand. For a second I can't breathe, and my whole body freezes. 'Together we'll get there. Now don't forget your tablets.' I pick up the little pot from the table, swallow my evening dose. 'I think it's about time we made a start.'

I swing my feet up onto the couch and he helps adjust the cushions so that I'm comfortable. He pulls a chair alongside me and wedges himself into it, his body too big, the chair too small. He's careful about how he sits, the open posture, the relaxed shoulders. He doesn't want to *force* me to open up. He said that not long after I arrived here. He leant down to my level, all smiles and gentle hands as I sat there wide-eyed and scared. 'You know I'm not forcing you to talk to me, right, Chloe? I don't want you to feel cornered. But if we work together, I know I can help you remember the things you've lost.'

But three weeks down the line I still haven't remembered anything concrete, and our sessions only seem to leave me feeling more confused and unsure. There are awards for his work on the desk in his study, so I know he's an accomplished doctor. I suppose it is possible that I am just too far lost, but there is also a part of me that wonders if this isn't doomed to failure.

'Don't you think this is a little bit weird?' I suggest as I settle into position. 'You're my father. I don't think people are meant to undergo therapy with their relatives.'

He shifts in his seat and smoothes out the paper on his little notepad. 'But Chloe, this is what I do. How can I stand by and not help you get through this?' He draws in a long breath, lets it filter silently through his nostrils.

'Perhaps I could see one of the other doctors I met at the hospital. Guy, maybe, the one who was here with you earlier.' I remember a bit more about when he saw me at the hospital, the idea of him sitting on the edge of the bed, smiling at me. 'Maybe he could help me instead.'

He narrows his eyes as if he is giving the notion some thought. 'Dr Thurwell? Well, I must admit he is a very good doctor, but I don't think it is suitable for you to start seeing him as a patient. He is my junior, Chloe. My mentee. I can take care of your needs, help you rediscover the past.'

'But we've been doing this for three weeks, and I still can't remember anything.'

He rubs a palm against his beard, his lips pink and pouty. 'Chloe, the human mind is capable of storing an incredible amount of information. It's all in there,' he says, tapping lightly at my head, 'little packets of data about your life. But the accident made it all a jumble. Things everywhere, strewn about like your drawers when you were a child.' Another offering from my past. Is that true? Was I a messy child? 'But the brain is remarkable. We can usually recall complex memories from childhood as if they happened only yesterday.' He snaps his fingers in front of his eyes to show the speed of the brain. '*Your* ability to recall has gone astray.

What we must do is reconnect the subconscious with the conscious, reducing your peripheral awareness by creating an environment whereby those hidden memories can rise to the surface. Reconnect the dots, so to speak. Hypnosis is a wonderful tool.'

So I lie back, tempted again by the promise of remembering my life. I rest my head against a cushion and gaze up into his eyes, the whites shining bright in the firelight, the shadows underneath dark and deep. Although I'm still not sure I trust him, he is seemingly my only hope at the moment.

'I want you to start by taking some deep breaths,' he says. 'Let's get you a little more relaxed. Concentrate on drawing air in through the nose and expelling it through the mouth. In through the nose, out through the mouth. That's right. No, Chloe, don't look at me. Focus on the pen.' He holds a silver fountain pen between his fingers. Black ink has leaked onto his skin, bled into the cracks on his fingers. 'Now just allow your body to rest into the rhythm of your breathing. That's good. In and out. Well done, but try not to blink so much. Very good. You're doing very well.'

After a while I feel calmer, and even a little sleepy. My arms feel heavy on the couch. I'm yawning, and the drumming of the rain against the window seems to resemble the crashing of waves against the shingle of a beach. Pebbles rolling in and out. Brighton, I think. Why do I know Brighton? Why did I think about it now?

'Now, Chloe. What can you remember about that night?'

'The rain,' I say. 'It was raining.'

'Very good. Where are you?'

'In the car,' I tell him. 'My head is hurting.'

'Keep going back. Keep looking, Chloe. What else can you see? I need you to go back as far as you can go, to the start of your journey. I want you to try to think back to the moment when you picked up the keys, when you got into the car. Can you do that for me, Chloe? Can you try to remember?'

I wake with a start. My eyes flicker open and I see his smiling face peering down at me. The fire has died down, only a few golden embers glimmering. The air around me has grown cold and dark. What time is it? How long have I been here?

'Well done, Chloe. How are you feeling now?'

I look round at the clock and see that it is a little after eleven. My head feels light, sloshy, as though it is submerged. As though I've been underwater. I lost myself, slipped into his dream world, the one he lulls me into each time we sit like this. I reach up and touch the dressing on my head. My father takes my hand. A wave of concern flashes over his face. 'What's wrong? Are you all right?'

'I fell asleep,' I say, pushing myself upright, looking at the clock on the mantelpiece. So much time has passed. Almost three hours. The dream comes back to me. The beach, the pier, my speeding car, and then . . . Nothing. What did I recall? I can't remember. 'Did I say anything? Did I talk during my sleep?'

'A little. Most of the time you were just resting. Listening. Nothing discernible. But you did very well, Chloe. You told me some simple details about the speed you were travelling, the weather conditions. All information that will be useful when the police want to talk to you.'

'The police? Do they still want to speak to me?' They had been to see me once in the hospital already. I remember little of what they told me, those early weeks a blur.

He stands up, pulls the edge of his shirt from inside his waistband. He has become more casual during the time I've been asleep. He has lost his tie, and his shirt is loose, unbuttoned to reveal a tuft of hair on his chest. 'At some point. But there's no rush. You really don't seem to remember much about that night. Still, perhaps that's for the best. It was a terrible accident.' He brushes a heavy hand over my sweaty brow. 'I'll fix us a cup of cocoa, how about that?' He goes to walk away and I push myself up, my arms heavy. Just before he slips from the room, he turns back to look at me with a smile on his face. 'Great job tonight, Chloe. I'm very proud of you.'

He might well be feeling proud of me, but somehow everything feels wrong, has done since I first arrived here. Two days ago, after the last therapy session I had with my father, I asked him if there was something he was hiding from me. I just have a feeling, as if something happened that nobody wants to mention. I asked him if we had argued before the crash, if there was a reason for me to be speeding that night. He told me that everything was fine beforehand. It was just a terrible accident, he said, distorted by a mind full of half-baked memories.

But deep down, although I can't explain how, I know that he is lying. There is something about my life before the accident that they don't want to tell me. I can feel it in their silence, my isolation, the way my mother and sister go out all day even though they seem to have nowhere to go. And until I can find out exactly what happened that night, I'm never going to be able to move forward. I'm trapped by a man who doesn't want to tell me the truth, and who with each therapy session seems only to confuse me more.

And if that's true, if I am correct, it means I'm going to have to find out what really happened on my own.

You said that you wanted to escape, that you needed a way out. And with that, what started off as a game became something that meant so much more. We stopped being about laughter and happy moments together and started being about something real that we could feel deep inside. I thought we started to be about us. I just didn't realise – and it makes me so sad to admit this now – that for you it was only ever about you.

Right from the first moment I laid eyes on you I knew it was different with you. That you were different. I could feel it in my movements, the way I held myself, wondering when you would look at me. I wanted to know what it would be like to touch a girl like you, to caress you and feel your hands against my skin. It was like a dream, Chloe. You were like a dream. I wanted right then and there to make you my wife.

You let me fall in love with you, and believe that you loved me in return. Would you still say that you love me now? Would you tell me still there is nothing else you think about? Do you remember that you promised me forever? Do you think about me when you go to bed at night? Do you remember anything about us at all? I can't stand the thought that you have forgotten me. Still, all I can do now is wait. Wait for you to remember. I have been reduced by your existence, Chloe, reduced to a beggar, forced to make do with empty promises of our broken life together. Sometimes I feel that's all that's left for me now. And sometimes, my love, I hate you for it.

4

My eyes flicker open, registering the pained look on my father's face looming above me. I have woken up screaming. I could hear myself in the final moments, when day and night are truly blurred, that moment when you are neither awake nor sleeping. His wrinkles are etched as deep as geographical fault lines, his voice shrill and urgent. The rain continues its assault against the window, streaming down the glass in the same way as the sweat runs across my face. Church bells chime to mark the start of another new day, the first of a new month. December: the last month of the year. Another juncture draws to a close.

'Chloe,' he says, hands pulling at my floppy body. He draws me in close to him. 'It was just a dream. You're all right now.' He strokes my wet hair away from my face and presses me into the soft flesh of his chest. My wounded head throbs at his touch. The scent of his deodorant is strong, his skin freshly showered.

'He was drowning,' I say as I try to escape his grasp. Our eyes meet; his are glassy in the pale light, his pupils black and bulbous as a seal's. 'He was drowning and I couldn't save him.'

'Who was drowning?' my father asks as he looks to my mother, just arriving at the door to my bedroom.

'I don't know. A boy. Oh God, I couldn't save him.'

'Oh Chloe, it was just a bad dream,' he says again, squeezing me tighter still. 'Look at you, you poor thing.' He smoothes his hand over the curve of my head. 'You're shaking.'

I scramble from his grip and push the sheets aside. Despite the weather, I am burning up. I can hear the sound of Jess moving around outside my room. My mother looks out into the corridor, ushers her away.

'I can't breathe,' I say, hurrying to the window. I throw it open, gasp for breath, the cold air a shock to my lungs.

Then my father is at my back, a hand rubbing at my shoulder. 'Dreams are nothing for us to be alarmed about, Chloe.' He shoos my mother away, and although she seems reluctant at first, she does as she is told. 'But you must rest, Chloe. You need to take your time, like Dr Gleeson told us, especially with that head wound. Don't rush to get up.' He edges me back towards the bed, plumps the pillows as I sit. I allow him to cover me and tuck the sheets in tight. 'Try to get some sleep.'

After my father's sessions, my dreams are always vivid. Last night it was a boy, faceless, drowning in the shadow of Brighton pier. I watched as he ran down the beach, ducking under the rafters. I was edging towards the water, scared to go in, desperate to save him yet powerless to do so. A couple of nights ago it was a car chase, me trying desperately to reach the car in front. I didn't see the boy's face that time either. I only saw his body, in the moments

27

before I woke. He was lying on a forest floor, covered in blood.

By the time I get downstairs, my parents have both gone out. I feel so jealous of their freedom, the ability to come and go as they please. Jess is in the kitchen, nursing a cup of tea.

'Morning,' she says, smiling. 'Are you OK?'

It is such a simple question, but one I feel overwhelmingly incapable of answering. Am I OK? I have no idea. I can barely tell her who I am or what I'm doing here. I feel like a cardboard cut-out of my previous self.

'Not sure.' She smiles and motions to a chair. I take a seat. 'It's all still a bit confusing.'

Out of the three of them, Jess has been the most relaxed with me since I came home. On the first day as I stood in the hallway, unsure how to act in surroundings I didn't recognise, I slipped off my jacket with Jess's help and then with some discomfort managed to wriggle out of my trainers. I reached down, held them up. 'Where should I put these?' I asked.

For a second she appeared puzzled, as if my question didn't make sense. Then she took them from me, tossed them underneath the round table that stood in the middle of the large hallway. 'Don't act like a guest,' she said, a sad smile crossing her lips. I didn't know how to tell her that a guest was exactly what I felt like. I was here in a house and a life that didn't feel like mine. What else was I supposed to do?

'Of course it's confusing,' she says. 'You can't expect to wake up from a coma and just slip straight back into your old life.' Even the word shakes me. Coma. It's just four short letters but seems infinitely huge. 'You'll get there. You just have to give it time.' She looks away, almost embarrassed. 'That's what Dad says, anyway.'

'It all just feels so alien. I wish I could get outside, go for a walk at least. That way maybe I would recognise something. I can't stand being cooped up in this house.'

She stands up, sets down her cup of tea. 'Well nobody is here to stop you. Why don't we go out together?'

'Dad said I shouldn't, remember?'

'Yes, but Dad's not here.' She flashes me a wink. 'Anyway, I'll be with you. I'll make sure you're all right.'

We slip on our coats and leave the house. The day is crisp and chilly, moisture clinging to my limp curls and woolly hat. We walk side by side up the driveway, able only to see a short distance ahead, not even as far as the treeline. When we arrive at the gate, I watch as she taps in the code, try to memorise the numbers. I say them over and over in my head. Then with a quiet beep the gate opens, we move through and she locks it behind her. That is all it took. Four numbers. We are out of the house, walking along the road towards Rusperford village.

As we walk, she tells me about her chemistry degree, about explosive lab experiments and how she wants to become a forensic toxicologist. A boy she is seeing and planning on dumping when she returns to university after Christmas. But I'm not really listening; instead I am looking around at the trees, the road, waiting for something to come into view. I'm enlivened by this liberation, my pain lessened and my spirits raised. I notice the church and the graveyard on my right, a cenotaph in the grounds just peeping through the mist. My world is growing. Across the road there is a hotel, the only visible part the sign at the start of the driveway. Have I been there in the past? I think maybe I have. I point to it.

'We used to come here sometimes at Christmas,' Jess tells me. 'Back when things between Mum and Dad were easier than they are now.' I gaze at the hotel, peeping at me through the mist. It is still only a sense of knowledge I have, an idea without proof. An illusion almost, like fog, there one minute and gone the next. I can't tell her anything about the hotel, like the decoration inside, or some funny anecdote about how Dad nearly choked on a sprout. I don't know anything specific, or even understand what she means about things with Mum and Dad. But I can feel my past in ways I couldn't before. We continue the walk in silence, my eyes hungry for more.

As we near the centre of the village, I realise that we drove this way from the hospital, but still it feels like the first time I am seeing it in years. There's a used-car garage and a hairdressing salon ahead. A small village green with a duck pond, a layer of mist clinging to the surface. We follow the road as it runs along the edge of the woods, and although I have been walking for less than ten minutes, with Jess's arm for support, the reality of my injuries begins to supersede my enthusiasm; I can feel my leg beginning to hurt, the headache growing underneath my woolly hat. I didn't bring the walking stick: a test for myself that I appear to have failed.

I stop for breath, hold onto a gate that leads to a small park. It feels as if my lungs might explode as I gaze across the wet grass towards the swings. Clouds form as I gasp for breath, drawing damp air into my lungs. Moisture clings to tree branches like jewels encrusted on spindly boughs. I notice some kind of wooden hut alongside the playground, a slide and a bench too.

And for a moment as I stand there, a clear thought comes to me, a vision of myself sitting on a park bench similar to the one in front of me. I am waiting for something, somebody perhaps. My nervous hands are so fidgety I have to trap them under my legs. It is summer, the scent of roses drifting by on a warm breeze. But Jess loops her arm through mine again, and just as fast as it came, the vision is gone.

'We used to come here as kids,' she tells me. I ignore her at first, searching the space before me for something that resembles the vision in my mind. Is it actually a memory? If so, from when? From where? 'Don't you remember?' she urges.

'Not properly. I have all these thoughts going round in my head, things I can't explain. I just wish I could remember something that would help me. Something solid.'

'Maybe I can help,' she says, shrugging her shoulders. 'That is, if you feel you can talk to me. You used to be able to. We used to be close.'

I think of the pictures from the family albums, the sight of us together in sibling unity, juxtaposed against the alien feel of her touch when she brushes against my skin. If we used to be close, that was in a different life. I was a different person then.

'I don't think I can, Jess. It's hard to open up to people I . . .' I stop myself, not wanting to offend her when she has been so good as to go against my father's instructions and bring me out.

'That you don't know?' Embarrassed, I nod, relieved that she appears to understand and that she isn't angry or upset. 'The thing is, Chloe, although you can't remember me, I remember you. Maybe some of the things you want to talk about are things we have already discussed. Maybe there is a history we share that could help shed some light on who you were . . .' She pauses, her turn to feel awkward about what she's just said. I notice her cheeks flush bright pink. 'I mean are. Who you are, Chloe.'

She fiddles at the handle of the gate, scratching at the paint with the edge of her nail. Even she knows the old me has gone. I used to think that there was a clear distinction between life and death: either you were here or you weren't. Now I know that you can be alive and still feel completely detached from the world.

'Anyway, I could help, I'm sure of it. You just have to be prepared to give me a chance.'

I look up. Could she be right? 'Really? So we were close?' It's hard to imagine all that shared history is lost to me. But maybe if I can find the courage to speak to Jess, open up to her now that we are alone, she might be able to help me discover something of the woman I used to be. The woman I still am?

'We used to trust each other, Chloe, talk about the stuff we wouldn't talk to anybody else about. At least before you left home.' She smiles, hops up onto the gate. It rattles under her weight. It's the only thing that breaks the silence. 'The sort of things we would have kept from Dad.'

'OK,' I say, glancing over at the play equipment. 'I feel like he's keeping something from me. Like something happened before the crash and he is trying to stop me from remembering it. Do you have any idea why I feel that way?'

She shakes her head. 'I was thinking more along the lines of telling you that you used to waste hours watching *Friends* repeats, or that you used to eat a whole tub of ice cream in one go. That sort of thing.'

More useless facts. 'That doesn't explain why I feel like this, though.' I'm anxious to say the next part aloud. I take a deep breath. 'He scares me a bit, Jess. I keep having these dreams, always the same thing. I'm sure they have something to do with the crash, but when I tell Dad, he just brushes it off. I keep dreaming about a boy. At first I was chasing him in a car, then he was lost out at sea. Another time I dreamed he was being buried alive.' That was before I left the hospital. 'I feel like something awful happened that I can't explain.'

'It did, Chloe. You lost your memory. That's the awful thing.' She hops down from the gate, loops her arm through mine again.

'I think it's something more than that.' I lick at my cold, chapped lips. 'Jess, please tell me. I didn't hurt anybody in the accident, did I? I didn't run somebody over?'

She is silent for a moment, and I'm sure I see a dampening of her eyes. She reaches out, strokes my face. She might be over a decade younger than me, but in that moment it feels as if she is much older. 'Don't you think we would have told you if something like that had happened?'

'Not if Dad told you not to. Please be honest with me. If you know something, tell me the truth.'

33

'Chloe, it was just a terrible accident, that's all. It was raining, and the place you crashed is notoriously dangerous.'

I feel so stupid in that moment, so helpless and naive. It seems that when you can't trust yourself, you can't trust anybody. 'I guess so.'

'Dad's difficult, yes, but he would have told you if something like that had happened, don't you think? Now come on, I don't want to tire you out. Let's get you home. I'll put the kettle on and we can curl up and watch some of those *Friends* repeats you love so much.'

We move off, Jess's arm through mine, her grip tight enough that it helps take the weight from my damaged leg. If I come out again, I must bring my stick, I think.

Halfway back to the house, I see a young woman walking towards us, moving fast, pushing a buggy. I look down to see a small blond-haired boy kicking about inside it, like the boy from my dream. And as she passes us, I can't help but stare, as if that little boy is everything I've ever wanted in the world.

5

When we arrive back at the house I go straight upstairs. I
open the drawer in the bedside table and pull out a pen and
an old bible. I open the book, see that just inside the front
cover I have at some point in the past written my name:
Chloe Daniels. As I flick through the pages, I recall standing
in church, singing a hymn, holding a book just like this, the
cry of a baby in the background. A memory, or my mind
playing tricks? I'm not sure. I grip the pen tightly and press
the tip against the first page. I write down the code from
the gate, then scrawl my name over and over. The letters
are shaky, almost childlike. But it is my name. That is what's
important. Chloe. Me. Still here. It doesn't take long before
I fall asleep.

I wake hours later to the sound of a car engine. I get up,
move across to the window and open it a little to have a look
at who has come home. I see my mother's white Range Rover
on the driveway, now back from the garage, her feet quick
across the frosty ground. The breeze bothers at the edge of
the heavy floral curtain so I close the window quickly, slip
back into the room. I am only wearing a light cotton blouse,
and I am cold. I need to find something else to put on.

I open the cupboards but the clothes are not mine, most of them either my mother's or cast-offs from Jess. Hand-me-downs travelling in the wrong direction. Everything in the cupboards feels wrong, because nothing really belongs to me.

I look down at the bag under the bed, the handle sticking out from where my mother disturbed it the night before. I drag it towards me, setting it on the edge of the bed. I pull on the zipper, peer inside.

Jeans, T-shirts and a couple of simple grey jumpers. Nothing immediately familiar. I find the set of pyjamas I was wearing in the hospital, a drip of blood on the inside of the left sleeve from where they changed one of my lines. I try to think back to the hospital, picture myself wearing these pyjamas. Even those days seem blurry to me now.

I rummage deeper in the bag and pull out one of the photo albums that my parents created for me in an attempt to make me feel like part of this family. I crawl onto the bed, setting the album down on my legs, and turn the pages one by one, taking in the images. In some of the pictures I am a child in the garden, fishing in the river, wearing a daisy chain I must have made. In others I am on holiday, part of a scene at the beach, a green and blue swimsuit with a badge sewn on the front for my achievements in the fifty metres.

As I turn the pages I grow, time fast forwarded to my teenage years in which I evidently became shy of the camera. In nearly all of the pictures from that time there is a silly grin on my face, an awareness of the photographer, an awareness of myself. In those pictures I have lighter hair, bleached either by the sun or by my hand. I look a bit like

Jess does now. There is a picture from my graduation ceremony after I finished at university, my parents flanking me
on either side. Jess is small in front of my mother, perhaps
nine years old. I wonder who took that picture. A well-
intentioned stranger, or somebody else from my past whom
I have forgotten?

I notice that the final picture of my graduation has
slipped out of position. Underneath there is another photo,
which has been hidden, the edge now exposed. I peel the
plastic cover away, take the picture out. In it I am sitting
in the kitchen, eating a slice of cake. There is a balloon
attached to the back of my chair, and Jess is standing beside
me pulling a stupid face. A knife in her hand, a cake set
before her on the table. I count the candles. Fifteen. Five
years ago. Mum is in the kitchen too, busy at the worktop,
a glass of wine at her side. But there are two more details
to which my eye keeps returning. Things that don't make
any sense.

The first is the ring on my finger, a simple gold band on
my left hand, glistening in the flash from the camera. It
looks like a wedding ring. The second is a little boy sitting
on my lap. I have my arms wrapped tightly around him,
my chin nuzzled into his neck, holding him close.

I look down at the ring finger of my left hand as a rumble
of thunder creeps across the heavy grey sky. The skin is dry,
the finger itself perhaps slightly thinner than its counterpart
on the right. Has a ring been sitting there? Was I married?
Am I married? If so, where the hell is my husband? And
who is that little boy? Is it the boy from my dreams?

The rain is really picking up by the time I get downstairs,

coursing down the kitchen window in waves, creating turbu-
lent shadows that shift across the walls. My leg is sore from
the effort of walking, my head throbbing. I call for Mum,
then Jess, and when nobody replies I sit down at the table
and wait. The light is fading further, dark descending despite
the early hour, leaving in its place the cool lustre of an
approaching storm. And then I see her, my mother, rushing
along the winding path of the back garden with her coat
pulled up over her head, caught in the sudden downpour.

She races through the back door, head down and shoulders
curled over, shrieking as cold rivulets of water drip from
her hair and run down her back. She is laughing to herself
as she pulls the door closed behind her. Then as she turns
and sees me, she almost jumps out of her skin.

'Chloe!' she shrieks. She catches her breath, laughs as she
shakes the water from her coat. 'You frightened the life out
of me. Jess told me you were sleeping.'

'I woke up. I was looking at the pictures you brought to
the hospital. One of the albums you made.'

'Oh?' she says as she locks the back door. She sets her
riding jacket on a black wrought-iron hook. I can hear horses
neighing in the garden stables. 'Anything new coming back
to you?' She sits down on a small bench, pulls off her muddy
boots. She puts the kettle on to boil before sitting down at
the table.

'You tell me,' I say as I hold up the picture that I have
taken from the album. She takes it from my hand. I don't
know if it is just my imagination, but in that moment it
looks as if she is worried. I see her swallow, an uncomfortable lump in her throat, her hands shaking with fear. She

appears on the verge of being sick. 'Who is that little boy?' I ask.

She takes in a heavy breath and sets the picture down on the table. She crosses her hands in front of her, plays with the band on her ring finger. 'Where did you find that?'

'It doesn't matter,' I tell her.

She looks at the picture again, pushes it away as if it's all too much. She can't look at me. Can't look at the picture. She moves to the door, then stops herself. She's scratching at her forehead, making it red.

'Just tell me, Mum.'

'I can't.' Eyes to the door. 'We should wait until your father gets home.'

'No,' I say, slamming my fist against the table. I'm up on my feet, aware of a blurring of my eyes, a thickness in my throat that makes it hard to swallow. It's the truth, I think. That's what I can feel choking me. I am close to some sort of truth for the first time. I'm about to find out what they have been keeping from me. 'I need you to tell me now. I'm wearing a wedding ring in that picture too. Am I married?'

Her hands are shaking as she brings them up to her face. She wipes her fingertips underneath her eyes, a tear escaping. 'I really think we should wait for your father to get—'

'Mum, just tell me,' I interrupt.

She slumps into a chair, hangs her head in her hands. I remain on my feet. 'No, Chloe. You are not married.' The scar on my head throbs with each beat of my heart. Her voice is all of a quiver. 'At least not any more.'

'Oh my God.' I begin to cry too, my throat burning, my cheeks hot. I feel like I might faint. Not any more? I was married? I had a life and a partner and a . . . I feel a cloud of dizziness approaching, so I cling to the table, palms flat against the surface. My mother moves to comfort me, steady me. I pull away. 'And the boy?' I whisper, my voice breaking, my whole body overwhelmed as I ask a question to which I think I already know the answer.

She gazes at the picture, tears streaming down her face. Yet she is defiant as she looks up at me. 'Chloe, I'm so sorry we kept it from you. That little boy was your son.'

6

Was.

Past tense.

I run from the room as best I can, the pain in my leg no longer present. Numb. I hear my mother, then Jess, calling my name. I stagger through the hallway, bumping into the frame as I open the front door and leave. I can't move fast, but still I am quicker than they are, edging towards the gate. I tell myself that I need to remember the code, that I need to escape, get out, get away from this place. They are liars and I don't want to be around them. But as I struggle up the driveway my mind is all muddled. What did I write down in the bible? What were the numbers? I stab at the buttons over and over but the gate remains shut. I grab it, desperate, rattle it as I hear Mum approaching behind me. I have to leave this place, but when I feel her hands on my shoulders, when I sense her effort to comfort me, I crumple to the wet ground.

We stay there for a good while, drenched by heavy rain, tears streaming from my eyes.

Once we are back inside, she tells me that my son's name was Joshua. That I had a husband called Andrew. She explains that when I woke up and couldn't remember what had happened, they didn't have the strength to tell me they had both died. Joshua was killed in the accident that somehow didn't take my life, and Andrew had passed away a week before. When I ask how Andrew died, she hesitates, an uncomfortable knot in her throat bobbing up and down in place of an answer.

'We're not sure, Chloe.'

'But you must know how . . .' I try to ask, but she shakes her head, rests a hand on my shoulder.

'Let's not go into all of that now. Your father is much better at explaining these things than I am. Let's leave it to him. But I can show you something that I think will help.'

In an attempt to pacify me she pulls another photo album from the cupboard, one that was hidden behind a box of old paperwork. Inside I see pictures of my life with Andrew, the husband I can't remember. I see myself caring for Joshua, a son I never realised I had. I see a life they've hidden from me for months. In the pictures we are laughing and smiling. In one, Andrew is in the swimming pool in my parents' garden, teaching our son to swim. My father is standing by at the side, his arms across his chest, watching the fun as it unfolds.

While I look at the album, my mother makes a telephone call, explaining the situation to my father. He is coming home, she tells me. Right away.

Jess hugs Mum and keeps telling her it will be all right. I want to scream at her: I'm the one she should be comforting. But when she tries to talk to me, reaching for my hands, telling me that she is sorry, all I can think is how beautiful my family was, the pair of them just like angels. They both had blond hair, tanned skin, as if Andrew might have shared some distant Scandinavian heritage with Joshua. But then there is another thought, one that quietens me, makes me cautious about what I say: that every single person in this house had the chance to be truthful but didn't take it. I thought perhaps I couldn't trust my father. I now know that I can't trust any of them.

I concentrate on looking at the rest of the photos in the album, taking in the details. I see shiny grey eyes, thin noses, pointed and well defined at the tip. They look so alike, this man and this boy. The loss of these strangers is like a pain in my gut, a twisting cramp spreading out like a wave. Even though I can't remember them in life, I can feel their absence in death. It is as if in their place something else has claimed me, a close relation to death that I know from this moment forth is never going to leave.

A little later, rejecting their kindness, I go upstairs to take a shower. I think maybe it will offer some relief, comfort in the heat of the water. But when I take off my clothes and stare at my body I see the evidence of my past. Silver scars run across the surface of my belly, red threads around the back of my legs. A little paunch, despite my weight loss after the accident. As I stand under the shower, allow the water to wash painfully over my head, I close my eyes, try to remember what it felt like to be pregnant, my life as a wife and mother. But as the steam swallows me up and the water streams across my face, it's a different memory that comes to me, arriving in broken flashes.

I remember the rain hitting the windscreen, the winding course of the road, pulling hard at the steering wheel. I remember the slip of the tyres on the slick surface. I was speeding, desperate. Crying, wiping my eyes. Wipers batting left and right. Losing control as I pumped the brakes, crashing into a mass of trees. The crash? The night I lost my baby?

I shut off the water and slip under the bedcovers, my skin still wet from the shower. I don't want the images of that night in my head. I shut my eyes tight, praying for a dreamless sleep that doesn't come. I stroke my right hand against my soft, wrinkled, empty belly. What else is there left for me to do now?

What else is left?

It's Mum who braves her way upstairs to find me. I am exhausted, my throat hoarse, my eyes swollen to the point of pain. I am silent. 'All cried out,' she tells me, as if I have no spirit left to put up a fight. She holds me and I let her, just so that I know I'm not alone. But even with her slight arms wrapped around my shivering body, I find no peace.

She picks out some clothes for me and suggests I get dressed. After she leaves I stare at myself in the mirror again, wondering who I am. Who I was before all of this. The same gaunt face that I came to recognise in the hospital as my own stares back at me. I still don't know it. I don't know the person behind these eyes. I might be less broken than I was when I first awoke, but my eye sockets remain dark and deep, my cheek and lip still red and scarred. My clothes are ill-fitting and loose. I have lost so much weight. But I no longer see the broken pieces of a woman who nearly died. Now I see the evidence of a car crash that stole my son's life. I can't bear to look at myself any more.

* * *

When Dad arrives home the three of us are sitting in the kitchen, our eyes dry but stained red from tears. I am quiet now, unsure what to say or do. I feel empty and numb. We hear the rumble of tyres as he pulls into the driveway, the heavy clunk of the car door. Mum stands up to greet him, first out of the kitchen.

'Come on,' Jess says to me, tucking her chair under the table. 'He'll want to talk to you now.'

He is quiet as he arrives in the house, but as I follow Jess from the kitchen, I hear my mother apologising, telling him that she is sorry for being so careless. She promises that she hadn't been drinking when she put the album together. 'No, absolutely not,' she says for a second time when he says he doesn't believe her. I watch her help him with his coat and gloves, putting them away in the cloak-room. I think of what Jess told me earlier, about the difficulties in their relationship, but I push the thought from my mind as their conversation trails off to a whisper. This isn't about them. This is about me and the things I have lost. They share a series of cautious, embarrassed glances as I arrive in front of them.

My father is hesitant at first, unable to even move, like his feet have sprouted roots and he physically can't shift. The space between us hangs like an abyss neither of us seems able to cross. I hold onto the table for support. I can feel his eyes upon me. He looks as if he could be sick. As if maybe he *has* been sick, so pale, so drawn. One hand reaches up to loosen his tie. Mum beckons to Jess and they hurry away into the dining room, closing the door behind them.

'Why didn't you . . .' I stammer, unable to find the words. I take a shallow, shaky breath. 'Why didn't you tell me that I had a child?' It comes out as a whisper, a voice as broken as my past.

He takes off his glasses, finds the strength to take a step towards me. He has aged since this morning. The weeks of dishonesty have taken a toll on him as well as me.

'Why?' I push. 'Tell me why.'

He stutters at first, his dry tongue desperate to wet his lips, moving in a sticky, serpentine motion. 'I'm very sorry that we kept the truth from you, Chloe. I thought perhaps it would be for the best.'

I shake my head and it loosens a tear. 'How could you decide that? What right did you have?'

'None,' he admits. He rubs at his face. I hear the dry skin of his hand grating against his beard. 'But when you couldn't remember them, it seemed somehow kinder. How could I tell you that people you had no memory of were dead?' He drags his fingertips across his sweaty forehead, the way he did in the hospital after I first woke up, worry burrowing its way inside like a worm. 'I just didn't know what to expect, or how you might react if I told you the truth. I was scared, I suppose, of how you would handle it.'

'But it was my right to know.' My chin begins to tremble. 'I needed to know, Dad.'

He walks away from me, circles a little before sitting on the bottom step of the stairs. He pulls his shirt from inside his waistband, loops his tie over the banister. 'If the truth be known, Chloe, I suppose I was scared you'd blame yourself.'

I swallow hard, the taste of blood rushing into my mouth from where I have nibbled nervously at the wound on my lip. 'Why would I have blamed myself?'

A moment of silence. Neither of us breathes. 'Chloe, I haven't told you much about that night because . . . well, we simply don't know the truth. But there was another car involved, and it is assumed that it ran you off the road.'

'I crashed because somebody hit my car?'

'Maybe. That's the hypothesis the police are working with. But who can be certain if you can't remember? The other driver is quite adamant that he isn't responsible for the crash.' He sucks on the stale air around us, air heavy with lies. What is he suggesting? 'You know that the police want to talk to you. I have been trying to stall them, telling them that you aren't well enough. I keep the gate locked so they can't just turn up in my absence and take you by surprise, but it's becoming increasingly difficult. I just don't know what we're going to tell them.'

I don't understand. It doesn't make any sense to me. 'I'll tell them the truth, Dad. If they want to talk to me, I'll tell them the truth.'

'But you don't know what the truth is, and I'm afraid the police won't see it simply as a case of amnesia. They'll think you are trying to hide something.'

'Why would they assume that?'

'Because on the night of the crash you left here in such a terrible state. You were finding it so hard, really struggling after Andrew's death. You blamed yourself, because only a few weeks before he died you'd chosen to leave him.'

47

Unlike the gradual remembrances in the shower, this fact hits me like a punch to the face. I left my husband? How can that be? We looked so happy in the pictures my mother showed me. Why would I have chosen to leave?

'You'd been living with us here for several weeks. You were sick of him. Of his drinking, his disappearances, and the effect it was having on Joshua. And then he died, and we just . . . well, we all thought that maybe he'd done something stupid. Then, only a week later, after leaving here in such a state, you had the crash and Joshua was killed. He went straight through the windscreen of the car. How could I tell you that, Chloe? Put that into words?'

I bring a hand up to my mouth, feel my knees buckle. My eyes glaze over and I hit the floor. He rushes to my side, cradles me against him. I don't fight.

'You say you don't remember what happened, but there are details of this accident that only you can explain.' He pulls me close, but all I can think of is Joshua, a child I can't remember, going through the windscreen of a car I crashed. 'I've tried to keep my mouth shut, Chloe, not tell the police anything they don't need to know, but it's hard to ignore the facts.' He shakes his head. 'My God, Chloe . . . you were so upset. You blamed yourself for Andrew's death. You kept saying that it was your fault, that you shouldn't have left him. That was another reason why I didn't want to tell you, because I didn't want you to have to mourn for a man you had mourned once already.

'And while it's true that there was another car on the scene, crashed off the road when the police got there, the owner of that car is adamant that he wasn't even there.

He claims his car had been stolen.' It's too much. I can't keep up. 'The prosecution will argue your case, but the defence will blame you as a way of reducing the other driver's sentence, say that you were upset, that you were driving recklessly. It's all so upsetting for us, Chloe. I want only to protect you.'

I don't understand what he's telling me. Surely I did nothing wrong. If a second car ran me off the road that night, where are all his doubts coming from? But then I remember the flashback I had in the shower, the rumble of a distant past making itself heard. I was crying in that memory, driving too fast. I was desperate, weeping, couldn't see for the rain. I *was* driving recklessly, wasn't I?

'Dad, I think I remember some parts of that night.'

He turns to me, eyes wide. 'You do?'

'Yes, I was driving, and it was raining.' I wipe my eyes on my sleeve. 'I was going so fast, and—'

He shakes his head, and I feel his grip tighten across my shoulders. My collarbone throbs under his weight. 'I don't think you really remember anything, Chloe. The brain creates images of things, attempts to put them in order when we cannot consciously do it ourselves. Right now I'm more concerned that the police want to talk to you and I don't know what we are going to tell them.'

'But it seems so real. If you help me, maybe I could remember more.' I have to know. I have to know if this accident really was my fault. 'We could go over what you know and what I remember, and together work out what happened and—'

He doesn't let me finish. 'Marriages go through difficulties, Chloe. Yours more than most. I don't know what happened that night any more than you appear to. But what I do remember is the terrible state you were in when you left this house. I know the police have their suspicions about your intentions.'

'My intentions?'

'You said you could never forgive yourself. That you couldn't live with the guilt.' He shakes his head, buckling under the memory. 'You were just so terribly upset.'

'What are you saying, Dad?' Is he trying to tell me I was so upset I couldn't concentrate, or that I crashed deliberately? 'Are you trying to tell me that I crashed on—'

'Don't say it. Don't let yourself imagine it to be true. When it comes to that night, all I know is that you not knowing what happened will make it easier to convict the other driver. He could have stayed. He could have helped you. But these flashes of 'memory' – he puts the word in bunny ears to make me understand that he doesn't really believe that's what they are – 'aren't going to get us anywhere. Especially not with the police. It would be better if you couldn't remember anything at all, because that way you can't incriminate yourself, can you?'

I shake my head, completely lost. I don't know if what he is saying is right. Is it possible that I wanted to crash my car? With my son inside? What kind of mother would do that?

'I'm right, Chloe, you know it. So that's what we'll tell the police, OK? Now that you know the truth I might as well tell them you are well enough to speak to them. But we must maintain that you don't remember anything. Not before, during, or after the crash. We would hate for them to draw conclusions, Chloe. We don't want to give them any reason to even consider taking you to court.'

'To court?' For a second I lose my breath.

'Of course. If they think you are liable, what's to stop them putting you in front of a jury? Could you imagine hearing the details of how Joshua died over and over again? It would be much easier if you simply can't remember anything at all.'

I can't concentrate on what he is saying. 'I feel sick,' I tell him. The swell of it rises in my stomach, a heaviness surging to get out. I see the image of my son flying through the windscreen, landing in the wet undergrowth, leaves stuck to his skin just like in my dreams. Real, imagined? I don't know. My fault? My choice? It's too much to process.

'You need to lie down. Let me help you.'

With his help, I make it up the stairs. I lie on the bed, the lights down low, rain pattering softly against the window. I stare at the picture of my family that I took from the album earlier and placed on the bedside table. What am I supposed to believe?

In the photo albums, we looked so happy. The life I was looking at in those pictures doesn't fit with the life my father described. Did I crash on purpose? I can't even begin to believe that to be true. Don't want to believe it. But if it *is* true, I now understand why my parents have been lying to me. Because if I tried to kill myself and my child, and I'm responsible for my husband's death, I don't deserve to remember either of them.

7

How many days have passed since that night I discovered I used to be a mother? I have no idea. Time has stood still like a stagnant pond, brackish and foul, unable to sustain life. I have been festering in this bed, slipping in and out of disturbing sleep littered with dreams of my dead son, listening to the sounds of family life continue around me. As if nothing has changed at all.

They bring meals and medication, sit on the edge of the bed and try to slip pathetic morsels down my throat. A plate encrusted with last night's untouched food still sits at my feet. People come and go, doorbells ringing, music and television. Last night I heard laughter in the hallway, the sound of the front door closing. I got up, peered from the window, saw Dr Thurwell leaving with an armful of folders. Discussing cases again. I stayed there to watch the red blur of his lights as he disappeared back to his own life.

On that day when he came to see me in hospital, sitting on the edge of my bed, he asked if I was feeling any better. He asked if I was looking forward to going home, and if I felt like I was making progress. Whether or not things were getting too much, and whether I'd had any thoughts about taking my own life. I thought it was strange at the time, his concern that I might be feeling low enough to kill myself. As far as I could see, I was doing everything I could to survive. But now I realise it wasn't strange at all: he assumed I'd already tried to kill myself once by crashing my car into a tree while my son was inside. Last night, as I watched him walking to his car, he turned back and spotted me, raised his hand to wave. I did nothing in return, edged back from the curtain, slipped back into the shadows. I didn't want to be seen by him.

But this morning my self-imposed isolation has come to an end. I can hear the heavy footsteps on the hallway floor outside my door, the brief knock, the handle being tested. My father stands in the doorway, his face cast in silhouette with the subtle yellow glow of the hallway lamp behind him.

'You remember what is happening today?'

I nod my head. His shoulders are slumped at the thought of what is to come. The police called to let us know they are eager to talk now that I am well enough. Just the idea that he has been delaying their case, keeping me locked up and out of their reach, makes me so nervous my limbs shake.

'Now that you know the truth, Chloe, I can't hold them off any more. Just keep in mind what we agreed. You don't remember anything.'

That morning after breakfast, Mum pops out to get her hair done, and returns half an hour later, neatly coiffed and ready for the police. Their arrival is tensely anticipated, rippling through the house in energetic waves since we all woke up.

Some of us haven't slept. The hallway floor has been mopped and what I assume must be my father's best suit is back from the dry cleaner's and hanging over the door to his study. The scent of winter roses drifts past me in waves. Air freshener. The smell makes me feel sick.

I remain on the sofa with my right leg up on a footstool while my mother works around me, plumping the cushions and setting a fire as if we were getting ready for Christmas Day. Dust circles the air. Jess is sitting with me, the television on in the background, a winter fashions special playing on *This Morning*. She asks me what I think of the outfits, tells me she thinks the polo necks make the models look chubby. She wants to make small talk, make her lies disappear. But I can't concentrate on the television. Despite what she probably thinks, I'm not angry with her. I don't have the strength. I may have intended to kill myself and my son. Nothing else has any meaning.

My father passes by as we sit there, peers around the door, regarding us with concern. He approaches, stops in front of Jess, blocking her view of the television. Only when she can no longer see the screen does she bring herself to look at him.

'We must create the right kind of impression, Jessica,' he tells her, looking down at her baggy pyjamas. 'Please go upstairs and dress appropriately.' She begins her defence but he holds his hand up to show his inflexibility. He watches as she skulks away and then turns off the television.

All morning I have been trying to decide what to do. Do I tell the police I can't remember anything about the crash like he wants me to? Or should I tell them what I think I know? That maybe I am to blame. That maybe I was driving recklessly. That perhaps I even crashed on purpose. My father told me three times last night and once again this morning that any flashbacks I might be having are all in my mind, that it is something he has come across many times with other patients. But the memory of being in the car that night seems so real. Tangible, almost. These snapshots of broken movement are like an old movie, or a flickering of light shining from the past. Like stars; not really there any more, yet still they can be seen. 'Just false memories, Chloe, the brain trying to get a handle on things,' my father tells me. The things is, I don't believe a word he says any more.

He sits down beside me, gives me a cursory inspection, his fingers meddling painfully at my head as he checks my dressing before his eyes settle on my face. I pull away, not wanting him to touch me. 'Are you feeling all right, Chloe?'

I nod, reach up to my dressing, pressing it to ease the discomfort. 'My head hurts.' My words are cold, sharp. I don't want to talk to him any more than I want to talk to the police.

'Are you anxious about the visit from the police today?'

'No,' I lie. He looks satisfied enough, but I know deep down he doesn't believe me, any more than I believe him. 'I'm going to go and get dressed too,' I say, attempting to get up. But I turn to see him shaking his head, reaching one hand out towards my arm.

'I think it's best that you stay as you are,' he says, straightening the neckline of the robe I'm wearing. He fluffs my hair, adjusts my hat to expose the dressing for all to see. I pull away, stare at him out of the corner of my eye. 'There's no point in hiding your injuries, Chloe. We want them to see how poorly you've been, not mistake you for a reliable witness.' He sits back, frustrated by my resistance. 'And there's no point looking at me like that either. I know you're upset, but I did what I did with your best interests in mind.'

He leaves, taking his suit from the study door, calling to my mother to find his cufflinks. The silver ones with the rubies in them. As he ascends the stairs he glances back just once at me, shaking his head with disappointment. But he doesn't realise that I'm scared; scared that he is right. That I'm the one who caused the accident, and that by leaving my husband I gave him reason to take his own life. Scared because I don't know how I'm supposed to live if my husband and son are both dead because of me.

8

My mother lets them in when they arrive. I listen as she takes their coats and asks if they'd like tea. They thank her, but refuse her offer of a drink. My heart is racing, no idea what I'm going to say. A few days ago I was just a woman recovering from a car crash. Now I'm a woman who might have been trying to commit suicide with her own child in the car. What kind of person am I?

'Head through that way,' I hear her say. 'You'll find her just in there.'

Their footsteps grow louder as they approach. They bring the scent from outside with them, that dirty smell of fog and winter that gets on your chest, delivers illness. Moments later two officers appear in the doorway, both wearing long winter coats. Their hair is damp, noses red, pink cheeks flushed against white skin. Cherries on cakes. One woman, one man.

The man is small in stature, his frame slight yet overweight. It makes him seem out of balance, leaning back like a pregnant woman might in order to keep herself upright. Did I stand like that when I was pregnant? Is that why I thought it? I vaguely remember him from the hospital, the deep parting and white-grey hair. He nods at my father. 'Dr Daniels, good morning.'

'Good morning.' My father walks over and holds out his hand. They shake and my father peers around to smile at the woman arriving behind. She is so different to the first officer: tall, young, delicate features. Her bright blond hair makes me think of Andrew and Joshua. Her face is narrow and angular; she has a cold look about her. She doesn't smile or speak, her gaze so strong I have to look away. 'Officer Barclay, right?' my father says.

'Detective Constable Barclay.' She reaches out, shakes his hand. 'Good morning, Chloe,' she says as she turns to me. Her wedding ring cuts into my skin as we shake. And with that a thought rises to the surface: where is *my* wedding ring? 'Nice to see that you are finally well enough to speak with us.' Still she doesn't smile. She makes me nervous: her attitude, the way she stands, feet firmly in place. I wring my hands together to stop them shaking.

'Welcome to you both,' my father says. 'Can we arrange for some tea or coffee for you? It's freezing out today.' There is a light frost on the ground, and the fog in the air is thick. You can't even see as far as the swimming pool. The chill has infiltrated the house, and despite the crackling fire, all the walls seem just that bit too far away for the atmosphere to feel cosy. I look over at Jess, sitting on a footstool, wearing a pair of tight jeans and a smart blouse: dressed as my father demanded. She is nibbling on the quick of her thumb.

'No, we're fine, thank you.' The male officer turns to look at me, a warm smile spreading across his face. 'Miss Daniels, good morning. I'm DS Gray.' I start to get up, struggling a little with my balance as I always do. Jess rushes to help me, and with her support I get to my feet and take DS Gray's hand. His palm feels cold and sweaty all at once. 'Please, sit down,' he says.

I tuck my robe under my knees as I sit, and just a moment later I notice my father pointing to my right leg. I set it back on the footstool, not sure whether it's for the good of my health or the sake of appearances in front of the police.

'My father tells me we have met before,' I say.

'Yes, twice, in the hospital,' DC Barclay says. She pulls up a chair and sits down. 'You don't remember us at all?'

'It was a difficult time for Chloe,' my father reminds her. 'She suffered an epidural bleed. She nearly died, Officer.'

Without looking at him she says, 'We are well aware of Chloe's injuries, Dr Daniels. That is, after all, why it has taken us so long to be able to speak with her, piece together her version of events.'

DS Gray takes over, lowering the tension. 'Of course we appreciate these things take time. But I must say, you are certainly looking a lot better than you were in the hospital.' When I study my reflection, inspect my injuries, I don't think I look well at all, and for a brief moment as I glance to my father, I wonder whether he isn't just a little bit disappointed by DS Gray's observation. 'It's a relief to finally have an opportunity to talk to you about what happened that night. We are really hoping to make some headway with this case, start to understand what happened.' I nod, swallow hard. 'I would like first of all, however, to offer my most sincere condolences for the loss of your son.' I can't look up and I don't say anything. He must feel the tension creeping back in, because he is quick to move things on. 'What we really want to try to establish is exactly what you remember.'

I think of my dream, the flashbacks. My certainty that they truly reflect that night. But then I think of what my father suggested: the possibility that I intended to crash.

'I don't remember anything,' I tell them, taking a split-second decision to do as my father has told me. I'm not sure I could take their judgement otherwise.

DC Barclay pulls out a pen and pad, crosses her legs, tapping her kitten-heeled foot like a metronome. Tick, tick, tick. All the while she looks at me, seconds passing, waiting for me to speak. Her pen poised, her face expressionless.

'Nothing about what happened before or after the crash,' I add.

DS Gray smiles, nods his head, as if my response has satisfied his expectations. 'Of course, we understand, Miss Daniels. But it is our job to try and glean from you what might seem like the most insignificant of details, and turn them into a case against the person we believe was driving the second car.'

I nod too, feel the need to reassure him, to come up with something. Funny how the police can make you do that. I feel like a child in the classroom, desperate to find the right answer, whatever that is.

My mother walks in, a tray of tea in her hands, and I'm grateful for the distraction. She sets it down on the table and pours two mugs, topping both with a splash of milk. We are all silent, watching her actions as if they are ceremonial.

'It'll warm you up,' she says as she hands both officers a cup. They thank her, take a sip, before setting the mugs down on the table. She looks to my father for approval, finds it in a curt nod of his head. DS Gray turns to me as my mother takes up position alongside Jess.

'All I'd like to do is pose a few simple questions, see what you can recall and what we can jog back into memory, OK?' I nod again and he smiles, flashing a set of crooked, stained teeth. DC Barclay seems to be noting down my every move, her pen scribbling frenziedly even when I'm not saying anything to warrant it. I try to keep still, avoid giving anything away. I realise I'm thinking as if I'm guilty. 'So, I'll start by asking if you can remember anything about the lead-up to the crash: where you were going and what you were doing on Ditchling Road.'

I try to think of Brighton and the roads I must have driven around time and time again. I think of our trip back from the hospital, know there was nothing that seemed familiar on that day. I only know what my father has told me: that I left this house desperate and upset. 'No, I'm sorry. It's like I said, DS Gray, I really don't remember anything.' I can feel my head pulsating, the throb of my brain against my fractured skull.

'You don't remember if you were upset or angry when you got in the car? I need to try to establish your mood, the conditions leading up to the crash.' He flicks through his notepad. 'Your father told me that you left here sometime after seven in the evening. Is that correct?'

'If that's what he said, then I suppose so.'

'And you can't remember where you were going? What kind of mood you were in?'

'Um . . .' I hesitate, glancing across at my father standing behind the officers with one arm on the fireplace. He shakes his head almost imperceptibly. I know what he wants from me. Silence. 'No,' I tell DS Gray. 'I'm sorry.'

'Do you remember anything about a second car?'

'No, I don't think so.'

'Whether it hit you or not?'

'No.' I bring my left hand up to my head, give my temple a rub. I'm struggling to find the words. The questions are coming too fast. The memory of driving recklessly on that night flies into my mind. I watch DC Barclay's tapping foot. I can't keep up. Tick, tick, tick go the seconds, slowing to a painful pace. I can hear her pen scratching against the surface of the pad.

'Everything all right, Chloe?' My father's voice. I nod, my eyes down. Jess edges alongside me, squeezes my right hand, but I don't grip it back. You're a liar, I think as I glance at her. You knew I had a son and said nothing. She smiles, but my face doesn't change. You're all liars, I think again.

'Chloe?' asks DS Gray.

'I'm fine.' I look up at him, then to DC Barclay. 'I'm really sorry that I can't be more helpful.'

DS Gray pauses for a sip of his tea, and DC Barclay takes over. 'Do you remember if you went anywhere between leaving here and arriving at the site of the crash?'

'I don't know.' I think of the flashback, of me driving in the rain. Where was I going? Was I crying? I feel like I was crying.

'And what about Damien Treadstone? Does that name mean anything to you?'

'No.' I answer fast. She makes me nervous, as though I

need to get this over with. Damien Treadstone isn't a name I know. But then again, when I woke up I couldn't even remember my own name. 'Who is he?'

'Damien Treadstone is the registered keeper of the second car found at the scene. He has been charged with dangerous driving. There is evidence to suggest he was trying to overtake on a section of the road where it would have been clearly dangerous to do so.' Her foot continues to tap and my heart beats faster and harder. I feel sick.

'What sort of evidence?'

'Tyre tracks, paint transfer from his car to yours. He is currently out on bail and denies all charges. But he hasn't got an alibi for his whereabouts that night. That's why it's so important we get your version of events, Chloe. Your testimony could make all the difference. He would have been driving a black BMW 3 Series sedan.' She waits for me to think. I reach for a tissue, wipe my eyes as I shake my head. 'There's no doubt that his car hit yours. If you could remember anything at all, it might really help our case.'

I can feel a lump in my throat, the bruising inside me swelling and choking. 'I don't know him, or anything about what happened.'

'And you're quite positive that you didn't have any sort of relationship with Mr Treadstone prior to the accident?'

'What sort of relationship?' my father asks, incredulous. They both ignore him.

'I don't even know who he is,' I tell her.

She reaches inside her pocket and hands me a photograph. It's a mug shot, a young man, bleary-eyed, with messy hair. I hand it back.

'I don't know this man.'

'And you can't tell us why you were driving along the Ditchling Road that night?'

'No.'

She takes a sharp breath in, lets it go. The fire crackles. 'Are you sure you're not keeping anything from us, Chloe? Protecting somebody?'

All at once my father steps out in front of her, putting a blockade between me and the police. Jess hugs me close as I begin to cry. I don't push her away; I welcome the comfort. I'm crying because DC Barclay is right. I am protecting somebody. Myself.

'I think that's quite enough,' my father tells the officers. 'Can't you see what this is doing to her?'

'OK, let's leave it there.' DS Gray stands up, turns to his partner, who puts her notebook away. They both appear annoyed. She's nursing a dissatisfied look, the corners of her mouth turned down in a frown. She has skinny lips, the kind that are particularly good at expressing distaste; she can't hide how much she hates me, how little she believes the things I say. 'I'm sorry to have to come here and go over everything like this, but the CPS is pushing for a prosecution, and anything you remember has the potential to be useful at trial.' He smiles at me, just enough to let me know that he is, in theory at least, on my side. 'It must have been a very nasty knock that you took.'

I sniffle back the tears. 'So they tell me.' Right now, my head feels like it is going to explode.

'Well, just focus on your recovery, but if you do remember anything I want you to let me know. Your doctor at the hospital told us that sometimes memory comes back in flashes, and over time. Really, Chloe, if there's anything at all you just give me a call at the station.' He hands me a card with his telephone number on it before he looks towards Jess, points a finger. 'You look after your sister now, won't you?' I slip the card in the pocket of the robe.

They turn to leave, walk through to the hallway. Just as I hear them arriving at the door I push myself out of the chair to hurry after them. Jess follows, anxious to stop me. By the time I reach the hallway DC Barclay is already outside, shrouded in fog and standing on the driveway. DS Gray is just moving through the front door.

'DS Gray,' I call, and he stops, turns back towards me. I feel the cold air hit, waking me up, drying my tears. 'Can you tell me anything about him?'

He closes his lips tight, let out a breath through his nose. 'Damien Treadstone?' I nod. 'Twenty-eight years old. Medical rep. Married. Not from around here. Lives in Maidstone, Kent.'

'Does he have children?'

He looks away, considers whether to tell me or not. He seems like he cares, like he doesn't want to cause me unnecessary pain. 'Yes. A son, two years old,' he tells me.

After they leave my father comes back through to the lounge, loosening his tie, letting go of the tension in his breath. My cheeks are warm from the fire, yet still my body feels cold. The name Damien Treadstone rolls around my head, a mixture of anger and sadness. Whose fault was it? Mine, or his?

My father sits down on the arm of the sofa, looks to my mother, who is sitting with her hands in her lap, not saying anything. 'That went very well, I think,' he suggests, and she nods her head like a dutiful dog. I realise I know, sadly, that of course she would do that. Jess was right. It's not easy between them, never was, my father always in control. He looks to me before setting a heavy hand on my knee. I glance up at his face, find him smiling, relieved, as if the worst of it is over. He winks at me, buoys me up with a quick squeeze. 'That was a very good start, Chloe.'

That night dinner is silent, the minced beef and mashed potato of a tasteless cottage pie sticking in my throat. Nobody is sure what to say, and every mouthful makes me feel sick. All I can think about is that I had a life I can't remember, and the people who should be helping me have done nothing but lie to me about it. They tried to keep my past a secret. How can I trust them with my future if I can't even trust them with the things that have already happened?

Mum begins clearing away the plates, her hands shaky and her focus lost, something I'm starting to see as normal. She knocks back the rest of her wine under my father's watchful eye before leaving the room, slightly off balance, the wine going straight to her head. She's been edgy ever since the police were here, her eyes darting all over the place, unable to settle. Jess too is up on her feet, helping with the napkins and place settings. They don't want to be around me, I realise, so they don't have to explain themselves. They are embarrassed, I think, guilt-ridden. Seconds later I am alone with my father.

'I know you are still angry that I kept the truth from you, Chloe.' I give him a sideways glance, lost for words. Still angry? Does he think it's that simple? I am experiencing every emotion right now. I don't even know how I feel. 'But please, do try to see it from our perspective. It was a terrible situation for us to be in.' He settles back in his chair, slips off his glasses. His other hand taps at the table. 'You must learn to forgive us, Chloe, so that we can help you move on. After all,' he adds, and this time I notice that his mouth curls up into a strange, affected smile, 'we are the only family you've got left.'

9

It is a horrible thought, the idea that this is it, that there is nothing else for me now. Have I lived the life I was due, destined from here on to linger in some sort of purgatory?

My father is still waiting for an answer, nibbling on the frame of his glasses. 'It's not just that you didn't tell me about them, Dad. It's the fact that even now, even though I have seen their pictures, even though I know they existed, they still don't mean anything to me.'

I have been trying ever since I first found out to remember something about our life as a family. The sound of Joshua's cry, the smell of his freshly washed skin. The feel of Andrew's hand on mine. But I can't recall anything. Even the things I think might be memories, like the image of me standing in church holding a bible, won't come into focus, won't reveal my son as an element of my past.

My father raises his eyebrows, slips his glasses back into place. 'Time, Chloe. Time is a great healer. And with time you will also begin to remember them.'

'I hope so.' It is obvious that time can work wonders; you only have to look at my physical condition for that. I am still a mess, with scars decorating my body, and according to my neurosurgeon, an ongoing risk of seizures and cognitive impairment for at least another two years. But time has allowed me to walk again, talk coherently, and leave the hospital. Still, I know none of these things would have been possible without some sort of intervention. If I am to remember, I must do something to help myself rediscover my old life. And I must do it not only for me, but for Joshua; only by revealing the truth of the life I lived before will I know whether or not I intended to crash my car. Whether I killed my son. 'But Dad,' I say, 'I feel like I need to be doing something towards getting well. I can't just sit in this house for the rest of my life.'

He tops up his wine, takes a sip. He seems relaxed. 'I totally agree, which is why you have a physio appointment tomorrow. Plus we can sit down together for another therapy session and see if you can remember anything more about your life. About your boys.'

I take a deep breath, knowing he isn't going to like what I have to say. 'It's not just physio or talking I need, Dad. I need to remember the past, and to do that I need to revisit it in any way I can.' He folds his arms across his chest as a light breeze skirts past the curtains. The fire crackles. 'I want to go home. To *my* home, Dad. Even if it's just for one day.'

He slips his fingers underneath his glasses, pushes them against his eyes to pinch away the tiredness. 'We have discussed this before, Chloe.' He takes a heavy breath in. 'Several times in fact.'

'I know we have. But you don't seem to understand how much it would help me. All I have from my house are the clothes you packed.' I pull with disgust at the twee grey cardigan I am wearing. 'It's as if I don't have a life of my own any more. I feel so alone, Dad.'

Since I discovered that I was once married with a child he has begun to tell me more about my life. He has told me how I studied law in London, and that afterwards I went on to work for a charity helping people with addictions; how I used to swim in the sea all year round. But none of these details feel real. They are elements of a life that no longer belongs to me. I can't go back to work, or head to the beach and dive beneath the waves. They are both lovely ideas, but untouchable, intangible. I need to understand who I was, and who I still am. Discover what part I played in this mess.

'I feel so unconnected to my own family. I need to go back,' I continue.

'We're your family,' he says. But he knows it is pointless; his words trail off into nothing and he reaches across the table towards me, takes one of my hands in his. 'Chloe, we must try to focus on the future.' It is his work voice, the sound of a stranger. This is how he speaks to me when I lie back on the couch and let him into my mind. It's the kind of voice that might soothe your pain as he roots around inside your skull. 'You'll begin to do that here with us.'

'But I can't remember anything,' I tell him. 'I need to go there. Don't you want me to remember my son?'

He brings his hand up to my face and smoothes the back of his thumb across my cheek. The pressure sends a shooting pain up into the wound on my head. 'I want you to think about this.' He speaks slowly, his words drawn out, cautious

as an animal coming out of hibernation. 'Have you considered how you might feel if, when you return home, you are
still unable to remember Joshua? What then?' I sit motionless, unsure how best to respond. 'At the moment you are
able to excuse yourself this failing, based on a subconscious
belief that the accident has resulted in huge gaps in your
memory. But what about when you see the place in which
you lived together? In which you bathed him, nursed him,
cared for him while he was sick. What if he still means
nothing to you then, what would you do? How would you
feel? I'm only trying to protect you, Chloe. You are very
fragile. We need to give things time.'

At that moment my mother enters the room carrying an
apple pie. The sweet smell seems out of place. Jess is behind
her holding four bowls and a tub of stracciatella ice cream,
whistling a tune that seems too cheerful for the mood of
the room. They realise something is up the moment they
walk in.

My mother looks nervous as she sets the pie dish down,
edging a small candle out of the way. She nibbles on her lip
and tries hard not to look at either of us. Jess hangs back,
lingering in the doorway.

'What's going on?' Mum asks eventually.

'Nothing for you to worry about, Evelyn.' My father pulls
a handkerchief from his pocket and offers it to me. I realise
I am crying, but still I don't take it.

'She's upset,' my mother says, still without looking at me.

'It's nothing.' He reaches for her arm, encourages her to
sit. 'She wants to go to her house. She'll be fine in a moment.'
He turns to me. 'It just wouldn't be a good idea. Not yet.'

I should have expected this answer. Still, I have to find a way to move forward, so I try something else. 'Maybe you're right,' I say. 'Maybe going to the house is a risk. But I can't just sit here like nothing has happened. I have to do something. I have to acknowledge they're gone. At least we should start organising the funerals. We can hold them here in Rusperford. They can be buried in the churchyard. Close to where I grew up.'

My mother stops slicing the pie before she's even finished with the first cut. Jess sets down the bowls and sits quietly in her seat.

'Please, Dad,' I say. 'I have to start doing something practical. It will help me to accept things, start to move forward.' I'm not even sure he hears me. Instead he just stares at my mother, a light shake of his head. She looks down into her lap. Her hands are shaking as if she is nervous, as if she has done something wrong. 'Dad,' I say, reaching forward. He turns sharply at the feel of my touch. 'Tell me where their bodies are being held so that I can start making plans.'

The mention of the bodies shakes my mother. She sets down her wine, reaches for the table to steady herself. My father turns to me, his face calmer.

'Chloe, you have been very unwell. You had a bleed on the brain. It's just not a good—'

'But they were my family. My son. It's my responsibility.'

Jess pushes back her chair, hurries from the room. 'Where are you going?' my father asks her, ignoring me. 'Jessica, you haven't been excused.' He leans across the table to get a better look as she flees through the hall. 'We haven't finished eating,' he calls.

'Oh Thomas,' my mother cries. 'Just tell her.' She is on her feet, her voice desperate. 'Just put an end to this, for goodness' sake. I can't stand it. I can't, I'm telling you. I'll break if it goes on much longer.' She starts to cry, her face red as blood rushes to her cheeks, her chest rising and falling so fast she is practically hyperventilating.

'Evelyn, I . . .' my father tries, but he is lost for words. He brushes his fingers clean, then sets down his napkin before guiding Mum into her chair. When he tops up her wine, she swallows it down. 'It's OK, Evelyn,' he says, his voice controlled, ordered once more. Work voice again. 'Just relax. Really, it's OK.'

She starts to mumble something, then looks up at me. 'I'm so sorry, Chloe.'

But it isn't her apology I want. I want to know what it is she is urging him to tell me. I want to know what my father is hiding from me. 'What should he tell me, Mum?'

'Chloe, not—'

'No, Dad.' A lucent glimmer of sweat washes slick across his brow. I take one more look at Mum but realise she is terrified, although I'm not sure of what. My father, or the truth? 'What did she mean, Dad? Whatever you tell me can't make things any worse.'

'Very well,' he stammers, his voice croaky. My mother rests her head in her hands, elbows on the table. 'Chloe, you can't begin to organise the funerals because they have already taken place.'

10

I am stunned and numb; I have no words. They have taken from me the last opportunity I had to honour my family. They are not only dead, they are now gone. Forever. It is over.

'We wanted to wait, wanted you to be there, but it was touch and go. We thought we had lost you too. They told us to go ahead, to prepare for the worst.' Now tears well in my father's eyes, threatening escape. They mirror my own. 'But I promise we can reconsider a visit to your house in a month or so. Once you're up to it. Come on now, Chloe,' he says as he reaches for my hands. 'Say something, won't you? Try to understand.'

Instead I stand up, walk from the table. The burning wood snaps at my heels as if it too wants to snare me back in. Shadows flicker up the walls. I walk towards the front door, open it without a sound, slip into the thick mist that has descended upon the house since the earlier rains passed.

I push through the fog, my scarred right leg burning with every step, winding along the driveway until I reach the edge of the graveyard that backs onto the front of our property. The soft grass is wet under my feet, leaving a residue on my trainers. Tombstones rise up ahead of me, grey lumps of rock shrouded in ivy, tinged black in places by the blush of moisture from the evening air. Are they buried here? Will I be able to find them? How is it possible that I missed my own son's funeral? But as I go to search for their names, I come up against the perimeter fence. In my desperation to leave, I had forgotten that I am enclosed on all sides.

I hear the boom of my father's voice coming from behind me, the rush of feet along the driveway. I inch away, staggering further into the mist as I weave in and out of a border of giant oak trees, desperate to avoid the two torch beams as they skip across the ground.

'Chloe!' I hear him call.

'Chloe!' my mother repeats. 'Where are you?'

I crouch behind a tree, wait for them to pass, their forms grey shadows in the distance. I am cold and shivering, the skin on my arms goose-pimpled and wet. I know I will have to go back to the house, but how can I when they have told such lies? How can I remain a part of their lives when they buried my son without my knowledge? When they took away my chance to say goodbye.

I turn when I hear something behind me, some movement through the wet grass coming from the direction of the church. At first I take it for a rabbit, or a fox, snuffling along the ground. But then I hear it again, footsteps too heavy and slow for a light-footed animal. It is a person, but it isn't my mother or father. The sound is coming from the other side of the fence, and I can see the faint glow of my parents' torches still a distance away.

'Chloe?' A male voice. Somebody who knows me. I stand

up, back away against the nearest tree. Fear grips me, makes my stomach turn. I look left and right but see nobody there, only the wispy tips of the churchyard willows dangling through the mist.

'Who's there?' I whisper. The trees answer first, their branches shivering against each other, rocked by a light wind. I feel raindrops misting my face. Then I hear the voice again, soft and cautious.

'I have to talk to you, Chloe.' I cling to the tree, the bark rough against my skin. 'Please don't be frightened.'

It's too late for that. 'I can't see you. Who are you?' I move towards the fence, and as I do, I see a hand stretch out and a figure steps forward, closing the gap between us, his face still in shadow. But then torchlight flares left and right, following the sound of my voice, and the stranger pulls back, disappearing into the mist.

The sound of urgent footsteps comes quick against the gravel as my parents rush up the driveway. Seconds later I feel my father's slippery grip taking hold of my arm. My mother is only a couple of steps behind.

'Oh God, Chloe. Look at you.' He grabs my face, his fingers investigating my head wound, turning my chin left and right. 'Who were you talking to? Are you hurt?' He whips off his jacket, draping it about my shoulders. My head feels set to explode.

In the distance I hear a car engine rev into life, the scuff of tyres on the road. I push past my father just in time to see the faint blur of two red lights, like smudges of water-colour paint. But my parents hold me firm as the car pulls away.

Who was that? What did he want?

'Get her inside,' my mother says, her voice close to panic. 'Quickly, Thomas.'

'Somebody was here,' I tell them, looking over my shoulder as they hurry me back towards the house, ushering me like a prisoner.

We erupt into the hallway and my father slams the door shut behind us, setting the security chain in place. Rain strikes the window. Upstairs, Jess's music is playing. I catch sight of my face in the mirror, my lips tinged blue, my hair stuck in damp clumps to my cheeks. My sodden hat drips from my mother's clasped hand. They push me to sit on the bottom step of the stairs as a crack of thunder splits the sky.

My mother pulls off my wet muddy shoes and runs to the living room, returning a moment later with a thick tartan blanket. My father pulls his wet jacket from my shoulders, showering me with ice-cold droplets. 'There was somebody in the graveyard,' I tell him again. 'A man, he knew my name. He knew me.'

'Don't worry about that now,' he says, shaking his head, his wet shirt stuck to his skin. He rubs at my arms, still surveying me for injury. 'It's just the churchyard. It's given you the creeps, that's all. There was nobody there.' But despite his insistence, I know that isn't true.

My mother sits down next to me and pulls me close, wrapping the blanket tight around my shoulders. She hands me a tot of something strong and I knock it back. Brandy, I think, as the heat chases down like fire to my stomach. She rocks me, tries to calm my nerves. And the way she holds me, the way I can feel the movement of her chest as she breathes; it's like being a child again. In that instant I remember falling down the stairs, breaking my ankle. I can even see the spot where I landed, the small break in the balustrade that was a result of the impact. On that day she cradled me in her arms just like she is doing now while we waited for my father to come home. The accident wasn't her fault, but still it happened in her care, and she accepted the guilt of responsibility, bore the weight of my father's judgement.

As I look at her face now, I realise there is something about the person who nurses you, who changes your nappy, who sings you lullabies before you are even old enough to know you're making memories. They imprint themselves on you, make their spirit part of your existence. Sometimes it is only a mother who can make things better. But with that knowledge comes an overwhelming regret: not only was I unable to save my own child, there is still, according to my father, a chance that I am the one who chose to end his life.

I turn to her, certain in this moment of maternal connection that she will listen, that she will believe me and understand. 'There was a man out there, Mum. He spoke to me.' But she just pulls my head into her body, holds me tighter still. 'He knew me,' I say, more to myself than anybody else.

'Hallucinations, Chloe,' my father says. Then: 'Why did you run off like that?' I feel his clumsy fingers needling at my shoulders, the left one still sore from the crash. 'We can help you through this, but only if you trust us. Isn't that right, Evelyn?'

'Yes, of course.' My mother tops up my brandy and I drink it down. 'It'll do her good,' she urges when my father tuts disapprovingly. Then she takes the glass and pours another shot, knocks it back herself.

'We'll talk more about this tomorrow,' my father is saying. 'Here, this will make you feel better, help you relax.' He hands me a tablet, and in my confusion I swallow it unquestioningly, with yet another glug of the brandy.

'But the car,' I tell them. 'I saw a car.' I look to my mother again, certain she will help after her display at the dinner table. She wanted me to know the truth, didn't she? Surely she wouldn't lie now. Not again. 'Didn't you see a car pulling away?'

'What car?' my father interrupts. 'There was no car. Tell her, Evelyn.'

My mother's left eye twitches, crow's feet extending towards her cheeks. She strokes my face, offers me a smile. My head is already feeling light. What was the tablet he gave me? 'No, Chloe,' she says, as calm as she can be. 'I didn't see any car.'

*You always said your parents were liars, that if they had
been truthful with each other it would have been easier from
the start. It was as if you thought they were to blame for
what you had become, as if there was some flaw that ran
through you, created by them, all the way down to a rotten,
decaying core.*

*But I disagree, Chloe, because without them you might
have become something else. Something I would have loved
less. I like your flaws, your needs, your weaknesses. They
complement my own. You smiled when I told you that,
but I came to realise that behind your smile, you were
hiding how you really felt. You pitied me, didn't you? You
thought me weak because I had accepted my own flaws.
You wanted to fight against yours, run away from who
you really were. You always hoped it would be different
for you.*

*But I never tried to hide anything. I told you over and
over how I felt inside. For me you had become something
palpable, a mass growing inside me like a tumour. No, that's
wrong. Like an organ, something necessary in order to keep
going. Something I never knew I needed yet couldn't live*

without. I could feel you in every heartbeat, every shiver of my skin. You became my life. My reason for being.

Without you I was empty.

I'm sorry that I said I wouldn't rest until I had ruined your life. I didn't mean it. It was just nonsense, I promise. I'm desperate, that's all, desperate for you. Doesn't love make you feel like that? Please try to forget that I told you I'd take everything you have. I didn't mean that either. Let's put all this nonsense behind us, start again. I'll forgive you too. I only want you to be happy. You told me you loved me once, and I know you still do. All we need is to be together. As long as you tell me that you are mine for ever, everything will be just fine.

11

After we've dried off, we settle down in front of the fire in the living room and my father tells me about the funerals. Simple affairs he says, the ashes scattered together from Brighton pier into the sea. A heartbreaking day. They tossed flowers into the waves, pink and purple gerbera daisies. Some yellow like the warmest sunlight. They will take me there, he promises, to say a proper goodbye. We'll take more flowers. Once I'm stronger. Once I'm ready.

He produces a simple gold band from his pocket and sets it down on the table. 'My wedding ring,' I say, picking it up, slipping it over my shaky finger. But I am quick to take it off again; it is strange to wear something to which I don't feel connected, though I get the briefest flash of what I think must have been my wedding day: Andrew in church, me walking towards him. My father takes the ring from me and I watch as he puts it on the mantelpiece.

'We'll just leave it here, and when you're ready, you can take it back.' He reassures me that soon enough the hallucinations will stop, that I will return to normal. I will feel better, he says. I will be able to move on. 'Now, Chloe, lie back on the couch. That's it, feet up.'

My mother is fussing around us, covering me with a blanket. My eyes are heavy, my head sore. I don't feel present. I am drifting again.

'Close your eyes and listen to my voice. I'm going to take you back. I want you to tell me what you can remember . . . Sorry, what did you say?' Is he talking to me? Did I say something? 'Yes, of course, Evelyn.' He's speaking to my mother. 'She's nearly asleep. Just stop your fussing and give me some space to put this right.'

That night I suffer a fitful sleep, my body fighting against the recurring dream. In it I am running through bushes, trees rising above me, searching a dense forest for Joshua. It is dark, approaching dusk, and at first I can't find him. A thorn catches at my head, tears through the skin. Rain washes into my eyes. And then all of a sudden he is there before me, lying on the ground blanketed in a layer of wet, sticky leaves. Moments from death. Blood covering his face. I see my car, crushed against a tree, as if I am reliving the accident at a distance, watching from afar as my son bleeds out into the rotting forest floor.

All night long I see the same thing, every time I close my eyes. It is the same dream as last night, but this time, when I wake up, something is different. It is as if I have brought the dream back with me over the threshold between sleep and wakefulness. I can still feel the chill on my skin, smell the rain. I can feel the tiny lacerations across my face and remember the way I sustained them when I fell into the undergrowth. Tonight it is as if what I see in my dreams is real.

I throw off the sheets, my head hazy, heavy like a hangover. Goose pimples shiver in waves across my body as I edge back the curtain and peek outside. Darkness stares back at me, interrupted by a street lamp near the distant church. The fog rolls along in the glowing cone of light like whitecaps breaking against a rocky shore.

I press a palm against the cold glass and streams of condensation rush away like liquid falling stars. Make a wish, I think, but what would I wish for if I could? My old life? Strange to wish for something I can't even describe. I have no idea what it was like; how it used to feel. Should I wish for a marriage to a man who my father tells me was a failure, who even before the accident I had decided to leave? I wonder if I should wish to become the person I used to be before the accident, but what's the good of that? She might have chosen to kill her son. I'm not sure I want to be her.

I grab an old robe of my mother's and wrap it around my body, slip my feet into a pair of her slippers. My leg feels better today, a little less sore than it did, as I creep downstairs.

I move past the front door, feel the draught as it sneaks through the frame, brushing at my bare ankles. I press down on the handle to my father's study, trying not to make a sound. As I am hit by the musty smell of old books, a memory jolts back to me, of sitting at my father's desk. School work on a winter's day, snow on the ground, a crow cawing. How things come back to you. How information can be triggered by just a smell.

I sit down in his chair, the leather cold against the back of my legs. The desk is old, like a captain's desk from an imperial ship. There is a monolithic statue to the side, glass, engraved with my father's name along the bottom. I read the inscription: *The Roberta Award of Excellence*. Next to it sits a picture of the four of us, the award in my father's hand. It seems familiar, although I'm not sure why. I stare at myself in the photo, my hair lighter, my face full and body curvy. I look along the bottom of the statue, find a date: just six months ago. My whole world has changed so quickly.

I turn on the computer and wait in the cool glare of the blue light. As I stare at my blurred reflection in the screen, I remember seeing myself in glass like this, a kitchen cupboard maybe, as I stand at a cooker warming up milk. A tartan settee somewhere in the background; the sound of a baby's cries. Me as a mother? My old home? It must be, but it remains heartbreakingly out of reach, just smoke from a previous life, a cloud.

A request for a password pops onto the screen. I try our names, lower and upper case and different combinations, but none work. I try the four numbers from the outside gate but that doesn't work either. I would try dates and birthdays if only I could remember them. When is my birthday? When was Joshua's?

'What are you doing?' His voice startles me. I peer over the screen to see my father standing in the doorway, leaning against the frame. He is dressed in a blue dressing gown with a red quilted trim, his hair all over the place, fresh from sleep. It is as if I have stumbled into the private life of a stranger, caught in a place I have no right to be.

'I'm sorry,' I say as I push myself to my feet. 'I couldn't sleep. I thought I'd mess about on the Internet.'

'Well, I'm afraid this computer isn't for messing about with.'

I nod, a hot flush of embarrassment spreading across my cheeks. Seeing him reminds me of the night before, a night that ended without a clear memory. What was that tablet he gave me? Did he start a therapy session just before I slept? It's a blur.

'I suppose you don't remember the day you managed to delete nearly all of my files?' he asks me.

'Really?'

'Yes. I lost a lot of work. You opened up an email, some-thing to do with Pokémon, if I remember correctly. It must have been a virus. I went ballistic,' he says, his eyes sheepish. The hairs prickle on the back of my neck, a memory I can't quite place. Just how furious was he? 'But I learned a valu-able lesson about backing up my work.'

'I won't try to use it again. I'm sorry.' I attempt to leave, a sudden urge to get out of the room. I step forward, but so too does my father, blocking my path with his oversized frame. He rests his hand on the chair. I have no choice but to remain where I am. He motions to the computer.

'Did you manage to get into it?'

'No,' I say. 'I didn't know your password.'

He swivels me around, his fingers digging into my clav-icles. The left one throbs. He edges me back into the seat.

'I'm disappointed, Chloe,' he says, pushing the chair forward, trapping me as the arms line up alongside the desk. He leans over my shoulder and reaches one pointed finger towards the keyboard. His beard tickles the side of my face, sends a shiver across my skin. 'You should have been able to guess the most important thing in the world to me.' I watch as he taps in the word FAMILY. 'There you go. But please, don't go rooting around in the documents. There are many confidential files in there, and it wouldn't be right for the patients under my care.' He gives me a pat on the shoulder, sending a bolt of pain down into my arm. The damp air is getting to the aches and pains that have set in since the accident. 'And whatever you do,' he adds with a wink, 'please don't open any emails.'

As he disappears into the kitchen, I open up Google. What am I hoping to find? Something about me, or something about the people lost to me? Something about the man who might have been responsible for killing my child? I start by typing my own name.

I get a mixture of results, most of which seem to spring from Facebook. There are a few people with the name Chloe Daniels, but I can't find any profile belonging to me. So instead I type in my sister's name, assuming she will have a profile and also that we would be friends. I search the list. No Chloe Daniels. But I do find my profile. My name is Chloe Jameson. Even the name I thought I had doesn't really belong to me. Something as simple as that and they kept it from me. But why wouldn't they tell me my married name?

And there is a picture: me with Joshua, exposed shoulders shiny against a blue sky. The intense blue gives me the impression I might have been on holiday when it was taken. It is recent, I think, judging by the fact that Joshua looks to be around eight years old, the age I know he was when he died.

I can't see much else on my profile because it seems I was a private person, most of it closed to strangers. I can't see my friends list, and only a handful of historical updates are visible. There are a few pictures of me, though, some with Joshua when he was younger; some of Andrew too. He looks fresh-faced, not at all like the drinker my father described. And we don't look like we were falling apart either. There is a picture dated only eight months ago, and we are together, smiling, and close. It is hard to imagine how behind those faces there are problems so severe that I wanted to leave my marriage. Leave him. Terrible enough that either of us would even consider taking our own lives.

My father walks back through with two cups of tea. He hands me one, then pulls up a chair and sits down next to me. 'What woke you?' he asks. 'The cold? More bad dreams?'

'I guess a bit of both.' I shiver as a draught winds in through the old window behind me, the curtains swaying as it brushes them aside. 'Why is it so cold in here?'

'Heating kicks in just after six thirty. Nobody is usually up at this time.' I look down at the computer, see that it isn't yet five o'clock. 'Care to tell me what was in your dream?'

'The usual stuff.' He folds his arms, waits for me to explain. 'The accident. I saw Joshua, lying on the ground. I couldn't help him.'

He takes a long breath. 'Perhaps that's my fault for telling you the details of what happened. Your mind has started working overtime, trying to piece together the facts. But don't worry about these dreams, Chloe. They'll pass. It is just the mind's way of trying to process everything you are learning. This is why we kept some of the details from you at first. It's a hard process of acceptance that you are going through.' He nods at the computer. 'Did you find anything interesting?'

Although I don't really trust him, don't know if I should be talking to him, he remains one of the only links I have to my past. Telling him might help me recall something important. 'I guess I'm looking for answers, trying to work out who I am. Or at least who I was.'

'You're the same person you were before, Chloe.' He nods his head. 'And did you find what you were looking for?' He peers over at the screen. 'Facebook? I didn't even know you had a profile.'

'Apparently I did. Chloe Jameson.' He doesn't react to that. 'I don't know the password, though, so I can't really see what I used to put on there. I'm just looking at some of the pictures, seeing if there's anything I can remember.'

'And?'

'Not much really.'

'Well, take your time. We'll get there.'

I look at the picture of me with Andrew, and then at my father. 'I'm not sure that I'll ever feel normal again. Normal for me was being married, being a mum. I can't go back to doing either of those things. I don't know what I'm supposed to be aiming for.'

'Life, Chloe. Work. The same as we all do.'

Something about his response gives me a surge of bravery. 'And what is my life like, Dad? Who are my friends? Why hasn't anyone got in contact with me from my past? What job do I do? I can't answer any of this, and you and Mum aren't exactly forthcoming. Being here just makes me more and more confused.' I can feel myself getting worked up. I know that somewhere in that Facebook profile there are answers, information that could fill in the blanks, yet it remains painfully out of reach.

'I told you about your job.' He pauses. 'You worked for the charity Fresh Starts. After your experiences with Andrew, you wanted to do something constructive. It's a rehabilitation charity. For alcoholics.' He drains his cup, sets it on the tray. 'But don't put undue pressure on yourself. I remind you again, it's all about time. In time I promise you'll feel better. But it's early for me. I think I'll get a bit more rest before I start the day. Don't tire yourself, eh?' He stands up, kisses the top of my head. But then he notices the picture of me with Joshua on the screen. Wrinkles form around his eyes as he smiles. 'What a lovely picture that is.'

I'm still smarting that as soon as I challenge him he makes to leave. But in this moment I can almost believe he is just a father trying to help a daughter he loves. 'I don't know where it was taken.'

'Well I can help with that,' he says cheerfully, as if this knowledge is such a simple thing. 'It's Brighton beach.' He points to a structure in the background, black lines that criss-cross each other and appear to stick right out of the water. 'That's the West Pier, the one that burnt down. We've got a picture of it in the hallway. The place where you are sitting is probably only a few minutes from your house.' He pats my arm and walks away.

A memory comes to me as I gaze at the photo. I see Joshua near the water's edge, smiling, a front tooth missing. *Look what I found, Mummy*, he says. Next he's in the sea, the gentle waves lapping at his ankles. He's pointing to something, a starfish, the edges blurry as I peer into the water. I wait for the turn in events, for him to head into the sea, to start struggling in the waves like he does in my dreams. But it doesn't come. This memory is just me with Joshua, something good. A happy memory.

'Dad, before you go.' He turns, one hand on the door frame. 'Do you think he knows where I am?'

My father edges forward. 'Who?'

'Damien Treadstone.' I see his jaw lock, his lips tighten, and he brings a hand up to stroke his beard. 'The driver of the other car.'

'I know who he is, Chloe. Is there some sort of issue?'

'Last night, I was sure somebody was in the graveyard.' He starts to protest so I continue quickly. 'They spoke to me, Dad. I keep thinking about it, and I'm sure I recognised the voice. Maybe it was Damien Treadstone. Maybe he tried to help me on the night of the crash. Maybe that's why I recognised the voice.'

He takes a shaky breath. I am making him nervous. 'If he'd tried to help you, Chloe, he would have called the police. You were found in the driver's seat of your car. You were unconscious, probably from the very moment of impact. I told you, what happened last night was almost certainly part of a hallucination.'

'Then why did it feel so real?' But it isn't just the voice. It's the dreams too, the sensation of being outside in the woods, my certainty that at some point I wasn't in my car on the night I crashed. Last night I dreamed of a car crumpled against a tree, me running through the forest looking for

Joshua. It all felt so real, so much more than a dream; it felt like a memory.

'OK, let's assume you're correct. Tell me why on earth he would come here looking for you.'

'Maybe he wants to convince me that he wasn't there at the time of the crash. That's what he told the police, isn't it?'

He shakes his head, looks away from me towards the window and the dark mist of the lingering night. 'Don't you remember that Dr Gleeson told us to expect hallucinations like these?' I can't remember any such discussion. 'There was nobody there in the graveyard. Don't you think I or your mother would have heard something if there was?' His voice softens. 'You wouldn't be the first person to see something that wasn't there after a bleed in the brain.'

'But I didn't just see him. I heard his voice.'

'Well, I'm no neurosurgeon, but if you can experience visual hallucinations, why not auditory?' He approaches, tapping the edge of the desk with his finger. 'Time, Chloe. Like I said. And plenty of sleep. You have to take things easy.'

I nod to reassure him. He gives me an appreciative smile and slips from the room. I watch as he ascends the stairs, his head low and shoulders curved in on themselves. He looks a hundred years old, the way he walks away from me.

After I hear his bedroom door close I turn to the keyboard, tap the name into the search box. There are plenty of Damien Treadstones in the search results, but the second image to be displayed is of a scared-looking man, no doubt the same police mug shot that DC Barclay showed me. I click on the link, wait for it to load.

The image comes into view: a brush of stubble, deep shadow rising into the pits of his cheeks, heavy eyebrows, dark circles under his eyes. His hair is a mess. I imagine him being dragged from bed as an officer reads him his rights, another cuffing his wrists. This time something about him seems familiar, although I'm not sure what.

But Treadstone didn't make it to bed that night. I read how he was picked up in Brighton city centre a couple of hours after the crash, mud on his trousers, his car and keys lost. He had been drinking, was over the limit. He had no alibi that could prove his innocence. I continue to read, steel myself for the details: how I was found unconscious, how it was a race to get me to hospital, drifting in and out of life, how my son was found . . .

But I can't do it. I'm not ready for a retelling. I don't want the gory details, or to face the reality of being truly alone just yet. I shut down the computer and stand up to leave. Then, as I push back the chair I knock into a pile of magazines, sending them tumbling to the floor. I lean down to pick them up, shuffling them back into order.

And there on the desk, hidden beneath periodicals and printed articles, I see an envelope sticking out. It is addressed to me, a house in Brighton, the letter torn open and crumpled and without doubt already read. I pull it out, see the details emerging before me, feel my breath as it catches in my chest.

It is a letter from Damien Treadstone's lawyer. They are calling me as a witness for his defence.

12

I toss and turn after that, my feet agitated and trapped in the sheets. At some point I must have dozed off because I wake to the sound of the front door closing a little before 8.30. I glance at the picture of me with Andrew and Joshua that I have propped up on the bedside table. I cross to the window and look down, see my mother heading to the car, calling to Jess. Again, I wonder where they are going.

A pale light bleeds through the windows and into the hallway as I walk downstairs. I can hear the crinkle of newspaper in the living room, the snap of a young fire, of splitting wood, the fizz of moisture. I'm not sure it will take. My father must hear the shuffle of my feet, because when I arrive in the doorway he is already folding up a copy of *The Times*. Outside, an echo of thunder rumbles through a ceiling of low grey cloud.

'You're still here?' I ask, the smell of burning wood rich in the cool air. 'I thought you'd have gone to work by now.' I sit down on the chair closest to the fireplace, the heat of the fire sharp against my bare feet.

He sets the paper down on the settee and flashes me a smile. His cufflinks catch in the overhead light, the ones with rubies that he wore when the police came. 'I have the day off. Your mother and Jess had some errands to run, so I thought it would be nice for us to spend the day together.'

'Where have they gone?'

'Brighton.' Thoughts of my house come to mind, the imageless place I once called home. Do my mother and sister go there? I try to visualise the seafront, the broken mental snapshots I took on the way back from the hospital when my father drove us along the promenade to breathe in the clean sea air. 'Jessica needed some books for next term.' He shakes his head, as if he is confused. 'How she can find chemistry such an interesting subject I'll never know. I absolutely hated it.'

I pull my robe across my knees. 'It would have been nice to go with them. All of us together.'

He peers at me over his glasses, a crease forming between his eyes. 'I don't think you are ready to go to Brighton, Chloe. It's not a safe place for you at the moment.'

I snort. I'm feeling brave today. Like I've nothing left to lose. 'What, and here is?'

For a moment he is silent, shocked. He rubs his right hand over the knuckles of his left. 'You don't feel safe?'

I have been thinking about that a lot since I saw Damien Treadstone's picture earlier this morning, the summons to take me to court. And my conclusion is that no, I don't feel safe. But not because he was here, or because he wants my help with his case when it goes to court. Rather why he was there on the night of the crash in the first place? Why were either of us there? And perhaps even more than that, why the hell didn't he help me? I know my father wants to explain what I heard in the graveyard as a hallucinatory moment of confusion, but after seeing Damien Treadstone on the screen, knowing he has been released on bail, I don't think I am wrong. He was here, wanted to talk to me, and I'm starting to doubt that it was a coincidence he was on the Ditchling Road on the night of the crash. I have to find out what he was doing there.

'No, Dad, I don't. I wasn't hallucinating the other night. Someone was in the graveyard, I'm sure of it.'

My father smiles, shakes his head. He moves over to the fireplace, grabs a poker to give a large glowing log a nudge. Flames flare red and bright, wood burns orange. I look up, notice my wedding band still sitting where he left it. Should I be wearing it?

'There was nobody outside, Chloe.' He leans one arm against the mantelpiece, sure of himself. 'I don't know why you are so convinced that—'

'Because I heard him, Dad.' I can't let him finish. How can he be so certain? 'And I saw him too. I wasn't hallucinating.'

He sets the poker down and sits. He sets his hand on my knee. I feel the scar on my right leg pull painfully tight, and in that moment, in that close proximity, some of my courage fails me.

'Chloe, he is not legally able to approach you. He is awaiting trial. It wouldn't be in his best interests.'

I reach into the pocket of my mother's robe, pull out the letter that I took from the study. I hold it out and he takes it from me. He unfolds the wrinkled sheet of paper and takes a cursory glance at it before hanging his head, resting it against one of his hands. He doesn't need to read the letter in order to know what it says.

'Where did you find this?'

'Does it matter? They are calling me as a witness. Why didn't you tell me?'

'We didn't want to worry you.'

'Worry me? Dad, are you kidding?' I am shouting, almost in a panic. I can't understand him. I don't remember much about being a lawyer, but I know you can't just decide to skip court when you are supposed to be giving evidence. 'What were you going to do when the trial started? Not tell me? I don't have a choice whether I go or not. It's not an invitation I can choose to decline.'

'I know.' He shakes his head and lets the letter drop to the floor. It flutters in the waves of heat radiating from the fire. 'I'm sorry.'

But his answer isn't good enough, and that knowledge makes me feel unstoppable. 'Damien Treadstone knows I can't remember what happened that night, and his lawyers think that if they can break me in court, the case will fall apart.' He doesn't say anything and I know he is thinking the same thing, which is probably why he chose to keep quiet. 'They'll ask me if I can remember him being there, and if I am telling the truth I will have to say that I can't.'

'We don't know what they are planning yet.'

'Yes we do, Dad. It's obvious. He's insistent that he didn't do it, and if I can't prove otherwise he'll get away with it, won't he?'

My father is breathing deeply; he seems irritated. Those moments of fear that I have felt in his presence have left me. But my certainty doesn't come without a stark reminder that there is a strong possibility I am to blame for all of this. That it was my choice to crash. My intention.

'And you know what I keep thinking? Why shouldn't he be cleared? Neither of us really knows what happened that night, so why should he pay for a crime if it wasn't his fault? You said yourself the police wondered whether I crashed on purpose. If I had intended to commit suicide, it would be unthinkable for Damien Treadstone to be held responsible, don't you think? I wish I had just died that night and got it over with, whether it was my intention to or not.'

He falls to his knees in front of me. His grip is so tight I flinch. His flailing foot knocks the letter dangerously close to the fire. 'Don't you ever say that. I won't allow it. It's a miracle you survived.' He pulls insistently at my arms. 'You have been given another chance, Chloe. Don't throw that away.'

'A chance without my husband and son,' I remind him.

'I've told you before, it wasn't all roses before the accident.' He lets me go. Just the mention of my husband is enough. Did he hate him that much? His breathing has quickened too, his voice raised. He stands upright, hands on hips. 'You don't remember, but it's been me covering your mortgage for the last eight months. We've been scrimping and saving to make sure you didn't lose your home, Chloe. Andrew skittered from job to job, leaving you to try and hold things together. He hadn't worked for the best part of a year, and you couldn't do it any more. Everything about your marriage was a disaster. You're better off without him.'

He sets his hands on the mantelpiece, braces himself against the edge. He has worked himself into a frenzy, years of accumulated rage. His shoulders are crumpled, his breaths staccato and quick.

He speaks slowly, yet still his words are tinged with anger. 'I know you think you must have loved him, Chloe, but Andrew was a drunk. He couldn't be trusted. I will not let you sit here wallowing in misery over a man who treated you so badly.'

'Are you forgetting that he also gave me Joshua? Didn't you love your grandson?'

He closes his eyes. When he speaks his voice is quiet, subdued, but somehow that unnerves me more than if he was angry. 'Of course we loved Joshua.'

'Then you should be grateful to Andrew, not happy that I can't remember him.'

Still he can't look at me. 'Chloe, please try to understand.'

'No, I won't.' I'm shaking, my voice trembling. 'I must have loved my husband.'

'No you didn't!' he shouts. He sweeps his hands along the mantelpiece. Two candlesticks and a vase of flowers crash to the floor, glass and porcelain smashing into pieces.

I am overcome with an urge to run down the garden, to the old mill. It's instinct, muscle memory; that's where I used to go, I realise, when I couldn't be here in this house, when my parents used to argue. His burst of anger has brought the memory of fleeing to the surface. But this time I go nowhere. I stay, stare at my panting father, his eyes rage-wide and pupils tight.

'You didn't love him, Chloe,' he says. 'You wanted to get

away from him, but you failed, and now look where we've ended up. I don't want you to suffer this tragedy for the rest of your life. Let Treadstone pay so that people don't see the real reason why Joshua is gone.'

'What do you mean, the real reason?' He turns away. Again there's the implication that I'm to blame. Mistake upon mistake resulting in my child's death. 'We don't know what happened that night. How can you insinuate that we should let him take the blame, as if I'm the one who caused Joshua's death and he's just a scapegoat? Nobody knows what happened. How could you make out it was my fault?'

He looks at the floor. Then he looks back to me, his face unflinching as he speaks. 'Because it's the truth, Chloe. Your poor choices are what led us here. If you had left Andrew the first time round, Joshua might still be alive.'

He takes a step towards me and I lean away from him in fear. His face is bright red, his jaw tight and set. In that moment I am sure he is going to hit me. But at the last moment he shakes his head and storms from the room, leaving me shaking and alone next to a dying fire.

13

I listen to the phone ringing downstairs, shrill and loud, begging to be answered. Then my father's sombre muffled voice, an agreement of some sort. I hear him coming up the stairs, the wood creaking under his weight. He knocks on my door, opens it without waiting for a response.

'I have to go to work, Chloe. Something very important has come up with one of my patients.'

I don't answer, don't know what to say. I focus on the edge of the pillow, the floral lace trim. A few minutes later I hear the front door closing, and for the first time in days I am alone.

I go downstairs and find the letter from Treadstone's lawyer propped up on the bare mantelpiece, the weak fire still simmering behind the guard. I stare at the debris of my father's anger, swept into a pile at the side. I crouch, search around for my wedding ring, but I can't find it amongst the broken china and wilting flowers. I grab a coat and step outside.

The fog is liquid as I walk through the back garden, ever changing, as if the land is breathing. Several times I have to stop, uncertain where I am going as I head up the path towards the river. I've left the light on in the kitchen as a guide for my return, but as I look back now, I'm not convinced I can still see it.

I push on, past the paddock, and the stable block full of horses. After several minutes of walking blind, I reach the clearing in the woods where the trees thin out and the river-bank slopes gently down, submitting to the edge of the fast-flowing water, the only break in the perimeter fence.

I stand there for a while, watching as the current rushes along in front of me, submerged reeds floating like silk scarves on a breeze. The river is wide at this point, chopped in two by a weir. I was expecting to see the bridge that led to the old mill, but all that's left are the remnants, dangling rotting and green in the water. The rest of the wood is black, charred like the old logs from a fire. I get as close as I dare to the fast-flowing water for a proper inspection, concluding that it is no longer passable from this point.

I decide to follow the river, certain that there must be another point where I can cross somewhere further upstream. But as I move through the forest, memories begin to surface, stirred into existence by my shady surroundings. It's the moisture on my skin, the way my hair is sticking to my face, bothering at my eyes. I recall the night of the crash, can almost feel the smack of the branches in my face, the sharp edges of broken wood tearing at my skin as I pushed my way through. And the feeling I get is the same as this morning when I woke from the dream to the sensation of cold air and the taste of rain. That night is coming back to me, just like my father said it would. My dreams are not just dreams, but memories of the life I used to live. Of the night I lost my son.

A little further along, knitted into the greenish brown of the undergrowth, I find a dilapidated stile that forms the start of a public footpath. I climb over, picking my way through heavy growth and overhanging branches. The rush of the river slows, narrows like a diseased artery, just as somehow I knew it would. I tread carefully, picking my way across the stepping stones, my left foot slipping into the cold water as I fail to balance on the slimy surface of the rocks. I haul myself to the other side. It's less than a minute before I see the mill coming into view.

My eyes scan the crumbling walls, the old wheel, its green bottom half just breaking the surface of the water. It's in a state of disrepair so great that I am sure one false move could bring the whole thing tumbling down like a deck of cards. The smell of damp wood and algae greets me as I step inside. Water runs down the walls, pours through a hole in the roof. The upper floors are disintegrating, giving a clear view through to the sky. Rotten boards are scattered at my feet in angry disorganised piles. Plants grow out from gaps in the walls, and light shoots through like a maze of brilliant lasers.

I tread carefully, gripping the dusty surfaces of the huge metal gears as I pull myself along, and after some effort I arrive on the other side of the room, where the vertical shaft disappears above. Drips of ice-cold water strike my face as I look up towards the hole in the roof. It's dark and difficult to see, but slowly my eyes adjust to the low level of light ebbing through the canopy of trees. And there, right along-side the vertical shaft, is the thing that a distant memory told me I would find.

One corner of the floor is lined with old flour sacks, the faded imprint of Willow's Mill a nod to the previous function of this broken-down place. A dirty floral sheet is laid over them; a sheet that the old me took from my parents' home and brought to this place. The edges are tinged green with mould, the years of damp leaving watermarks across the rest of it. Despite how it looks, I duck beneath a thick wooden beam to take a seat, shuffle about to make a well for my body. And as I sit, I remember how this place used to feel to me, how I used to come here with Andrew. I remember him when he was no more than a boy, when he was my escape from the life I lived with my parents.

This was the place I ran to when I needed somewhere to hide. It is enclosed on two sides by external brick walls from which sections of mortar are now missing. The other two sides are bordered by giant wooden beams, creating an open box no bigger than a small double bed. On one of the beams sits an old knife and fork set that I stole from home, and next to that a blue plastic beaker. An old Pony Club badge clings to a splinter in the wood. An unopened carton of juice, the sheathed straw loose because the glue has dried up. I pick it up and turn it over, the expiry date from over ten years before. I place it back on the beam, alongside a faded unopened packet of crisps. The objects are a testament to my time here, just like the carving of my name in the wood of one of the beams. *Chloe Alice Daniels*. And alongside that I see two sets of initials, bound by a crudely shaped heart. *CD* and *AJ*.

When I was young, I used to send messages to Andrew to join me here. I was only fifteen when we met, but I can recall sitting here in the cold and damp, the security I used to feel when I nestled against him, my head resting on his shoulder. It was an escape from the shouting and crying and fighting at home. It was always so simple with him. Back then at least.

But now I know that I left him, a decision that resulted in his death. I have his blood on my hands, the taste of it in my throat.

14

I leave the mill and the ghosts of my past, head back towards the river. I cross, the mist still thick this close to the water, and begin to pick my way through the trees, push on towards the house. Everything is growing against me, so I double back, follow the easier path in the opposite direction towards the road, my plan to return to the house via the village.

As I emerge from the trees it is still, quiet, the villagers hibernating for the winter. I'm thankful for the solitude; I must look a mess, with twigs in my hair and leaves stuck all over my boots.

The only sound apart from my footsteps is a car behind me, the headlights on full beam, casting me in a strange yellow glow. The driver seems anxious, perhaps because of the weather, his speed too slow. I pick up my pace to get out of his way, but as he passes, I lose my concentration and slip off the edge of the kerb, twisting my ankle as I fall to the ground.

And a memory of my past momentarily descends over the present. I remember lying in a road like this, the grit of the tarmac beneath me, the screech of tyres as a vehicle sped away. I think I was in a park, the sound of a lawnmower revving in the distance. Hedgerows rising up all around me, the smell of roses carried on the heat and humidity of summer. Is this memory from the day of the crash?

I pick myself up and head back towards the house. But as I near the gate, with the oak trees peeping through the haze of fog, I stop. A man is fiddling at the latch, a briefcase at his side. He keeps pressing the buzzer over and over.

He turns when he hears me, greets me with a wide smile, all teeth and finely lined eyes, as if he has spent a summer at the beach. He reaches down to pick up his briefcase, the other hand up for a wave as he ambles towards me. He is underdressed for the weather, wearing a light jacket and a scarf draped casually around his neck. Even in my mother's thick woollen coat I am freezing.

'Hi,' he says. 'How are you?'

As he approaches, I realise it's the doctor who was here the other night, the one who works with my father and whom I met at the hospital once before.

'Hello again,' I say. 'Dr Thurwell, right?'

'That's right. I wondered if you'd recognise me.'

'You're the only person I've seen other than my family in the last week or so.' I offer him a smile. 'You were here the other night.'

'Yes. Your father and I often meet after work to discuss important cases. It's part of my training.' He pauses as I shiver from the cold. 'Chloe, if you don't mind me asking, just how long have you been out here? You look freezing, and very pale.'

'I went for a walk.' I look down at my wet clothes, a smear of mud on my coat. 'I fell over.'

He slips off his jacket and offers it to me, cautious and slow as if to demonstrate he poses no threat. Like somebody might approach a stray dog they were trying to help when they really didn't want to get bitten. 'I don't mean to speak out of turn, but I don't think you should be out here after everything that's happened.' He motions to my head. 'Why don't I give you a hand getting inside?'

It takes a while to remember the code for the gate, and I have to make several attempts before I manage to open it. We enter the gloom of the hallway, my face cold, my fingers blue. I hand him his jacket and he shivers a little as he threads his arms back into the sleeves. He has to rub his hands together in an effort to warm up, and I find myself doing the same.

His hair is short, a dark chestnut-brown, the curls picked out by the moist winter air. He is younger than I assumed now that I see him close up, probably not much more than mid-thirties. The cut of his suit reminds me of my father's: a classic fit, not too fashionable, designed to make him appear older than he is, more credible. He looks kind, with soft features, and there is something about him that I like, something reassuring. That same feeling he instilled in me at the hospital. His smile, I think. Maybe that's what it is.

He catches sight of himself in the mirror, pulls a face of mock-horror. He flattens out the kinks in his hair as best he can, running his fingers through the thick curls. I remain by the door, watching his movements. 'Is your father here?' he asks.

I shake my head. 'He's already left for work.' I hang the spare keys back on the hook, and throw my coat over the banister. 'About an hour and a half ago.'

He presses his lips together in disappointment. 'I just came from there. I thought he'd taken the day off.' I see him gazing at my cheek, scratched no doubt on a tree branch. Then he looks down, notices my hands. 'You've hurt yourself,' he says.

I hold out my hands, let him see. I can feel myself cast in his shadow as he inspects the damage, my small hands swallowed up in his. I look down at my palms, which are dirty with grit, two grazes on the heels that appear wet and weepy. 'And what about here? May I?' He lets go, reaches up to touch my chin. When I don't resist, he tilts my head back, lifts my hat. His touch is light and I feel the quickening of my heart as he moves in close.

'Does it look OK?' I ask.

'Your head looks fine, but we need to wash the wounds on your hands,' he says. I can smell his aftershave, something rich and spicy. I avert my eyes, aware of his proximity. He has another look at my hands, pointing to a small black lump near my wrist. 'That's a piece of grit. Come on, let me help you wash it out.'

We go to the kitchen and he turns on the tap, tests the temperature of the water. He guides my hands underneath, flicks out the dirt and debris as the warm water washes over the broken skin. I stare at my ring finger as his fingertips move over it, the place where a wedding ring should be. He takes a wad of kitchen roll and bandages it around my hands.

'It'll be fine,' he says. 'It's only superficial. But if you've got some antibacterial cream, it wouldn't be a bad idea to put a bit on the cuts.'

We exchange an awkward smile and he takes a step back, as if he realises he might have overstepped the mark. My cheeks feel warm, embarrassed. It isn't his presence that makes me feel that way. Not even his touch. It's my vulnerability, my reliance upon him. He's a relative stranger and yet I need his help; that's how little of myself I have left.

'I remember you from the hospital,' I say. 'You came to talk to me not long after I woke up. You asked me some questions.'

Does he remember? A little wrinkle appears on the left side of his face as he smiles, almost as if he's embarrassed. 'You remember that? Indeed I did. I came to complete an assessment.'

'But you're not a neurologist. Why did you have to come and see me?'

He looks away awkwardly, pushes his hands into his pockets. 'It was nothing, Chloe. We just wanted to see how you were feeling about everything, that's all.'

It takes a while to realise what he means, the pieces fitting together one by one. To understand the reason a psychiatrist would come to assess me. 'It was a suicide risk assessment, wasn't it? Because people thought there was a chance I crashed on purpose.'

He takes a big breath in, looks to the ceiling. His eyes meet mine. 'Yes,' he says quietly. 'But honestly, it was all just part of the process. I never believed that theory for a second.'

15

I sit down at the table while he dries his hands on a tea towel. When he looks up at me, his expression is sad. 'Chloe, I want to say how sorry I am about everything. I mean, really, I can't imagine what you must be going through.'

'Thank you.'

He shifts awkwardly, puts his hands in his pockets. I point to the briefcase that he set down next to the kitchen door. I don't want to linger on the past now, the possibility that what happened was not only my fault, but intentional.

'Did you want to leave something for my father?'

'Yes. He needs to review a set of notes ready for a departmental meeting tomorrow. He asked me to drop them off. He obviously didn't realise he'd have to go into work. Will he be back soon?'

'I've no idea.' I think of his anger this morning, not sure I even want him to come home. 'Do you want to call him?' He nods, reaches for his phone. 'You might as well use the house phone. You won't get any reception out here.'

I stay in the kitchen while he makes the call. After a few minutes he comes back in from the hallway.

'He'll be home soon,' he says. 'He asked me to wait with

you. I'm sorry, but I mentioned that you had slipped over outside, and . . . well . . .' He knows he has dropped me in it. 'I think he felt guilty that he went to work and left you here alone.'

'You don't have to stay if you have other things to do,' I say. 'I'm fine.'

He lets go of a heavy breath. 'You've had surgery for a bleed. Your father's right, if you hit your head when you fell, then—'

'Really, I'll be fine.'

But he shakes his head, pulls off his scarf, touches my arm briefly with gentle reassurance. 'I'm more than happy to stay.' He nods towards the kettle. 'I take mine with milk and one sugar.'

I boil the kettle and set out the mugs. It sparks a reminder of another kitchen, making tea for somebody else. Who was it there with me? Andrew, in our old house, while things were still good between us?

Dr Thurwell – Guy – must notice the difficulty I have with my coordination, because when the kettle clicks off, he gets to it first, helps me finish the job. I am grateful for the quiet, easy assistance, and we sit together at the kitchen table, where he tells me what he can about the risk assessment. He says that he knew it was a waste of time from the moment I spoke to him.

'I just knew immediately you weren't the kind of woman to crash a car on purpose. I was aware that you had fought your way back when all the odds were against you. I knew you weren't someone who would just give up.'

His words bring such relief that I can barely articulate it. But then a few minutes later my father calls, asks to speak to Guy. He is needed back at the hospital after all. He tells him to leave the notes on his desk and return as soon as possible.

I open the door to the study and we step inside, that familiar smell in the air, everything old and troubled by dust. I can feel it in my throat. Guy gazes around at the books, the piles of papers. He casts a look over the desk as he sets down the brown file, notices my father's Roberta award.

'I always used to wonder what people did with these after they took them home.' He picks up the glass trophy, then puts it back down as he notices the picture of me with my sister and parents next to it. 'Wow, look at you here,' he says as he picks up the frame, holds it with a smile. 'What a great photo.'

I reach across, take it from him, set it face down on the desk. I don't want him to see me like that. I don't want him to think of me now as a shadow, a lesser version of someone else. He looks embarrassed.

'I'm sorry,' I say.

'No,' he says, hands up. '*I'm* sorry. I didn't mean to upset you. It's just a lovely photo, that's all.' My hand is still on the frame, but he reaches towards it, momentarily rests his hand on mine. He wants to look again. 'May I?'

I let go of it and glance away as he gazes upon the face of the woman I used to be. After a moment he sets it back upright in the place it was before. 'It's a lovely photo,' he says. 'Don't worry. You'll get back to normal soon.'

'I hope that's true.'

'Of course you will. Your father will help you. He's an expert when it comes to memory. If anybody can help you, it's him.'

I sit on the edge of the desk. He is still looking down at the photo. 'An expert in memory?'

'Yes,' Guy says, surprised, as if I should have known. 'That's his speciality, if you like. Experimental psychiatry. In particular, memory and its formation. That's why he won this Roberta award a few months ago. He wrote a paper about the creation of false memories and how you could use them in the clinical setting to ease the burden of past traumas. He proposed that if you could provide somebody with an alternative history, just a few subtle changes, then the trauma would cease to be so debilitating. That actually the patient would learn to believe in the memory construct and eventually be able to leave the trauma behind.' He lets go of a breath. 'Amazing stuff.'

'That sounds like science fiction,' I tell him, still trying to process what he's said.

He laughs. 'Yes, only it's not. It's a proven fact. The mind does it all the time. Like when you lose your keys and you're so certain that you put them in one place, and then they turn up somewhere else entirely. The mind is malleable, Chloe. Open to suggestion. Your father hypothesised that by creating false memories under hypnosis, you could get a person not only to believe in something that had never happened, but also to forget something that actually had.'

'What?' A cold shiver runs down my arms. 'Hypnosis?'

'I know. He's quite a remarkable man. Anyway,' he says, 'I really should be getting back.'

114

He picks up his briefcase and heads towards the door. The hall clock shows he has been here for nearly an hour. He steps outside underneath the wisteria that clings wet and barren to the frame of the porch. The sound of falling rain intensifies; water pools in muddy puddles on the driveway.

'Listen, Chloe, your father said that your mother should be home soon anyway. You just get yourself back inside. It's freezing out here. But you need to give me the code to get out.'

I do as he asks then watch as he follows the driveway, pulling up his collar to protect his neck from the rain. After a while he turns back to face me, smiling, before he disappears into the fog. Seconds later the red lights of his car are disappearing into the distance. The chill is so strong it stings my eyes.

I close the door and walk to the living room, stare at the mess on the floor. I have never asked myself what exactly it is my father does at work. But memory specialist? Is it possible that he is using me as part of some strange treatment plan I know nothing about? I have to start taking charge of the things that are going on around me. I have to grow to be more than a remnant of the person I once was.

I start by picking through the broken china to find my wedding ring. I want it back, that connection to the old me, that woman in the photograph who was beautiful and radiant and who impressed people just by the sight of her. When I can't find it, I grab the letter from the mantelpiece and go to the phone to call Damien Treadstone's lawyer. I want to warn him that his client was here at the house, get it on record before my father organises another therapy session, tries to convince me it was all a hallucination.

I find it difficult to control the thoughts going round in my head as I stare at my old address on the letterhead. I can't remember the place that I used to call home. Can barely even picture it save for a few sporadic flashbacks. Why can't I remember the old me? My son? My husband? My life?

I dial the solicitor's number. A secretary picks up, tells me that Treadstone's lawyer is at lunch, unavailable. I leave a message asking him to call me back, giving her the number written on the base of the phone. Even as I hang up, I know he won't, and I wonder how bad it will look when this effort at contact is raised in court.

I gaze at my reflection in the hallway mirror. I notice a fresh drip of blood on my cheek, so I grab a tissue, push it up against the wound. The phone begins to ring. I snatch up the receiver.

'Hello?' I say.

'Is that Chloe?' A woman's voice. Nobody I recognise. 'I'm Alison, and I'd love to talk to you for a moment if you have time.'

Alison? Do I have a friend with that name? Does this voice belong to a person from my past? Nothing comes to mind.

'Are you calling me from the lawyer's office?'

She laughs. 'No, Chloe. I'm calling you from *The Argus*. I want to interview you for a piece we are running about you and Damien Treadstone, get your version of events regarding what happened that night.' I glance across at the magazine rack and see an old newspaper lying there, *The Argus* printed across the top. 'I thought you'd want to tell your side of the story. After all, it's only fair we give you the opportunity to speak to us before we write about your accident. Plus it's quite something for you to be called as a witness for the defense, when really you're the victim in all this.'

I hang up, or at least I try to, but I miss the telephone base and feel my legs go weak. My eyes fuzz over like they're suddenly filled with water. A trickle of blood creeps down my death-pale face. I'm going to faint, I think as I reach for the table. Seconds later I hit the deck, the last thing I see is the bloody tissue scrunched up in a ball on the parquet floor.

16

As I hit the floor the memory comes to me, my old life crossing paths with the new. Something jolted perhaps, knocked back into place. I am in my old house, my old bed. The sheets are cold, and I am alone. Early-morning sun is already creeping over the horizon, enough to light the room. Outside I can hear the frenzied gulls as they fight over the fish shoaling in the shallow water.

It is near the coast, a small house with two bedrooms and one large room downstairs that spreads into a neat kitchen and small dining room. I can see it now, the way the light catches the kitchen cabinets, that place I can recall warming milk. The rear window affords a slim view of the sea, framed between the walls of two other houses. And on that morning, the sky is on fire as the sun rises over the pier, bathing the water in a golden haze. It should be beautiful, but I have long stopped finding the beauty in such days; Andrew should be there. I have no idea where he is.

The floor is covered with a scattering of plastic toys and miniature cars. I collect some of them, toss them into a large wicker basket underneath the stairs. It was one such toy that led to the argument last night. Andrew stepped on one of the tipper trucks, the sharp edge cutting the underside of his foot. He stormed out, hasn't been home since.

Despite the early hour and the lack of sleep, I feel alert, wide awake, as I do most mornings. It is more a sense of vigilance than anything else, a little like a soldier asleep in a war zone, never sure if this is the day I will wake to find an enemy gun thrust in my face. Gladiatorial awareness from the second I open my eyes.

I get Joshua up and dressed. I watch as he performs his daily ritual, checking each room, under the beds, inside the cupboards. He never asks where his father is, not now. He just conducts his own circuit of the house, looking in each of the rooms. If he finds him in our bed it is a good day; on the sofa a cause for concern. When he can't find him at all, that's when he is the quietest.

We drive west along the seafront that morning, watch the waves rolling in to shore, gentle and submissive as they break under the pier. It is a call to swim, a glorious day, the sun painting the surface of the sea a brilliant white as it rises in the sky. The stucco hotels loom tall on our right, and the early holidaymakers are out walking on the promenade, serenaded by the call of gulls. I listen at the traffic lights to the tap, tap, tap of somebody hammering in a windbreak.

I drop Joshua at school and continue towards work. Piles of paperwork await me as I walk into the sweaty office at Fresh Starts, the heat of an early summer. I sit down, open the window as far as it will go, gasp at the cool air. I can smell grease and chips, the saltiness of the English Channel. I glance over at the others. George, one of my colleagues, waves at me. But nobody stops for a chat, or includes me in the office gossip. I keep myself to myself now. It's easier that way, limits the need for explanations. Everybody knows about my problems with Andrew. You can't share in the office gossip when you are the subject on everybody else's lips.

At lunchtime I slip out, grab a sandwich stuffed with pastrami from the Italian deli I go to every day. I walk down to the beach, peel off my summer dress to reveal a plain black swimsuit underneath, and step into the water, the waves lapping at my feet, comforting and calm. I breathe the sea air as I wade in further, the cool surface swelling around the soft stretch marks that appeared on the tops of my legs midway through my pregnancy.

Gulls circle overhead as I swim, the water washing against my face. It feels good, a relief from the humidity, the headache I have been nursing all morning beginning to relent. But the day is changing, a storm brewing out at sea that promises a downpour later, the clouds deep and grey on the horizon. I can feel it coming, the sky a little darker, the breeze a little cooler as I sit wrapped in a towel on the shore.

I like the changeability of the coast, the strength of the sea. It is a comfort to see the seasons change, feel the passage of time. Even on the coldest of days I bring Joshua here, both of us wrapped up in thick winter jackets. We sit on a bench where we can feel the spray from the water, sipping from a flask of hot chocolate, watching the relentless push of the waves. Andrew never comes with us.

'The world is always working on a new day, Joshua,' I told him once, on one of those days when I could feel the weight he carries on his shoulders. The weight of having a parent who drinks, who disappears for days at a time. 'Don't ever think that one bad day means the next has to be the same.'

He looked up at me and blinked, and a tear streaked down his freckled face. 'But every day is the same, Mama. Nothing ever changes.'

17

I wake to the sound of screaming, a shrill note of confusion and despair.

'Oh Chloe,' wails my mother, tears smeared across her face. 'What happened?'

In those first moments, I'm not sure. The dream of being with Joshua at the beach is still with me, so strong in my mind I can almost smell the salt water. It's my old life, right there, still lurking beneath the surface. It gives me renewed confidence that I must be able to remember other details about the person I used to be if only I try. But as I look up to see my mother's familiar red hair dangling over the telephone clutched against her ear, the past is gone, a memory turned to dust.

'Peter?' she cries into the phone. 'Peter, Chloe's hurt. She's bleeding. She's . . .' She pauses, and I imagine Peter – whoever he is – telling her to slow down. 'Well I don't know. How could I know that? Please just come and see her.' She is getting irritated. Desperate. 'Please, Peter. I can't get hold of him and I don't know whether to call an ambulance. He won't be back for hours. You have to come. Chloe, don't move,' she instructs. 'Lie back down. Peter's on his way.'

I recognise Peter as soon as he arrives. He's the resident doctor in Rusperford. It's the flushed cheeks and messy hair; I've seen him like this before. I remember that he once became the talk of the village after being suspended. He came to the house red-faced like now, demanded to speak to my father. I recall the two of them arguing on the driveway, my mother having to separate them before it ended in a fight. In the end, Peter left, shouting about it being my father's fault. I can remember my parents arguing about it afterwards, my mother telling my father that the allegations were false. Something about fraudulent prescriptions and misuse of opiates.

'Chloe, hello. How are you feeling now?' He removes the saturated tissue that my mother has been holding to my bleeding wound, before helping me to move through to the living-room couch. 'Do you remember what happened? Did somebody do this to you?'

I shake my head. 'I cut it while out walking. On a tree branch. I fainted, that's all.' I try to sit forward but find that everything feels fuzzy, my head a fug of delirium. I look up at my mother. 'A journalist called, wanted to talk to me. Honestly, though, I'm fine. You didn't give me a chance to explain.'

'But what about all that?' she asks, pointing at the pile of broken china on the floor.

'That was something else,' I say, and she shares a look with Peter. I know they both understand who is responsible for it. Neither of them asks me any more questions after that.

Peter opens his black bag, pulls out some fresh gauze swabs and begins dabbing at my cut cheek. 'Can you pass me that saline, Evie?' he asks. My mother hands him a small vial. He inspects the label and snaps off the top, squirts the contents at the wound. The saline runs over my face, and I notice a few pinkish drips falling on my jeans. 'And I think Chloe could use a glass of water. Why don't you fetch her one?' My mother heads into the kitchen.

'I'm sorry to send her away,' Peter whispers once she has left the room, 'but she doesn't do too well with things like this.' He pulls a small pack from his bag. 'It's quite deep. You need a couple of stitches. Are you feeling brave?' He takes my lack of resistance as a positive sign and pinches out a crescent-shaped needle from a sterile pack with a pair of forceps. He holds onto my face and I grit my teeth as he pierces the skin around the wound. By the time my mother arrives back with the glass of water, he has completed three quick stitches and has got a fresh dressing in place. 'That should do it,' he says. 'Those stitches will dissolve in due course, but you might want to call by the surgery at a later date for me to have another look.'

'Stitches?' my mother cries, water sloshing from the glass. 'Oh goodness me, Peter. Was it really that bad? I should've been here. I shouldn't have—'

'Everything is fine, Evie. Relax. Chloe didn't feel a thing, did you?' I shake my head. The pain of the needle was nothing compared to the pain of when I awoke in hospital.

After asking me a few questions about the time and date, recording my blood pressure and providing me with a prescription for some extra antibiotics, which he assures me are a precaution rather than anything else, he makes his excuses to leave. My mother follows him out. I can't see them from where I'm sitting on the couch, but I can hear the mutterings of conversation, just too quiet for me to make out. I'm sure it must be about me, and determined to avoid any more secrets, I stand up and head towards the hall.

As I arrive at the doorway, the pearly light of an early winter's afternoon is just strong enough to illuminate the tableau. My mother looks anxious, sad maybe, her head hanging down against her chest. Is it about me? Is my injury worse than I think it is? But then Peter reaches towards her, a gentle hand brushes against her cheek. It's nothing really, just the briefest of moments. But still, it's something I didn't expect. Something illicit. I can tell by the way she raises her hand to his, as if she can't bear the thought of him letting go. But I'm stunned not only because of this exchange, but also because of the feelings it stirs within me. I have been in the same situation, I think, the comforting touch of a hand that shouldn't have been on me. A hand that belonged to somebody other than my husband. My cheek feels alive at the mere thought of it. I slip back into the room, sit quietly on the couch.

My mother follows me in just a few minutes later. 'What a fright you gave me,' she says. But I say nothing, my mind still a jumble. I'm trying to remember what it is that I've remembered, what part of my life this sensation is linked to. And who. But I can't reach anything more concrete. I feel blind to the truth. 'I think we both need a nice cup of tea. What do you say?' I nod my head and force myself to smile.

I dream of you, Chloe, do you know that? In my dreams we are together, just you, me and Joshua. Doing normal things. Last night I dreamed of Christmas, of him coming downstairs and opening his presents. It's because I saw some fairy lights; I guess they set me off. On another night, before you tried to end things, I dreamed of us all at the beach. You know that thing he does where he stacks pebbles into tiny cairns, like a hill walker marking a route?

I watched him once, playing with the rocks as you were sitting there near the shore. He built five different piles that led you across the beach, under the pier. Remember? It was June, I think. Maybe early July. You never told me what he led you to, of course, but after you left the beach I wandered down to the shore, found a starfish. I like to think that's what he showed you, on that bright sunny day when you looked so sad. What had happened to make you blue? Why didn't you let me make things right?

That hurt, you know, seeing you like that and not being able to do anything about it. I felt useless, as if I had no power. So I kept that starfish, tucked it in a drawer at home where it shrivelled up and dried out. When I look at it now,

I'm reminded of my failings, times you've been sad when I wasn't there to make it right. I'll never let that happen again. Once we are together again, I promise I'll never let you go.

18

About fifteen minutes after Peter leaves, Mum returns to the living room clutching a silver tray topped with a pot of steaming tea. She pours, hands me a cup. Outside, a light wind disturbs the surface of the swimming pool. The fog swells against it like rolling mist.

'How's your head feeling? Any better?'

My head is still sore, but I'm not thinking about that. All I can think about is what I saw. But I don't know how to broach what just happened. What am I supposed to say? I have so many things to ask, so many answers to demand. I look up, see her nibbling at her lip, fiddling with a button on her skirt.

'Well?' she asks.

'I'm fine, Mum.' In that moment it's the only answer I can find.

'Are you sure, because if you are in pain I can always ask Peter to—'

'No,' I snap. I look to the mess on the floor and know that we don't need him to come here again. I think I am starting to remember the feeling of being a child in this house. My father's dominance, the way he ruled the roost.

My parents arguing late at night when they thought we couldn't hear. I can't remember anything specific, but rather am aware of a desire to get out. I recall the dream I was having before my mother arrived home: the memory of Joshua, the effect Andrew's absences were having on him. How the dysfunctional nature of our families has left its ugly mark. Blocks of my past are starting to fit together, the picture coming into focus. I realise I don't like the things I am seeing.

'Mum, I'm tired. I need to go and have a lie-down.' She nods, smiles, watches me as I leave the room.

I'm halfway up the stairs when I hear her. 'I'm not sure what you think you saw, but it's not what it looked like.' Her eyes are kitten-wide when I turn to look, desperate for understanding. 'I knew as soon as I walked back in that you'd seen us. But it's not what you think.'

'Then what is it?' She looks at the floor. 'I saw the way he touched you. I know what that touch . . .' I stop myself. Do I really know what that touch means?

She moves forward, sits on the bottom step. 'When I saw you on the floor, I panicked. He was the first person I thought of. But it was all over a long time ago.'

'Whatever it was, it didn't look very over to me.'

'It barely even began,' she says quickly. 'It was so brief. You were still at school.' She takes a moment, straightens her collar. 'But feelings never die, Chloe. They are always there, even when it ends badly.'

I descend a few steps, sit alongside her. 'Did it end—'

'There's nothing between us,' she interrupts. 'But I have to ask you whether you are going to tell your father.'

129

'Maybe he already knows,' I suggest, thinking back to the argument between my father and Peter in the past.

'I don't mean about the affair. I mean about Peter being here. Your father wouldn't want to think that he had been in his house.' Is that confirmation that he knows? 'I'm sorry to ask, Chloe, but perhaps if you could remember how things have been between your father and me over the years, you'd understand.'

I edge forward, close the gap between us. Part of me wants to comfort her, but there is also a part of me that holds back. She has been telling me lies since I arrived in this house, keeping the truth from me. I allow myself to wonder now if she has done so willingly, or whether her hand was forced.

'I can't remember anything specific,' I say, 'but I think I understand what you mean. I remember that I couldn't wait to leave. I was always running away, looking for an escape.'

'And you found it in Andrew. That's why you married him, built a life away from us. I found my escape in Peter, brief as it was.'

I feel woozy, but it has nothing to do with my head wound. Instead it's that feeling I first got when my father told me my husband and son had died. It's the knowledge that everything has changed, that things can never be the same as they were before those last words were spoken. I have lost my escape. Had given it up before the crash by leaving. And it's a terrifying thought, because it's easy to leave when you know you can go back; less easy to see the severity of the problems once a person is dead. Could we ever have found a way to make things work if Andrew hadn't died?

'Nothing changes by running away, Mum.'

130

She nods. 'I know,' she says as she looks away, ashamed. 'But sometimes it's easier just to forget than it is to try and face up to things.' She starts to cry then, her flushed cheeks sunken and lined. It's like looking at the mess of my own marriage. 'Your father was a tyrant when you were younger, Chloe. He blamed me for everything.' She shakes her head. 'There were times when I felt like I didn't even know myself.'

'But with Peter you did?' I ask. She sobs even harder at that, and I know the answer is yes.

After several minutes she stands up, brushing tears from a puffy red face. 'I need some air, Chloe. I'm going to take one of the horses out for a ride.' She looks over to the window at the fizz of rain as it beats against the glass. 'You used to enjoy riding. Maybe you could put a hat on and come and walk one of the others, just a stroll around the yard. I'd be happy to help you, like I used to help Joshua. He did love it when you came to stay here, Chloe.'

I look up at her eager face. I think of her lies, the way she withheld the truth. But in this moment, with the knowledge of just how much she has suffered at my father's hands, I can't summon the strength to remain angry.

'Mum,' I say as I rush to reach her. 'I won't say anything.' It isn't relief I see on her face, but rather a sadness that it has come to this. 'I need to ask you something, though. So that I can understand.'

'OK,' she says, her head bowed.

'Did you love him?'

For a moment she doesn't say anything. I see her swallow hard before she looks up and stares me right in the eyes. 'Yes,' she says, brushing her hair away from her face. 'I do love him.' And I realise that I'm not sure if either of us really know who she means.

That afternoon I walk one of the small horses out in the paddock. My mother trots alongside me on a horse called Prince, her green wax jacket dark with rain. It chills my skin as it falls. We don't talk much, and based on the tracks left in the soft ground, I'm sure she keeps a purposeful distance.

We eat alone that night, just me, Mum and Jess. Dad is late home from work. And I'm glad; I don't know how to face him, knowing that I am now lying to him. I wonder if it's his guilt that is keeping him away, anxiety about his outburst, fear about the lies he has told me. Fear of where to go from here. All evening long I think about what Guy told me, the experiments my father has written papers about. Memories removed, memories created. I need to organise the facts in my head, so I write down what I know. At least that way when tomorrow comes, what I know today is solid, fixed in a moment of time. But although dinner is quiet and I have things on my mind, the fact that it's just the three of us seems to ease the tensions in the house. And despite my lingering anger at the pair of them for all the lies they've told me, I listen as Jess talks about her new books, and I tell her how I scared Mum half to death by fainting in the hall. They both seem to find the retelling of events hilarious.

But that night as I lie in bed listening to the sound of the rain falling outside, the occasional call of a roaming gull, it isn't my mother or Andrew or even Joshua on my mind. It's Damien Treadstone and his family. I think of it as my parents' fault, the way their problems have left their mark on me. The way I needed to escape, and did so by marrying an alcoholic. The way Joshua was already being affected by the problems in my marriage. And it was Joshua who paid the ultimate price, problems and weaknesses passed down from generation to generation. Can I allow the same level of destruction to tear through Damien Treadstone's family as it has through mine, when I don't know if he is really to blame? When I don't even know if he was there?

Although I'm not sure of the exact events that night, there is a seed of doubt in my mind that is beginning to grow. I have such vivid memories of moving around in the woods that I am sure I must have been awake at some point. I remember being out of my car. I was awake enough to see Joshua lying lifeless on the forest floor. That wasn't just a dream, or a nightmare. I can't explain how I ended up back in the driver's seat, but I know this: I was conscious at some point, and I don't remember Damien Treadstone being anywhere near me. I can't ignore these memories, pretend I know nothing like my father wants me to. I'm sick of the lies and half-truths, even if in their absence the blame ends up with me. I can't let this go as far as a trial. If I'm to blame for the accident, I have to take responsibility, not run away like I always used to. I can't allow another family to end up being destroyed.

I get up and retrieve DS Gray's card from the pocket of my robe. I stare at the number, brush my fingers over the flat blue lettering. Tomorrow, I decide, I will go to the police and tell them what I know.

19

I'm running, slipping on leaves, the branches of trees smacking me in the face. I fall down an embankment, the freshly broken bark of a tree gouging into my right leg, cutting it all the way from my ankle to just above my knee. Joshua is ahead, lying in the dirt, barely moving, rain falling across his body. I hear him call me.

Mummy.

I wake shaking, my fingers reaching down to my leg, my skin slick with sweat. I run my fingers down the length of the thick red scar. The wound I was dreaming about is the same as the one I see before me now. These dreams are pieces of that night. I have to start putting my old life back together, and maybe DS Gray is the one to help me do that.

I sneak out through the back door, use the code at the gate, calling a taxi from the village shop. I close my eyes as we drive through the countryside. It's overwhelming seeing the world before me, so large in comparison to what I've been used to over the last few months. I feel lost. I pull DS Gray's card from my pocket and study it: his name, the number. Anything rather than look outside. I wonder where

Ditchling Road is, the place I lost my son. I don't know, but I know I'm not ready to see it.

The roads are quiet until we arrive in Brighton, our only companion the constant downpour of rain. The driver pulls up outside the police station and I hand over the twenty-pound note I took from my mother's purse on the way out.

I gaze up at the building as the taxi pulls away: all angles and harsh edges, big, white, and aggressive. It seems brutal, designed to intimidate. Water streams down my face as I look up at the clouds swelling above. Rain forces pedestrians to fight with umbrellas, shelter under porches and porticos. I hurry towards the entrance of the police station and step inside.

A slim uniformed officer leads me through the corridors, dark and narrow, claustrophobic and tight. As he walks, I keep my eyes on the back of his head, studying the sharp haircut, the neat outline of his clothes. The sight of his neck stirs a memory of looking at the back of a man's head, the hair blond and wavy, hanging around the neckline in slick, greasy clumps. It's Andrew's face I see as he turns to me, smiles. It's a sad smile, laced with disappointment. The flashback is from near the end. Tainted memories. He had probably lost his job by that point. I used to believe that if only he could get another job, then everything would be all right. That if he had to go to work he wouldn't be able to drink. How I pinned my hopes on ifs.

I can feel my heartbeat beginning to race, as if the walls are closing in on me as we move deeper through the maze of corridors. The echo of it grows louder, stronger with every beat. The officer's shoes resonate as he walks. I can

barely breathe as people pass, dashing by with hurried footsteps. Did I rush about like this when I was working, making
demands, following orders? Did I have a life as rich as this?

We arrive outside a blue door, and the officer who is
escorting me knocks twice. I hear DS Gray call for us to
enter, and any thoughts of my old job evaporate, like water
under the glare of a hot summer sun.

The office is small, only just big enough for a desk and
one visitor's chair. It smells of coffee and sweat. A filing
cabinet stands on one side of the room, folders piled high
on top. Other files are stacked on the floor. Too much work.
The young officer closes the door behind me and DS Gray
motions for me to sit.

The walls are unbroken, no windows, so everything
sounds dull and echoless, like a small Parisian hotel room.
Why do I think that? Have I been to Paris? Post-it notes
and photographs cover sections of the wall. Somebody has
made an effort to string up a garland of tinsel over the top
of a poster about a Christmas party. Was it DS Gray who
did that? It makes me warm to him if he did; that effort
in an unexpected place. The party is to be held at a place
called The Fountainhead, which I think sounds vaguely
familiar.

'It's a nice place,' I hear him say. I avert my eyes when I
realise he is staring at me. 'Do a nice roast on a Sunday,
too.' He gazes up at the string of green tinsel and shakes
his head. 'I was the mug that suggested it, so I got left with
the organisation.' I smile, unsure what to say. 'Anyway, email
sent,' he says as he hits the enter key with a show of enthusiasm. 'I'm all ears.'

He sits back in his chair, folds one awkward leg over the other, squashing his thigh against his ample stomach. He seems uncomfortable, unable to fit into the chair properly. He edges back and after a bit of manoeuvring finds the sweet spot, laces his fingers together over his protruding gut. He snaps one thumbnail against the other.

I can hear people in the corridor on the other side of the wall, hurried footsteps, distant laughter. 'It's about Damien Treadstone,' I say. I have so much I want to tell him, so many things that I have learned or remembered. I don't know where to start, but I'm aware of a need to be cautious. 'I've been called as a witness by his defence.'

He rocks on his chair. 'I know that.'

The thought of having to stand up in court makes my skin crawl. 'Considering I can't remember what happened, what does he expect me to say?' I feel guilty, aware that I'm not telling DS Gray the entire truth of what I think I know. There are so many possibilities running through my mind, potential explanations of what happened and why I was there. Most significantly, I'm almost certain that at some point I wasn't in my car that night. But this has to be taken one step at a time. I have to understand first what Damien Treadstone wants before I give too much away. I only have a little knowledge, and so I hold on to it, protect it with my life.

'Well for a start you can't testify to his presence. I'm guessing he is rather hoping that once you see him there on the stand, you'll admit that you don't remember seeing him at the scene of the accident. That would be very good for his defence.'

I think about Damien Treadstone's son, the idea of what lies ahead for his family if he is found guilty. 'DS Gray, do you believe him when he says that he wasn't involved?'

He chews on his lip, still flicking one thumb against the other. 'It's not my job to believe him or not, Chloe. It's my job to collect and collate the evidence as I find it. The courts will decide if he is guilty.'

'But if he's innocent and is telling the truth, he'd be desperate, right? He'd try anything to get me to help him.'

'Such as?'

'Like finding a way to talk to me.'

He shakes his head. 'Legally he cannot approach you.'

'What about illegally?'

He sits forward in his seat, rests an elbow on the desk, his chin in his hand. He chews on an already bitten nail. 'Are you telling me he's tried to approach you?'

'He came to my parents' house.'

He thinks about that for a moment, rubs his face with his hand. 'That's a very serious allegation, Chloe. Were you able to identify him clearly?'

'He was in the graveyard next door. I was walking in my garden. When my parents arrived, he ran, drove away.'

'But did you see his face?'

'I heard a man's voice. I'm sure it must have been him.' I think back to that moment, the blur of red light disappearing into the fog. If only I'd seen his face. I realise that I can't truthfully testify that he was there. I look up, find DS Gray waiting on my answer. I shake my head. He stands, sits on the edge of his desk and folds his arms, his backside edging piles of papers out of the way. I feel hot, sweaty, pull at the neckline of my jumper. I can't breathe in here.

'Chloe, here's the thing. What you've just told me doesn't make much sense. Besides the fact that you can't identify Damien Treadstone visually, only a feeling you had that it was him, why would he call you as a witness and then try to approach you? He would know it would be detrimental to his case.'

'I didn't say it made sense.'

He lifts piles of papers until he finds a pack of Nicorette gum, flicks a tablet into his mouth. I am hit by a sudden urge to smoke. Was I a smoker in my previous life?

'I know you've been going through a difficult time,' he says as he chews, an off-mint smell drifting through the air. 'Especially with the loss you have suffered. But you're smart, I think, Chloe. I know you used to be a lawyer.' There it is again, the implication that my previous life is over. Used to be. Was. Done. 'But while Damien Treadstone might be desperate, he is most definitely not stupid.'

He leans over and opens a drawer, pulling out a file. From it he takes a picture and passes it to me. It's Damien with a woman I assume is his wife. Between them the little boy who has facelessly plagued my thoughts since I decided to come here and try to do the right thing. She looks nice, his wife. Smiley and neat. His son is plump, happy. It's one of those pictures people get done professionally when they first have children. White backgrounds and happy smiles. Do I have these kinds of pictures? I feel sure I must have. Somewhere.

'Why are you showing me this?' I say, tossing the photo down onto the desk.

'Chloe, Damien Treadstone is a twenty-eight-year-old married man, and the father of the boy you see there. He works for Meditec as a rep, supplying catheters and lithotripsy equipment to various hospitals in the south-east. He has no criminal record, and an excellent reputation in his work and private life. He's an active member of his local church, and two years ago he spent six months as a missionary working in Uganda. No matter where I dig, I can't find anything to discredit him. He's like a goddamned saint.'

A bead of sweat trails down my back. 'So you don't believe me when I say he came to the house.'

'It's not that I don't believe you, but I want you to see the bigger picture, and what we are up against.' He chews hard on his gum. 'Like I've told you before, Damien Treadstone claims that he wasn't even in the car at the time. That it was stolen prior to the accident.'

I feel desperately out of my depth, kicking about in the open ocean with no sign of the shore in sight. Like I am drowning. Like the boy in my dream. 'Is there any evidence to support that?'

'Well, he has no alibi. He claims to have been in Kemp Town at the time of the accident, drinking in a bar after finding that his keys and his car had been stolen. But we can't place him on CCTV, and nobody who was working in the bar that night can remember him. His car was found at the scene, keys in the ignition. We checked for prints, came up with nothing. Interestingly, not even Damien's. But when we picked him up, he was inebriated, his trousers were covered in mud and he had a cut on his forehead. We also found evidence of paint transfer from his car to yours on the rear wing, driver's side, which would support the theory of a collision prior to you leaving the road.'

'Well surely that all goes against him?'

'Right, yet still he insists that he wasn't there, and he hasn't deviated from his statement once. Plus, in addition to your amnesia and inability to place him at the scene of the crash, there is other evidence that his defence team will be focusing on. For example, your injury pattern.'

I pull my coat around me, try to cover my right leg. DS Gray's eyes instantly slide towards it. He knows what marks lie beneath my clothes.

'For a start, there's your position in the vehicle upon discovery. You were found in the driver's seat with your seat belt fastened. You seemed to have careered off the road and travelled almost fifty feet down an embankment before hitting a tree. Logically, you must have been wearing your seat belt otherwise you would have been thrown from the car like Joshua.' He pauses briefly, and I am grateful that he feels awkward about bringing up my dead son. 'Yet when you were admitted to hospital, you were found to have sustained no trauma consistent with a seat-belt injury. No skin abrasions, no broken ribs. Not even any bruising to the chest.'

And in that moment I can picture myself in the car, trying to unclip my belt, fumbling about in an attempt to escape. I was definitely wearing my belt when I first woke up, just like DS Gray tells me.

'Then there's your direction of travel. You claim to have no memory of what happened after you left your father's house, but when the crash occurred, you were travelling *towards* your father's house. You had been in Brighton, it would seem. But what had you been doing? Who had you been with?'

He shakes his head, flicks another tablet of gum into his mouth. 'There are inconsistencies, Chloe, and such discrepancies cast doubt on Damien Treadstone's guilt, which is the very reason his defence wants to call you as a witness. It's not what you can tell them, it's what you can't.' He reaches down for a mug of what looks like cold coffee and knocks it back with a wince. 'To be quite honest with you, nothing you've told us makes much sense. But it's not just that.' He pauses, his fingers tapping at the desk. 'There is one other thing that none of us can yet explain. We were rather hoping you would be able to help us, but you claim to have no memory of what happened that night.'

'What is it?' I ask. When he doesn't answer, I stand up. 'Please, DS Gray, just tell me.'

He takes a long breath, and the sickly scent of coffee mixed with mint wafts over me. He swallows hard. 'The dress you were wearing on the night of the accident was covered in blood.'

'Well it would be, wouldn't it? I hit my head. My leg was cut.' But I stop talking when I realise that he is staring right at me, his face expressionless. My anxiety level shoots up.

'When we look at blood in forensics,' he says slowly, 'we look at the kind of pattern it leaves. If it was your blood, running like you suggest from your facial injuries, then it would create what we call a passive stain. What we found on your dress was a pattern of staining consistent with blood transfer by direct contact.' He gives me a moment to take that in. 'But Chloe, it wasn't just the pattern of staining. It was the blood itself. It didn't belong to you. I'm sorry, but I have to tell you that the blood we found on your clothing belonged to Joshua.'

20

For a long time I can't find any words. DS Gray helps me back into my chair, and I sit still with only the background bustle of the police station to break the silence. At some point DC Barclay comes in and DS Gray shoos her away. I can't stop thinking about all those tears I've cried, lamenting the fact that my son died alone, that I failed to comfort him while he was in pain. Now DS Gray is telling me that he may have died in my arms.

The blood we found belonged to Joshua.

'Can I get you something to drink?' I hear him ask. He moves awkwardly at my side, shuffling left to right in the minuscule space. I hear the sound of water behind me, the chink of glass against glass. He turns to face me with a small beaker, pushes it into my right hand before edging it towards my lips.

'Thank you,' I say, and he sits down on the edge of the desk again, closer to me than he was before. He takes out a handkerchief from his pocket and gives it to me.

'You see, that's why it doesn't make sense to us, Chloe. There are inconsistencies in both stories, yours and Treadstone's, and the facts, as much as they are facts, don't help us to draw a logical conclusion. What I would like to do is—'

'DS Gray, I remember what happened.'

He stops mid-sentence, his mouth open as if somebody has paused him. He leans forward, and I see his eyes widen in anticipation.

'You remember?'

I take a breath, tuck my hands between my knees. I shift in my seat and try to sort what I know into some logical order before I speak.

'Well, sort of. Not everything, but something. Something I haven't told you yet.'

He stands up, moves back to his chair and opens a drawer. He takes out a sheet of paper and picks up a pen from his desk.

'I remember being in the woods, seeing my car. I was trying to get to Joshua. I thought at first it was just a dream, but now I'm sure that what I'm seeing is a memory. I can see Joshua on the ground, I'm trying to reach him.'

He picks up the file and roots through it. He pulls one sheet out, sets it before me. It's a photograph of my car crushed against a tree. What else must be in that file? I want to know, to see. Does the truth lie in there? Can it tell me if I intended to kill myself and my child?

'I know this must be difficult for you,' he says, 'but can you tell me where Joshua is lying in your memory? Where do you expect us to have found him?'

I look down at the image in front of me. DS Gray glances away, perhaps as a mark of respect. My memories are coming back to me drip by drip, like the rain on that cold, dark night. I point to a small clearing alongside a rocky outcrop. 'Here,' I tell him, moving my finger along the ground that I know Joshua died upon. 'With his feet pointing towards that tree.'

He nods, looks embarrassed as he places the picture back in the file. 'Well, I think you can be confident that your memory is real. That is indeed where he was found.' He writes something on the sheet of paper, draws a line underneath it. I can't read what he has written, his handwriting little more than a scrawl. Perhaps that's intentional. 'What else? Do you remember getting out of the car? How you ended up back in it?'

'No. I only remember running, trying to find Joshua. It was raining, getting dark. I remember falling down an embankment, cutting my leg. That's why I came here today, to tell you these things. I wanted to tell you that at some point I was outside my car that night, and I don't remember seeing Damien Treadstone. I can't be sure he was there.'

He nods, takes a breath. 'I appreciate your honesty, Chloe. Every detail is vital if we are to understand what happened.' He covers his mouth with his hands, rubs at his face again. 'Tell me – and again, I'm sorry if this is difficult, Chloe – what was your relationship with your husband like before the accident?'

I sigh. How can I answer with any confidence? All I know is what my parents have told me. 'Complicated, I think. My family tell me he was a drinker, that I'd left him. That I'd taken Joshua to live with my parents.'

'That is my understanding of the situation too.' He writes something else, nibbles the end of the pen. 'Do you think he was angry with you for leaving the marriage?'

'Maybe. More likely upset, from what my father tells me.' It's hard to admit to knowing that Andrew might have killed himself because I left. 'I think he probably didn't want to lose me.'

'And yet he had lost you, hadn't he?'

My cheeks grow hot, my head light. I feel like DS Gray is blaming me, that he too believes my leaving is the thing that pushed him over the edge. 'My father told me that things with Andrew were making it too difficult for me to stay.'

'I wasn't suggesting you were at fault, Chloe.' He smiles. 'Quite the opposite, in fact.' He glances down at his notes. 'Everything about the scene of the accident – the way the ground was disturbed, the presence of the second car – supports the theory that another person was there. But what if it wasn't Damien Treadstone? What if it was somebody else, somebody who had a motive to be there? Somebody who was angry with you? Your husband, perhaps. It could explain a lot of things.' He sets his pen down.

I shake my head. 'That's impossible.'

'Why? Like I say, he had a motive to follow you. You said yourself he could never let you go. I know he tells us that he has an alibi, but we still haven't been able to corroborate it as yet. That means that it's questionable.'

'Questionable? How can it be questionable?'

'Every alibi is questionable, Miss Daniels.'

I sit forward, one of my hands on the desk. 'But my husband is dead, DS Gray.'

He rocks back in the chair, the legs complaining under the weight. 'Pardon?'

'Andrew,' I say, almost shouting. 'He died a week before the accident. That's why I was so upset that night. I blamed myself.'

'Who told you that?'

'My father.'

DS Gray is shaking his head. 'Chloe, I spoke to Andrew Jameson only two weeks ago.' I sit back, open-mouthed, waiting for him to speak, to fill in the blanks I can't hope to complete myself. 'Mr Jameson claims that on the night of the accident you were supposed to be meeting him, only you never showed up. So if it turns out that Damien Treadstone is telling the truth, I know who my next suspect would be.'

What did you think? A few little lies and it would all go away? That I would go away? Chloe, you have no idea.

But what I'm not sure about is to whom you've been lying the most. Me, or yourself? When we're together, I feel your presence, the way your eyes flicker when I get close, when my hands touch your body. And that last time, when you rolled over in bed, looked into my eyes and asked me one simple question: how can we be together? It cut through me, hearing those words. I thought you already knew the answer, but even so, I bit my tongue and answered with a smile. I told you the simple truth: easily. I knew you didn't believe me.

But what I didn't expect was for you to tell me it was over. Over, you said, like it was nothing. That you were leaving, going to live with your parents, and that I wasn't to contact you. How could you bring yourself to do it, end everything we had together? I could have been there for you, Chloe. Joshua too. I just wish you could have seen that I could have been a good father. I've made you so many promises, but still you don't understand. All I needed was one more chance, but you wouldn't let me show you just

149

how good I could have been. Somehow you still think you're better on your own.

But without you, Chloe, I can't survive. Without you I might as well be dead.

21

Andrew is alive. Andrew is alive and he is a suspect. I sit
on the wall outside the station. I'm shaking, can't catch my
breath. I blink as I try to work out what I think has happened.
But for a while I can't get past my first thought: how can
he be alive when my family told me he was dead? And more
to the point, where the hell is he? Why isn't he looking for
me? Rain beats down, and at one point a women under a
large umbrella stops in front of me.

'Excuse me, are you all right?'

'I'm fine,' I tell her, and she moves away looking doubtful.
I look around; more people are close. I have to move, leave
this place.

I stand up, pace the pavement in tight circles, try to piece
together what I know about the day of the crash. Realising
I need to find some sort of shelter from the persistent rain,
I find a bus stop next to the station, perch on the edge of
a wet bench. Suddenly a vague memory comes to me of
being in a park, sitting on a bench. Was it the night of the
crash? I feel as if I was waiting for somebody, but who?
Could it have been Andrew? Then the memory shifts and I
see myself driving in the rain. Running through the woods.

Searching for my son. The trees, the dark. Joshua, lying on the ground. But what the hell happened next? How did I end up back in my car?

At no point can I picture Andrew or Damien, or arrange the individual pieces of that night into any logical order that explains things. I can't tell the story of how I lost my child. But I am becoming ever more certain about one thing: I had no intention of crashing with Joshua in the car. All along I have felt it, the doubt that I could do such a thing. Now I know that at some point on that night I held him close to my chest, tried to make everything right. I know with certainty that I didn't mean to kill either of us. Otherwise there is no way that his loss would hurt as much as it does.

I know something else too. My father is still lying to me. Andrew, my husband, is alive. It is impossible to believe that my father doesn't know that. He even told me he had arranged Andrew's funeral, thrown flowers from the pier. My mother and Jess must also know. My whole family, for crying out loud. How could they lie about something so important? Is that what my mother wanted my father to tell me that night in the dining room? Did she want him to tell me the truth?

I leave the bus shelter and walk aimlessly despite the pain in my leg, passing shops and people and places I don't know. I wish I had the letter from the lawyer with my address on it so I could go to my house. If I could find it, I would never leave it again. I want to lock myself in and stay there forever; hide away, pretend the rest of the world doesn't exist. But I can't remember where it is. Close to the beach, my father said when he saw that picture on Facebook, but no matter how many roads I walk down, none seem familiar.

The rain is beating down, my clothes getting wet through. I stand on the seafront in the shelter of an awning, a little shop selling Brighton rock. The ruined pier sits to my right, the other one further to the left. But the shop owner is watching me and I can't stay here forever. I need somewhere to go, somebody to go to. But I have nowhere and nobody. Not a single friend I remember who I can call on. I can't go back to my parents' house after learning of their deceit and lies. And I can't go home, because I don't know where home is. Does such a place even exist for me any more?

I find myself at Palace Pier, standing next to a kiosk that sells vinegary chips in cones with wooden forks. Garish lights flash above me, the pier illuminated and blurry in the thick wet air. I listen as the waves crash against the shore, echoing underneath the wooden slats as I walk. I pass a sign that promises all the fun of the fair, ancient shelters, peeling paint. The smell of rotting wood. The obnoxious buzz of amusements rounds on me, loud and caustic, songs playing on top of songs, mixed with the din of games and cheer. A lone man feeds coins into a twopenny slot. Another shoots baskets. Gulls swoop. I stumble on, and suddenly the sight before me raises a memory of my past, hitting me like the rain, heavy and consuming.

Shall we get our fortune read?

It is Andrew's voice I hear, and although it's only in my head, I can picture him as he was then, all those years ago. His hair bleached by the sun, the scent of his old sweater as I leant in. A teenager. I see the kiosk at which we once sat, the old gypsy with her crystal ball and headscarf, bracelets that jangled as she moved. He was a sucker for things like that. He loved the machine you put a penny in too, which spat it back out with the image of Brighton pressed onto the surface. We did it every time we came to the pier, I think. I remember that now, just like it was yesterday. Where are all those old coins now? Lost, no doubt, along with the memories we once took the time to make. I wish I could remember something more solid, rather than these snapshot postcards of the past.

I walk further, past Horatio's Bar, down to the helter-skelter and the colourful horses of the merry-go-round. I go as far as I can, brace myself against the railings at the end of the pier. The waves grow louder. I look out to sea, the place where my father told me Joshua's ashes were scattered. Is that even the truth? I can't believe anything they've told me any more.

Because he didn't stop there, did he? Oh no. He told me it was my fault. He implied that Andrew killed himself because of me, and that Joshua was dead because of my mistakes. How could he do that? To his own daughter. A father is supposed to protect his child, not lie and manipulate her. He wanted me to believe that I could have chosen to kill my child. It's unimaginable, and yet the truth. I gaze over the railing at the white swell of the waves, feel the spray on my face. And as I stand there, the wind buffeting my body, I can't help but wonder if it wouldn't just be easier if I ended this now.

But instead I sink to the floor, my body flat against the wet boards of the pier. I let one hand slip through the railings, reaching down towards the water, towards the place where I can only assume Joshua's ashes are. They should have waited, I think to myself, before they held the funeral. They should have waited for me to say to goodbye.

They should have told me the truth.

By the time I leave the pier, the light is fading, another weather front moving in, clouds swollen and grey out at sea. I know I have to confront my father, tell him what I know. He won't be able to lie to me then. I walk through the streets, asking for directions from strangers, until I find the clinic where he works. It's a large place, an old Victorian mansion, which even has some patients who stay overnight. I move through the unmanned reception, following the signs to my father's office. I climb the stairs, the pain in my leg eased; I can't feel anything any more. I am going to demand the truth. I am going to make him tell me the truth. But before I reach his office I see Guy standing in the corridor, talking to a nurse.

'Chloe?' He smiles at first, a set of notes in his hand. 'What are you doing here?' Then he notices my pale face and red eyes. I am shaking from the cold. Maybe anger. His smile disappears. 'Chloe, what's wrong?'

'Where's my father?' I demand. He hands the nurse the set of notes and pulls me aside.

'He's already left.' His voice is low. 'And in a hurry, too. Something about a problem at home.' I'm close to tears again. I need the truth and now my father is gone. 'Chloe, tell me what's wrong? What are you doing here alone?'

'He's lying to me.' I feel Guy edging me towards a seat. 'No!' I shout, the eyes of the nearby nurses suddenly upon us. They think I'm a patient. I must look crazed. 'I have to find him. He has to tell me the truth.'

I'm close to breaking, so I don't stop him when he takes hold of my arm, firm but not in a way that hurts, and leads me towards the door. 'Not like this you don't,' he whispers as we walk away from the crowd of onlookers. 'Let's talk in private.'

We walk until we find a quiet corner with a deep window-sill. We wait for a small crowd of people to pass. They're laughing, cheerful. The sight of them makes me feel sick; the thought of everything I've lost, all the untruths I've been told. After the last of the group disappears around a corner, Guy turns to look at me.

'It's all lies,' I tell him. 'Everything he has told me is a lie.'

'What are you talking about?'

'My husband's alive, Guy. My father told me that he killed himself because of me, but he didn't.'

He stands back, runs his fingers through his chestnut hair. I notice a few white strands creeping through at the temples. Then he reaches for my hand and gently pulls me to my feet. He starts walking, taking me with him. 'We can't talk about this here. Not when it concerns your father. Tell me everything in the car.'

He guides me down a rear staircase, quiet and away from the crowds. We exit into a gale, the rain eased, and cross the car park. In the car, before I can stop him, he calls my father to explain that I am with him. That we are on our way back. To that house, to that place where they have blinded me to the reality of my life. Reality, I think, laughing to myself. What even is that? It means nothing any more.

22

To my surprise, as we drive into Rusperford, Guy doesn't turn left past the church, the road that would take us to my parents' house. Instead he turns right into the Old Ghyll hotel, a sprawling outcrop of Tudor elegance nestled on the edge of the village, where, according to Jess, we sometimes used to eat at Christmas.

He pulls open the weathered wooden door and I listen as it grates against the uneven slate floor of the porch. I know instantly that I have heard that noise before. We sit at a table next to a roaring log fire, the smell of burning wood strong and heady. A Christmas tree twinkles behind me, decorated with rich gold ribbons and clusters of fir cones decked with bells. Underneath there are presents without names, and all around me I hear the gentle hum of contentment: the clatter of plates, the chink of glasses, the crackle of wood as the fire burns and the wind lures the flames up the chimney. But disappointingly, despite my certainty that I've been here before, no specific memory comes to mind.

'I know you want to speak to your father, Chloe, but let's take a break here first, OK?' Guy sets down two glasses of red wine. 'I didn't know what you would want.'

I sip the wine, feel the rush of alcohol, the warmth as it hits my throat. The tingle of the flames is sharp against my skin, and I'm grateful for the comfort after spending hours in the cold. Guy takes my coat and loops it over a hook on the wall behind him so that it will dry in the glare of the fire. He pulls his chair close. 'Now, what the hell happened today? You weren't making any sense earlier, and your father sounded frantic.'

'I'm not sure where to start.' I can feel myself getting upset again. He reaches across the table and covers my hand with his own. His skin feels warm, his touch heavy. Protective almost.

'Just start with what happened today.'

At first I hesitate. But then, as I begin by telling him how I sneaked from the house, all the details come streaming out. I tell him everything my father has told me: that my husband died, that I had left him and that it was my fault he was dead. I tell him how my father withheld the fact that I have been called as a witness. I tell him what DS Gray told me regarding the inconsistencies at the crash site, the police's doubts, and how Andrew is still alive. About Joshua's blood being found on my clothes. That my father led me to believe it might be my fault that my son is dead. That I killed him.

Guy picks up his red wine and knocks it back. I fiddle at my hair, try to cover up my dressing with my woolly hat. I feel like I have just confessed, that feeling of immense relief. It's surpassed only by the worry concerning how my confession will be received.

He rubs his chin, then sits back in his chair, his fingers woven together like a basket. 'That's quite a lot of information.

Why would he lie about something so massive? It's not like he could keep it up. You've been called to court, for goodness' sake.'

I nod to agree. 'Why would he even say it in the first place? He told me they had scattered Andrew's ashes. That there had been a funeral.'

He pulls at his hair, runs his hands through it. He looks as confused as I feel. 'I'm not sure, but you yourself told me that your husband was perhaps a difficult man. That you had problems and that he was a drinker. Perhaps he was trying to protect you. If it *was* your husband in the other car, he might have a point.'

Is it possible that Andrew is a threat I need protection from, and that my father's lies are designed to stop me looking for him? I haven't experienced any flashbacks to give me cause to fear my husband. But then again, I remember almost nothing from that time.

'But it's not just what my father said, is it? It's what the police said. That the accident doesn't make sense.'

'Tell me again what you mean by that. What did DS Gray say exactly?'

'That my injuries weren't consistent with me wearing a seatbelt, but that I was wearing one when they found me. That I had Joshua's blood on my clothes. It doesn't make any sense to me. But the scary thing is, I know he's right. I know that I got out of the car that night. I can remember walking through the trees, the rain. I can remember Joshua on the ground . . .'

I break off, and he waits patiently while I blow my nose and wipe my eyes.

'The most likely explanation is that this Treadstone character is clutching at straws,' he says. 'His car was there. It had the keys in it. Let him call you as a witness. Let them throw anything and everything they like at you. I don't think it matters, because all you have to do is tell them what you know. There is more than enough evidence to place him at the scene of the accident.'

'Do you think I should have kept quiet about what I remembered?'

'I didn't say that. But your memory isn't clear, and if he is guilty then he deserves to pay for what he did. It's not fair that he might go free on the basis that you can't remember what happened. From what you've told me, I'd say the evidence is stacked against him. Plus it most likely was him in the graveyard the other night.'

And whilst what he says makes sense, and up until a few hours ago I would have agreed, now I can't help but wonder if it could have been Andrew calling my name that evening.

'I guess you're right,' I say. I glance down at myself, at my hand-me-down clothes and wet shoes. In contrast he looks so well put together, a nice shirt with a pullover on top. People must be wondering what the hell he is doing with me. I look as if I have just been saved from drowning, pulled to the shore and gasping for desperate breaths. 'I feel so stupid, you having to bring me home like this.'

He is shaking his head. 'I don't see it like that. I was happy to help. I understand what it means to lose somebody you love. I know how important it is to take time to grieve for something you can't have any more. Something you can't change.' His eyes glaze over, and I reach across and touch his hand. It's instinctive, a need to comfort. It draws him back, his eyes meeting mine. 'My brother died when I was young. It's hard to get over something like that. Still hurts now, even years later.'

'I'm so sorry.' I like the contact, the connection, no matter how small, to another living person. But at the same time it makes me aware of the people around us. The hotel is full. Are they watching us? Am I doing something wrong, here with a man who isn't my husband, now that I know my husband is alive?

'Look, I'm so grateful for today, for your help and kindness. But I really need to speak with my father,' I say. 'I have to face him.'

'Sure.' He nods, finishes his wine, stands up. 'Come on, I'll drive you there. But if there is anything else you need, just call me, OK?' He searches in his pocket, finds a pen, scribbles on the back of a beer mat. 'Don't hesitate. Even if all you need is a friend. You seem like maybe you could do with one.'

He grabs my coat, holds it up as I slip my arms through the sleeves. I feel his hands run across my shoulders, smoothing the material into place. And to my surprise, I feel a pang of desire wash over me. It has been so long since I've been touched by anybody other than my family, felt the pressure of a man's hands against my skin. I can barely even remember what it feels like. I think of that sensation I got when I saw my mother so close to Peter, the way his hand reached to her face. Who was the last man who kissed me? Can I really be sure it was my husband?

I take a step away, embarrassed by my feelings, and slip

the beer mat into my pocket. A minute or two later we are back in his car and on the way to the house.

When we arrive, the gate is open, a police car on the driveway. The blue flashing lights remind me of the accident. The lights are on in the windows of the study and dining room, and somebody must hear the car approach because when Guy pulls up my father is already at the door, running towards us.

'Oh Chloe, we were so worried,' he bellows, rushing forward, taking me in his arms. He holds me so tight I can hardly breathe. I try to pull away but can't.

'Good evening, Dr Daniels,' Guy says as he gets out of the car.

My father holds me out in front of him, ignoring Guy. 'Why did you leave without saying anything? We were frantic. How did you even get out?'

He waits for my answer but I don't offer anything, don't want to even acknowledge his stupid questions. How did I get out? Why does it seem that the only thing that bothers him is that I outsmarted him? 'I went to speak with the police,' I say. 'Then I came looking for you. Guy found me by chance.'

'Oh yes,' he says, indignant, still daring to be angry with me. Still ignoring Guy. He doesn't yet realise that I know he's been lying. 'We know about the visit to the police. What was all that about? These two won't tell us anything.' He points towards two uniformed officers stepping from the house. 'She's back,' he calls, and one of them gives a weary nod of the head. How tired of my amnesia they must be.

My father thanks them, and after a quick check that I'm all right, they get in their car and drive away.

'Oh Chloe, you're back.' I see my mother hurrying towards me from the house. As she approaches, I turn away from her. She appears so disappointed in that moment. She thought we had become closer, united by collusion. But you can't fight on two separate fronts. You have to pick a side.

As if to shift things on, get the situation contained, my father turns to Guy. 'Well, thank you so much,' he says, moving forward to shake his hand. 'How lucky that she saw you. I'd love to ask you in for a drink, but Chloe must be tired.' But the way my father looks at me out of the corner of his eye, I know he has realised that something is wrong. He is no longer quite as confident as he was.

'It's no problem. I really should get going anyway,' Guy says. He waves at me, nods towards my father. 'I'll see you tomorrow, Dr Daniels.'

We enter the house, the cool light and chilly air sucking me back in. The whole place feels like a lie, and it doesn't matter what Guy tells me about my father's best intentions, or his desire to protect me. It doesn't matter if my relationship with Andrew was falling apart. What I needed when I woke up was the truth.

My father turns to face me as I stand inside the door. 'Evelyn, bring a blanket,' he says as he closes the door behind me. He tries to shuffle me out of my coat, fiddling at my zip which he can't seem to manage in his haste. 'You're bloody freezing. Evelyn,' he hollers again, sharper this time. 'A blanket, now.' And then he mutters something about the fact that if he'd have been at home this morning this would never have happened.

I push his hand away and step back. 'What is it, Chloe?' I look straight at him. 'You're a liar, Dad.'

He is frozen to the spot. I can see the fear flooding over him, into his lungs. He can't breathe for it.

'What?' he says, stepping away, his hands on the hall table, bracing himself.

'I said you're a liar. You told me Andrew was dead.' He opens his mouth to protest, but changes his mind. He realises there's no point in lying any more. That I know. 'He's alive, Dad. The police spoke to him two weeks ago. Why did you lie?'

He moves from the table towards the stairs and sits down on the bottom step as my mother comes through from the kitchen. 'What is it?' she asks. 'What's going on?'

Where is Jess? I want her answers too. She told me I could trust her, yet she has been lying since the day I arrived.

'You all lied to me,' I say. 'You lied about Andrew, about the fact that he is still alive.' My voice is rising, my words building to a crescendo as I turn back to my father. 'Why did you do it? Why did you tell me he was dead?'

He takes a deep breath. My mother stands watching me, tears in her eyes. I see Jess in the living room doorway, her head hanging in shame. It is my father who speaks.

'Because, Chloe, I wished he was.'

The trouble was this, Chloe: I started to blame you, and it made me hate you. They say, don't they, that there is a fine line between love and hate. I don't think that's true. I think love and hate are part of the same thing, the balance always swinging, more in favour of one than the other at any given time. It's all about expectation. Because when we love somebody we start to expect, make demands, and then we get let down and love starts to morph into something else. We expect the person we love to protect us from harm. But when I needed you, you weren't there. You always let me down. You always ran away. That's why we are in this position now, this awful fucking position where I feel like there's no way out.

Because now you want to leave me behind like something discarded, scraped from your shoe and tossed to the ground. You think there's nothing left, no reason to stay. What is it? The excitement's gone, peaked and faded, a firework on the way back down to earth? That's it, isn't it? Is it my fault, because of my problems? I think it might be. I could feel it in the way you rested against me that last time, not as close as you were before, your leg after we made love like wood at my side instead of threaded through mine like silk.

But I can't handle being away from you, Chloe. I can't cope on my own, not any more. When you leave, it makes me hate you, and then I miss you and love you more than I ever did.

Almost, at least.

And there it is again, that balance.

Love and hate. Love. Hate.

Now on my own, waiting for you to come back, I wonder if I've ever known which emotion I felt more strongly when it came to you.

23

'What?' My hands are shaking. I can't believe it. 'You wanted him to be dead so you just told me he was?' I look up to see my father's set jaw, irritation that he has been caught out. He appears resigned, but not in the least bit sorry.

'Chloe, you don't understand.'

'No,' I say. 'I don't.' My mouth is dry, the taste of metal on my tongue. My head throbs. 'Tell me why you wish he was dead.'

He takes a long breath, and my mother stands motionless. 'Chloe, there is so much you don't remember. His disappearances . . . the problems when he was there. The number of times you called me desperate for help.' He looks to me for understanding, finds none, my face a portrait of expectation. 'Don't you remember any of it?' he begs. 'How many times I've been there to rescue you because he came home drunk and angry. He was a horrible drunk, Chloe. You remember that I told you I've been paying your mortgage?' He looks up, defiant now. 'I saw a chance to help you make a clean break. I took it.'

'Help me? You told me he killed himself because of me,' I say, horrified. And for the first time in the conversation I can see that he feels a shred of shame, a sign of doubt over what he's done. His chin drops towards his chest and he steadies himself against the table.

'A mistake, Chloe.'

'A mistake? Is that all you can say? Why would you do that?' He doesn't answer. My voice becomes weaker as my strength begins to leave me. 'How could you let me believe that?'

'I just . . . I saw a way to end it, that was all. I thought that if you felt guilty over his death then you wouldn't question it. I thought you would leave it in the past. I just wanted you to move on.'

I begin pacing again, leaving wet footprints on the floor. 'Dad, Andrew is my husband. I had every right to know that he was alive. That I was married. You had no right to keep it from me.'

'I know, Chloe, but I was just trying to save you. That's all. I did it for you.'

'For me? What were you trying to save me from?'

He glances at my mother, then down at the floor. When he looks up again, he has puffed his chest out, making himself large. Perhaps that's the only way he can convince himself that what he did is right. 'From the pain of a marriage that was no longer working,' he says quietly.

As he continues to speak, the memories begin to come back to me, snippets from the past, hurried and urgent. I watch him confess and I know with total certainty that his disapproval of Andrew began the moment he caught us together at the old mill when we were little more than kids.

It was a Friday night, I recall. I was up in my room trying

to finish off an assignment for English literature, an essay on forgiveness for our study of *The Tempest*. U2's *Joshua Tree* was playing low on the stereo. I heard my father complaining about something, my mother's response. Their voices were muffled and I couldn't make out what they were saying. It was nothing new: another argument, tacked onto the back of those we'd survived throughout the week. I turned the volume up and lay down on the bed, my eyes closed as 'With or Without You' played out. I picked up my phone, sent a text to Andrew.

THEY'RE ARGUING AGAIN. MEET ME AT THE OLD MILL??

A short while later I heard the beep of an answer come through.

HEY BABE. BE THERE IN THIRTY MINS XX

I closed my eyes and buried my head under the pillow. It was about twenty minutes after that when I heard a knock at my door. I knew it must be my father. He was the only one who knocked, waiting at the threshold for permission to enter ever since the day I started developing breasts. They had become a natural and insurmountable hurdle between us, a fact for which I was grateful. I sat round on the edge of the bed, lowered the volume.

'Come in.'

I was taken aback when he opened the door. His face was drawn, his eyes red. I had never seen my father cry, but I had no doubt he had been crying. His hair was all messed up, and his cheeks were flushed pink. There was a small tear in the neck of his shirt, his skin exposed.

'I need your help,' he said. I was so shocked by his appearance that I got up, followed without question. I licked my lips but my mouth was dry, my tongue scratchy as I trailed behind him, filled with a sense of dread.

I had seen my mother in all manner of states by that point: head in a toilet bowl, in bed for days, bloody from where she had fallen and hurt herself. They were moments that spoke of the fragility of our lives. Although she held it together for most of the time, we all knew, even Jess, who was no more than four years old at the time, that there was always a disaster just waiting to happen. We all knew that there was a chance we might open a cupboard and find a bottle of something stashed in there instead of toiletries or food. We had learned to ignore it, shove the bottle back, pretend it wasn't there.

I looked out through the large gable window, a view to the night. It was cold, past dusk, the light disappearing behind the thick wall of Willows Wood. The brightest stars were already shining, the sky was that clear. There was no wind, the air so still I could hear the rush of the River Mole even though we were some distance away. How I wished I was there. But instead I was standing with my father outside their bedroom door. He stopped, turned to face me with one hand on the handle. His fingers gripped it, skin tight over bone.

'I need you to do something for me.' He looked at his cuffs, let go of the door handle to twist the left one back into alignment. 'I need you to talk to your mother.'

'What about?' I asked. We weren't speaking a huge amount

by that point, instead choosing to interact from a safe distance: a note left in the kitchen, a text message to confirm pick-up times for weekend piano lessons. I always thought it best to give her a wide berth. That way I could avoid the polar extremes of her moods.

'She is packing a bag,' he said, standing up straight and taking a step back to view himself in a mirror on the wall. From the shake of his head I assumed he didn't like what he saw. 'She intends to leave us, Chloe. Apparently she has somewhere better to go. But we cannot let that happen. I cannot allow her to leave this house. To leave you. She is your mother. She belongs here.'

Despite the fact that I was nodding in agreement, the first thought that came to mind was that perhaps if she did leave it wouldn't be so bad. It wasn't that I didn't want her around. It was just that I thought her not being here might be best for everybody. Herself included.

I had so many questions when it came to relationships. I couldn't figure out how they worked. Were individuals bad, full of problems, or was it different combinations of people that caused the fights? If she left, would she stop drinking? Or would she become free to drink as much as she wanted without intervention from her family or a reason to limit herself? If she left, would my father become a kinder man, or would he divert his angry and manipulative attentions elsewhere? Towards me, perhaps? Worse still, towards Jess?

'What do you want me to do about it?'

'I need you to tell her that she has to stay. That you need us both. That if she were to leave, you wouldn't be able to cope.'

It seemed so unfair, a toss-up between me and her. Because really it was Mum who couldn't cope. That was why she wanted to leave. She had to get away, perhaps in order to survive. I understood that, just a little. But there was a selfish part of me that didn't want to face the prospect of everyday life without her.

'And tell her that Jess wouldn't be able to cope either.' His voice was a whisper now; he was nodding his head, turning to open the door, pushing me through, without waiting to see if I had agreed to do what he asked. Did he even care if I had agreed or not?

I stepped through, could hear her movements inside. There was a bag on the bed, clothes strewn about like there had been an explosion. A bottle was standing on the bedside table, something clear, half-empty. I looked left, then right, couldn't see her. There was a low-level lamp shining against the far wall, casting a blood-orange glow across the bed. And that was when I got my first glimpse of her, as my eyes trailed to the corner of the room.

She came sneaking out on all fours like an animal, un-identifiable in many ways as my mother. My father touched the light switch and she cowered away as the overhead light went on, too bright for her eyes. I turned, looked at him. His face was tight, his jaw locked. I knew in that moment that he wanted the light to dazzle her, make her flinch. A brief moment of guiltless retribution.

'Go on, tell her what you wanted to say,' he ordered.

I took a few steps forward. 'Mum?' I asked, as if I wasn't even sure it was her. Her eyes were swollen from tears, streaked with make-up.

'Chloe?' The realisation that I was there seemed to spur her on. I turned to glance at Dad, but he was looking away, unable to keep his eyes on Mum or watch what she was doing. I crouched down by her side. She was trying to stand up, wobbly on unsteady legs. 'What do you want to say to me?' she asked, her words slurred, voice cracking.

I put my arms round her and lowered her gently to the soft yellow carpet, then sat down next to her. Her face was close to mine, her breath pungent and poisonous.

'You can't leave, Mum.' God, I felt so guilty. 'I want you to stay.'

She reached out to touch my face, made contact with my cheek. Her hand was warm and sticky. She started to cry. 'Chloe, I—'

But I interrupted her. I wanted her here. Needed her. I knew it in that very moment, when I decided to put my own life above hers. I looked across at the bag on the bed and I knew I had to change her mind. 'I need you here, Mum. Jess needs you. You can't leave us.'

'You'd be better off without me,' she sniffed. 'I have to leave, for all our sakes.'

And then it was my turn to cry. 'Please, Mum. I can't do this on my own.' She knew what I meant. She understood that I didn't want to be left alone with him. 'Please?'

And that was all it took, one word from child to mother. She nodded, and a tear fell onto her skirt, a dark blush on the cream linen. 'OK, Chloe. Please stop crying. I'll stay, I promise.'

I heard my father moving, his weight as it disturbed the edge of the bed. 'Chloe, I'd like to talk to your mother alone, if that's all right with you.' He spoke as if I had a choice. As if I'd dare to challenge him and make a demand of my own.

She nodded, touched me lightly on the leg as I stood up. I walked with my head down towards the door. I glanced back only once. Mum was staring at me, watching me as I left. Was that gratitude that I needed her in her eyes, or resentment that I'd asked her to stay? Perhaps it was a bit of both. Just as I closed the door behind me, I heard her ask, 'How could you?' I hoped her question was aimed at him rather than me.

I headed towards the top of the stairs, knew I had to get out. I heard a door open behind me as I descended the first few steps. I didn't intend to look back until I heard a little voice.

'Can I come with you?' I turned to see Jess standing in her doorway. She was already dressed in her coat and shoes, her eyes wide and pleading.

I shook my head. 'No, Jess. Go back to bed. It's past your bedtime already.'

She took a step forward. Mittens swung on elastic. 'But I'm ready,' she said, holding up her hands to show me.

'I said no. I'm going to meet Andrew. It's grown-up stuff.' And with that I turned, ran down the stairs, and out through the back door.

The air was freezing as I burst into the night, my skin cold and goose-pimpled. I ran up the garden, my breath fogging the air. I crossed the bridge to the old mill, where I huddled under the sheet, waiting for my saviour to come. He arrived only a few minutes later. He didn't ask questions, and instead just slipped beneath the sheet next to me. I crawled into his arms, felt his strength and comfort. I have no idea how long we were there before one of us spoke.

I told him what had happened and he listened in disbelief. He pulled me in closer still, my head cushioned in his neck, his pulse strong against my cheek. A crow cawed in nearby Willows Wood.

'Your family make mine look normal,' he laughed, but it was bittersweet, laced with the knowledge that it wasn't quite true. I had been to his house, knew they were far from normal.

'What am I going to do?' I asked, sure that he would have the answers.

And he did. His lips were warm on my skin as he kissed me, his fingers cold as his inexperienced hands fumbled at my clothes. I was still wearing my school uniform, so he pulled my jumper up and over my head, pushed his hands underneath my blue shirt. I shivered, yelped. He stopped for a second, looked me in the eyes, then whispered, 'Stay here with me. Together we'll be fine.'

It was an empty promise, a mark of what was to come. But in that moment, it was all I needed.

Before long we were both half undressed, and I was lying back on the flour sacks with his body pressed up against mine. My eyes were closed, my fingers gripping tight to his shoulders as he moved up against me. It was our first time. I was shaking, but this time not from the cold. I could taste his salty skin as my lips brushed against his shoulder. I felt warm, comforted. And then I heard a loud click, and my eyes flicked open.

'Get off her,' my father said, motioning with his gun for Andrew to move aside. I recognised it as the gun he took shooting. Clay pigeon, wildfowl. Andrew scrambled off, tried to fasten his trousers. My father leant down, grabbed my arm, pulled me to my feet as I tried to cover myself with my half-open shirt. He looked at me, at my bare skin, and then away in shock and disgust. I wanted to get out of there, drag him away, but he was still pointing the gun at Andrew. He pressed the end of it against his forehead. Andrew froze. I heard the horses neighing in the distance.

'Dad, please,' I said, but I could only watch as his grip on the gun tightened. He pushed me away and I staggered back against a wooden beam.

'If you come near her again, I will kill you.'

Andrew said nothing. Didn't move. My father didn't flinch either. For a moment we all just stood there as the floorboards creaked under our weight. Then my father turned to me. 'Get back to the house.'

I shook my head. I wanted to say no. I wanted to protect Andrew as he had tried to protect me. 'What are you going to do?' I asked.

My father's voice was so calm, so quiet. 'I said get back to the house.' I looked to Andrew, who nodded. I had never seen him so defiant. He didn't even look scared. Maybe he was used to bullies too.

I backed away, stood waiting just the other side of the bridge, trying to dress as quickly as I could in my gathered clothes. My father emerged a minute later, the tip of the gun dragging along the ground. He arrived in front of me, towering over me. 'You'll not see that boy again.'

I swallowed hard, tried to speak. 'Dad, I—'

He slapped me across the face with such force I fell to the ground. My cheek stung like ice and fire all at the same time. He had never struck me before.

'If you think I'm going to let you become a slut like your mother, running around after men, you can think again.' He gripped my arm and pulled me to my feet, marched me back towards the house. I wanted Mum, wanted to tell her that we had to get away from him, that we should leave together. But after begging her to stay, I knew I couldn't ask her to leave for me.

Later that night I watched from my bedroom window as he doused the bridge in petrol and set it alight, taking away my escape route. His wheels of control already firmly in motion.

A while later, once the flames had died down, once all that was left was a trail of white smoke to signal the destruction of my sanctuary, the start of a new reign, he came to my room, standing in the doorway as I lay in bed. I didn't want to react, give him the satisfaction of acceptance or rejection. To him, from now on, I wanted to be nothing. In turn he chose his path too, stepping towards me, touching my arm. He squeezed it, letting me know that he was in control. I knew he meant to hurt me.

When he spoke, it was quietly and without emotion. 'There are no lengths I wouldn't go to in order to protect you, Chloe. I will never let you forget that.' And then he kissed me on the forehead and walked away.

24

It lasts at least two hours, the screaming and wailing, shouting and crying. I round on each one of them in turn, accusations and threats: threats to leave, threats that they'll never see me again. Threats that I'm going home. All this time he was telling me that I might have been responsible for Andrew's death, that I might have chosen to crash my car on purpose. It was all bullshit. The worst of all lies.

'I'm not staying here,' I say, as much for myself as them. 'I can't be here with any of you.'

'Chloe, don't be silly. It's freezing out.' My father rushes ahead of me, stands with his back to the front door. 'You have nowhere else to go.'

'I have my own home, Dad.' I see my mother crying in the background. 'I had my own life.'

'You can't go there. Stay here with us. I'll help you, Chloe, I promise.' He steps towards me. 'Besides, you can't be alone.'

'Why not? You leave me alone all the time. And anyway, maybe I won't be. Andrew might be there. After all, it's not like he's dead, is it?' Another moment of shame crosses his eyes. But I see now his only regret is that he has been caught in his own lie. And a thought comes to me. What if I had gone to my house and found Andrew there? What would my father have done then? 'Tell me this,' I say. 'What did you think was going to happen further down the line?'

He seems confused. 'I don't understand?'

'I mean how were you going to keep this up? How could you expect to maintain this lie without me finding out?'

He waits, raises a hand. I shy away from it, but still he brings it to my face, cups my cheek in his massive palm. 'Oh Chloe. You poor thing. You really have no idea who you were married to, do you? It's easy enough to maintain a lie if the person involved is complicit.'

I take a moment to catch my breath. 'What do you mean?' My words arc quiet because I think I already know. I just don't want to believe it. 'I'm not complicit.'

'Not you, my love. Andrew. One cheque, that was all it took. I left it blank.' He shakes his head. 'But every penny was worth it if it bought you your freedom.'

And that's the moment I can't take it any more. My eyes feel hazy, my head light. I have no fight left, no energy. I sink into a heap on the floor, and after a while, and a lot of fuss on my mother's part, my father is at my side again.

'It was an opportunity for you to make a clean break from a man who did nothing but ruin your life,' he says. 'It was for the best, Chloe. You are better off away from him.'

He scoops me up unchallenged, carries me to bed. I lie there for an indistinguishable number of hours in the dark, alone. My mother knocks on the door a couple of times, begs to be granted access. At some point she comes in, gives my head a wipe with a cool towel, tucks me in and kisses me on the cheek. My father too. I feel the squeeze of a blood pressure monitor and it gives me a lucid flashback to the hospital. I am lying supine in bed, a man hovering over me, touching my head. I see my father, recognise his beard. 'I'll make it all better, I promise you, Chloe.' Then I'm asleep again. Lights come on, go out. I slip away, lost once more.

I stir when I hear the floorboards outside my bedroom creaking as somebody passes over them. It's Jess, I think, the footsteps too quick to belong to my mother, too light for my father. It's only Jess that doesn't ask permission or knock on the door. She opens it, steps in, closes it behind her. She sits down at my side, the mattress sinking, her presence disturbing my position.

'I'm sorry, Chloe. I feel like I lied by default.' I wonder how she's got the nerve to say that. By default? She lied to my face when I told her about the boy in my dreams. She could have told me about Joshua, yet she said nothing. But my thoughts are patchy. I can't quite focus on telling her how I really feel. She brings the cold with her, a chill across my skin. She wipes a tear from her cheek. 'They lied to me too at first. By the time I found out the truth it was too late, and I thought if I told you then it would only make things harder.'

'You lied,' I tell her, suddenly finding my voice. The words come out fast and jumbled, but in my head at least they make sense. 'Not by default. You should have told me. You had the choice to tell me, but you took his side.' I feel her nodding her head in quiet, desperate agreement before she stands up and walks towards the door. I speak just as she reaches for the handle. 'I've come to expect lies from him. I'm beginning to remember the way he used to behave, his need for control. But you? You said we used to tell each other everything, Jess. You told me that you hoped I could trust you again. How can I trust you if you're prepared to lie to me about something as important as this?' She fights back tears, clings to the door for support. 'You should have told me what you knew.'

She turns to face me. 'And if I did, would you tell me what you know, Chloe?' Her words are enough to silence me. 'I heard you talking to Dad. I know you can remember parts of the accident, that you're searching for your old life as if you still loved Andrew. You aren't telling us the truth either, so you have no right to demand it from me.'

'I did love Andrew,' I protest, sitting up.

She shakes her head, irritated. 'Whatever you say. But you of all people should understand that sometimes it's better not to know the truth. That sometimes lies hurt less.' And with that she closes the door behind her, leaving me alone again in the pale light of the bedside lamp.

My mother bustles into the bedroom the following morning while I am still asleep. She draws back the curtains and smiles at the day outside as if nothing the night before happened the way I remember it. Do I remember it? She turns around with a cup of tea in her hand, the steam rising in front of her face.

'Good morning,' she says. She's bordering on skittish, her fingers tapping at the edge of the mug. I notice that despite the early hour, she has done her hair, make-up too. She has painted the rims of her eyes dark and her lips pink and glossy. A meshwork of fine lines attests to a life spent outside, and at the hands of my father. 'It's a beautiful day.'

'I don't care about the weather.' I pull my knees in tight to my chest with the covers draped over me. 'I'm leaving this place today.'

She shakes her head, smiles at what I can only assume she takes for my naivety. 'Try to be reasonable, Chloe. Last night you were out of control, trying to run away. But that was last night, and today you are better, I can tell. And outside the air is crisp and the day is new. Every day is a—'

I stop her because I suddenly know what's coming. A memory of lying here in this bed, my mother sitting beside me on the edge, making meaningless promises. 'A new day. Yes, Mum. I've heard it before.' I recall how it became her motto during my teenage years, after that night I begged her to stay. Later I adopted it as my own, used it to comfort Joshua after Andrew had had a particularly heavy night on the booze, promising that the day ahead would be different. It never was, and Joshua knew it. What a way to spend a life, a catalogue of broken promises, dashed every time by the one person who was supposed to love you the most.

'In which case you should be starting to believe me by now.' She smiles and sits down on the edge of the bed, setting the mug of tea on the bedside table.

'Believe you? Are you kidding me? I'm leaving, Mum, getting out of this place. You lied to me. All of you. I can't be here any more.' She looks away, embarrassed. 'He told me I was responsible for my husband's death.'

'I know, and I'm so sorry.' She reaches for me, her hand

on mine. 'I wanted him to tell you the truth about Andrew. I promise I did.' Her words give me hope, but then I catch the silence of the briefest pause. There's a 'but' coming. 'But then when your father reminded me of everything you had been through with Andrew, I thought maybe it would be for the best if you simply couldn't remember. Anyway, you know how he is, Chloe. I didn't dare go against him.'

A layer of sweat glistens on her brow. How I can be angry with her? It's true that my father has complicated and controlled both of our lives.

'Maybe you thought what you were doing was for the best, but now I'm telling you it wasn't. You know the right thing to do would be to tell me where Andrew is.'

'But he took the money, Chloe. Why would you want to find him?'

'I need to work out what happened that night. I need to know why I didn't show up when I was supposed to meet him. You know he's a suspect, don't you?'

Her eyes widen. 'A suspect? Andrew?' She looks away, thinks about it for a moment. 'Well, he always was very volatile. He was no good right from the start.'

But I know now that this isn't true. I have remembered some things about the man I married. Those moments we shared in the old mill; our trips to the pier. It's not much, but it's enough to know it wasn't all bad. And when I stood on the pier and looked back towards the beach, I remembered something else. The dream I had, of being with Joshua overlooking the water. I am certain that was the same day I decided to leave. It was the same day Joshua told me that every day was the same, that nothing ever got easier. I made the decision to leave that very night. But I didn't leave because I hated Andrew. I left because we all deserved something better. Nobody more than Joshua.

'Anyway, suspect or not,' my mother is saying, 'there are more important things to address right now. Get yourself up and dressed. Your father is waiting for you downstairs.'

'I'm not going to—'

But she doesn't let me finish. 'Chloe, you have to.' And in that moment, there's none of that team spirit she was searching for last night. 'If you don't, he'll just come up here and get you. The outcome will be the same either way.'

25

At first I thought that perhaps Mum was under his spell, going along with his plans through fear. But now she doesn't seem scared at all. I'm shaking as I watch her leave, terrified of the idea that what is happening here is unstoppable. That I don't have a choice. I don't trust her despite her assurances that everything will be OK if I just let them help me. I don't trust her when she says she's on my side, that my father is to blame, that she is simply following orders.

I dress in warm clothes and a sturdy pair of trainers. When I arrive downstairs, I walk into a scene of relative chaos, consistent with what my mother told me earlier. A general lack of order that feels wrong: dead flowers scattered across the hallway table, a water spill that nobody has bothered to clear up. A few coats hang limply over the banister and another, mine from yesterday, lies in a mucky heap on the floor.

'Where are they?' I ask as my father looks up from his newspaper. He's sitting on the velveteen couch, a bloodstain still noticeable on the cushion like a dirty brown smudge from where Peter treated my wound. The fire crackles as it burns. My head feels like a helium-filled balloon, the after-effects of whatever he gave me last night slow to leave my system. I'm aware now that I'm moving that I don't feel entirely with it.

'Jess is out with a friend.' I remember her visit last night, the insinuation she made that I was keeping secrets. What does she think I know? 'And your mother has just popped to post a letter. She'll be back soon. Why don't you take a seat? It's important that we start to work together, get you feeling better after last night's little outburst.'

I perch on the edge of a stool. 'My husband is alive and you told me he was dead. How did you expect me to react?'

'Well I never expected you to find out,' he says, this time it would seem without any shame at all. 'After all, Andrew took our money, Chloe. He left you.' He sighs, nods his head as if he can't get over the awful facts. 'But I agree it was most unfortunate that you had to find out that way.'

'I think that's a bit of an understatement, don't you?'

He closes his eyes briefly, flippant as he speaks. 'Not really. After all, we were only following an agreed course of treatment. But I promise I can help you begin to feel better. I was doing very well at one point until the police started meddling and your mother let that old photograph slip through.' His words are soft, resigned, and yet still they sound like a threat. He rests his elbow on the arm of the sofa, one hand on his chin. 'We need to get back on track, Chloe.'

I'm not sure what he is suggesting here, but all sorts of thoughts are running through my mind. I thought at first he was a passive liar, somebody who was taking advantage of the situation, using my amnesia to soften my pain at losing my son, to exclude a problematic husband from my future. But the way he is speaking now, I feel like he has some sort of plan. Get back on track? What is supposed to have been agreed? Whatever it is, I want no part of it.

'I was rather hoping we'd have something positive to tell your mother when she arrives home. I think it would be good to try to make a start right now. There's no point in wasting any more time. But you know that reconsolidation therapy only works if you are willing. *Are* you willing, Chloe?'

'Willing to do what?' What is he talking about? 'What is reconsolidation therapy?'

He sighs, frustrated. 'You know all about it, Chloe. We discussed it right at the start, when you first woke up. We made an agreement.'

'I don't remember.'

'That doesn't change the fact that we discussed it. Reconsolidation therapy, Chloe. A proven way to move forward, to compartmentalise your feelings about the traumatic events of the past. It's about putting those difficulties behind you and finding a better future.'

It sounds a bit like the blurb on the back of a self-help book. False promises. 'Cut the bullshit, Dad.'

He clenches his jaw, then stands, sets the newspaper back on the chair. 'Reconsolidation therapy is a way of dealing with post-traumatic stress, Chloe. It enables the patient or client to resolve their anxiety, move past whatever is holding them back. We discussed our options and you thought it would be for the best if you couldn't remember what had happened. In some patients it actually facilitates a complete erasure of the traumatic event.'

'You're trying to tell me I chose this? I would never have agreed to that.'

'I can assure you that you did. Isn't that easier than having to deal with your loss? Your grief?' He pours a small glass of water and opens the drawer of the antique bureau. He produces a small childproof bottle, taps out a tablet and offers it to me. 'Let's not waste any more time.'

'What is that?' I ask.

A flash of disappointment crosses his face. He holds out the tablet, expectant and waiting. Eventually he relents. 'It's propranolol. You've been taking it before each session,' he says with a sigh. 'It simply lowers your blood pressure, helps speed the process along. Now come along, lie back on the couch.'

'I'm not taking that.'

'So what *are* you going to do?' he almost shouts before getting himself under control. A moment of frustration. 'Leave this place? That's what you told your mother, isn't it?' He sneers, almost as though it's a dare. 'And go where? With whom? You're not ready to leave this house, Chloe. You cannot be alone this soon after surgery. Now come on. It's high time we made a start.'

'OK,' I say. He hands me the tablet, the glass of water, waits for me to comply. I place the tablet on my tongue, then, as I bring the glass up to my lips, move it to the side against my teeth, manage not to swallow it as I take a small sip of water.

'I'm pleased you've finally seen sense, Chloe. We can soon have you back on track. It really is so much better if you can't remember either of them.'

'Dad,' I say, just as he is sitting down, making himself comfortable. While he isn't looking, I take the tablet from my mouth, push it between the cushions of the settee. 'Could you do me a favour before we start?'

'What is it?' he asks as he looks up.

'I'm cold. I left my jumper on the bed. Would you get it for me before we begin?' I rub at my scarred leg. 'I'd go myself but my leg is sore today.' He smiles, pats me on the head, his hand cold and damp.

When I hear the creak of his footsteps on the stairs, I stand up from the couch, grab the lawyer's letter from the mantelpiece and move towards the hallway. I take whatever money is left in a small bowl on the table, a few coins, then slip through the front door, under the dripping arch of wisteria, and run up the driveway as fast as I can. Within a minute or so I'm out through the gate, on my way to Rusperford. I reach into my pocket, pull out the beer mat with Guy's number on it. He told me to call if I needed help, and I've never needed it more than now.

26

I wait outside the village shop, hiding in the shadow of a hedge. The rain is pouring down, my hair soaked through, the dressing coming unstuck from my head. It's about fifteen minutes before I hear the slowing of a car, see it pull up alongside the kerb, the tyres sending streams of water rushing over the pavement. The windows are misted over, the bonnet steaming as heat rises from it.

At first I'm not sure whether it's Guy or not, so I wait, watch from behind the sparse privet hedge as a shape stretches towards the passenger window. I've already seen my father drive past once, cruising along slowly, searching for me. But as a hand slaps against the glass to clear a porthole in the mist, I see Guy's familiar dark hair. At first he hesitates, and it is only when I step out from the shadow of the hedge and into the downpour that he leans over, opens the door.

'I wasn't sure if it was you,' he says as I duck into the car, hood pulled tight over my head. 'Have you been waiting long?' He pushes at his sleeve to glance at his watch. 'I got here as soon as I could.'

'No, it's fine.' I have so much I want to ask Guy about: the medication my father tried to give me, the therapy techniques he's been using. But although I'm the one who called him for help, I'm not sure I trust him enough to just blurt it all out; there's still the possibility that he might turn around and take me back to my father, like he did when I turned up in the hospital.

'Look at you, you're soaked. Let me help you out of that.' I turn to face him, notice that his cheeks are pink from the cold, his hair drying into a mass of wayward curls. He helps me pull my coat out from underneath my body before tossing it over to the back seat. I reach around for my seat belt as he sits back, his eyes on my face, taking in my frozen features. I wish he would get going. 'You look better,' he says eventually. He flicks on his indicator light and pulls out. My sense of relief is massive. We are on our way at last.

We leave Rusperford behind, moving into the stark winter landscape of southern England. The trees are all bare, skeletons of what they were in the summer, branches gnarled and intertwined like nests of spindly fingers. The hedgerows aren't much better, damp and brown, naked in parts. The landscape feels like me somehow: empty, ripped bare of its vitality and life. It's just surviving, waiting for a new season to come and bear fruit. It will be months before the first shoots of spring make an appearance.

We pull onto the A23, heading south. Traffic roars past us, rain coming at us from all directions. We drive through villages, the rooftops of distant houses just visible over the fences and clouds of spray from the road. 'How are you feeling about today?' Guy asks.

'Good,' I tell him. When I called him from the payphone to ask for his help, I told him not to mention the trip to my father; that he thought it was too soon but that I felt I needed to do it anyway. Guy said he understood. And now I'm here in his car, on the way to my old home. Anxiety grips me as a flashback of the crash comes to me, the similarity of the conditions, the memory of heavy rain and my careless driving. I don't want to think about the accident right now and everything I possibly did to cause it. 'But I'm also nervous,' I continue. 'I'm anxious about what we might find.'

'Do you think there is a chance your husband will be there?'

'I hope so.' Guy presses down on the accelerator. 'But part of me is scared that he will be there too.'

He seems surprised. 'Why?'

'Because it only raises more questions. Like why he was prepared to accept my father's money in order to leave me alone. Why I meant so little to him.'

As we drive, it's impossible not to wonder what Guy thinks of all this, this plan to return home in search of a resurrected husband and a lost life. I'm sure he is used to his patients rambling on about their complicated situations, but I don't want him to think of me as one of his patients. Because Guy has been on my mind for other reasons as well. I like the way he looks at me, the way he touched me in the hotel, how he made me feel desire. It's a guilty feeling, but it's human. I want him to like me, think of me as more than a charitable good deed. It's the fact that he seems like a full, complete person; I want to be part of something like that, instead of being wrapped in the lies and fakery of my family. It's not even sexual. Not entirely. Just sitting here with him now is enough; he makes me feel alive for the first time in months.

I watch him as he drives, the car speeding over the South Downs, a landscape of muted green hues tinged silver by the rain. The angle of his jaw is set low, square and distinct. His eyes are a deep brown, his lashes long and dark. After a while he notices my gaze. 'Everything's going to be all right,' he says, like a dependable old friend.

We arrive in Brighton, and Guy pulls up by the side of the road, buses and cars sailing past. Seagulls squawk relentlessly overhead, as if they are driven by anger. I crack open the window, breathe in the smell. It's strange, but I don't feel as I expected to feel coming here, knowing my house is only a short distance away. I'd expected to feel anger towards my father, resentment like I did while I was in my parents' house, wondering about all the things I'd lost from my life. But instead all I feel is sadness, an overwhelming sense of pity for the person I used to be. Because I realise that in a small house somewhere nearby I once lived a life consumed by difficulties that left me unable to appreciate what I had. And now with Joshua gone it's too late to get it back.

'Did you hear me, Chloe?' Guy asks. He's speaking to me, but I'm lost in the thoughts of my wasted life. I turn to face him. He's looking at the screen of his phone. 'I was saying I've had five missed calls from your father in the last twenty minutes. No doubt he's looking for you.'

I wonder if I look as nervous as I feel. 'Are you going to call him back, tell him where I am?'

He sits back in his seat. He doesn't look at me during those few agonising moments while he decides what to do. 'Well, I should.'

I take a chance. 'But you're not going to?'

'If you ask me not to, then no. But Chloe, do you want to explain what's going on?'

As we sit there amidst the sound of the cascading waves and the rumble of busy traffic, I tell him what I believe. What I know. And only as I say it aloud do I realise the extent of it.

For a moment he is quiet as he processes what I've said. Then he turns, looks at me. 'That's quite a lot to take in, Chloe, and quite a stretch of the imagination.'

I can see all manner of thoughts running through his mind: am I crazy, is this going to cost him his job, and is it possible that I'm right?

'Listen, let's just focus on what we know, see if your husband is here. Try not to think about the things your father has told you, or what he might be doing. I know he has made some mistakes, but I'm sure he's not trying to modify your memories.'

'Is that what you really think?' I ask. He swallows hard as he looks away, and I'm not remotely convinced that he believes what he has just said. 'You're sure he's trying to help me, even if I feel he isn't?'

'What else would he be doing? He's your father. He loves you. Nobody who loves you would try to hurt you.'

Is that true? Is love binary like that? Or is there a scale that tips between joy and disappointment, altruism and selfishness?

'I just don't know any more. I'm so confused by it all. My mind feels like a mess.' We sit for a moment in silence, both of us unsure what to say, and I wonder if he is regretting getting involved. 'I don't mean anything by it when I speak like that, Guy. It's just so hard not to be angry with him.'

'I understand. But try to look at it from his perspective. He knew that your old life was very difficult, and then you woke up and couldn't remember a thing. He hoped for something better for you, that's all. Perhaps he hoped for some*body* better for you as well.' He senses my frown. 'You had left him, Chloe. Remember? You were planning to create a new life. Maybe your father was just trying to help with what he thought you wanted.'

The windows are steaming over again. Guy uses his sleeve to clear a patch of condensation, peers towards the grey haze of a non-existent horizon. In the near-distance I can hear the waves breaking against a shingle shore, the call of the gulls. I suddenly recall the mornings when they would wake me at first light with their petulant conversation. Memories of an empty bed, of watching Joshua search for his father, just metres away from here. Home. If only I had another chance, what would I do? Stay and make it work, or search for something better? For some*body* better, as Guy put it? I just don't know any more.

Guy turns to me, and his hand finds a place on my knee. 'It's only a matter of time before you start to remember more about the life you used to live, which in turn will give you the freedom to move on with your future. One way or another.'

It's easy to profess morality when you're happy, Chloe. And I know you scoffed at the idea, but I always thought of myself as a moral person. Sure, I know I've made mistakes, but I've paid for them. Oh, how I've paid. And while you might laugh at that now, you knew it once. You knew that I was worth something to you, and that our life together meant something to you as well.

But you just don't have a clue, do you? You follow your routine of waking, working, swimming, and complaining about how marriage is so damn hard, but you have no idea what I'm going through. What it means to be alone. To want to get back to the life you used to share with the woman you love. All I want is to get you back, Chloe. Do I even exist in your world any more?

I've been there for you. I've loved you when nobody else would. When you cried about the mess of your life, I wiped your eyes. There's nobody for me but you, Chloe. You're everything to me. I don't think you realise that you have made me like this. Do you? You told me it would be forever, and I believed the things you said. Now you want to take that away from me. You want to leave. How could you even think that? How do you fucking dare?

So I'm sorry, but I can't do this. I can't stay away from you. I won't stay away from you. We are made for each other, Chloe. I love you. Why can't you see it. You. Me. Joshua. Perfect.

I will not let you make this mistake, finish what we have. I will not let you end us. And if you try again to kill this life we share, I promise you, Chloe, with everything I have, that I will kill you first.

27

We wait for the buzz of the pedestrian crossing and then fight our way through the crowds of shoppers leaving the Sainsbury's Local. Seeing the place triggers a memory of picking up bread and milk, painkillers if and when Andrew had a rough night. Yes, I remember that. We edge into the mouth of a narrow side street, ripe with the smell of meatball sandwiches coming from a nearby deli. People rush along around us as we negotiate the uneven surface of the road, the tarmac formed like a dirty patchwork quilt. The paintwork on the surrounding buildings is dry and flaking, colours faded. In places whole chunks of plaster have come away from the walls, exposing the bricks beneath.

We arrive at the front door to a depressing little building. It's narrow and old, positioned alongside a back-street bar called West End Nights. A crack runs up one side of the wall. I look up at the dark, inky window above, and then down at the lawyer's letter in my hand. I realise that I know this broken-down house in desperate need of attention. But time, it seems, has put a degree of space between me and it. It's like seeing an old friend and not being able to quite believe just how much they've changed, or falling out of love and seeing all those flaws you have long since denied. Did I really live here in this dingy, dismal place? I look at Guy for reassurance, and he reaches down, takes my hand. I know I did. This house before me is my home.

No garden exists to pretty up the front; instead there's just a small path that merges with the road, bordered by a set of double yellow lines. Two vehicles are parked with their hazard lights flashing, making the road near impassable for other cars. A hanging basket at the side of the front door contains the remains of a dead clematis plant, chopping back and forth as it is taken by the wind. A gull circles above us, swoops in close, then soars over the rooftops as it heads back out to sea.

Guy braces himself against the wall, hands in his pockets. His hair blows about in wayward tufts, tousled and curly in the moist salt air. I knock on the door. Wait. No footsteps, no light. I knock again, hear nothing. Nobody is home.

'Maybe we should come back later,' I suggest.

But Guy tucks himself in close to the door, then lets a screwdriver slip from his sleeve. He checks once over his shoulder before fiddling the flat end into position alongside the lock. I hear a car door closing and turn to see one of the parked cars pulling away. When I look back, the front door to my house is gaping wide open.

'You broke in?' I ask as I peer into the dark corridor beyond.

Guy smiles, standing back. 'It's your home, remember?'

I step over a few splinters of wood and into the narrow corridor. The door is loose but still functional, so Guy closes it behind us. I move along the shadowy tunnel, the smell of something rotten getting up my nose. Everything about the atmosphere is stale. It's harder to be back here than I thought, and I can feel my breathing quickening. I hear Guy flicking a switch behind me, but we remain in the dark. It's as if the place has been tarnished, marked in some way by the things that have happened. It has become a mausoleum of my life, a testament to everything I have lost.

'I think the electricity is off,' he says, heading towards the kitchen, which connects via a peninsula of cupboards to the lounge. He opens the door of the fridge and pulls out a mouldy loaf. The scent of sour milk fills the air. 'Definitely off,' he says as he drops the bread into a nearby bin, wafting the air with his hand. It must have been there for the best part of three months.

I am standing with one hand on the back of the tartan sofa, feeling the texture underneath. I must have sat here thousands of times. Yet nothing feels like mine. But when I look down, see one of the scatter cushions lost to the floor, I remember Andrew sleeping here. I used to wake up to find him passed out in this very spot, the image so stark in my mind. The thought that I might never see him again is enough to make me feel sick.

Guy picks up the phone, listens to the receiver. 'Still connected.' He comes up behind me, making me jump as he touches my arm. 'Are you all right? What is it?'

'This place smells,' I tell him, unable to admit to the surfacing memories, the odours of blood and vomit, the messes I had to clear up. He smoothes his hands across my shoulders and down my arms in a protective way. For a moment I can feel him behind me, the heat of him, before he moves to open a side window for some air.

I walk to the rear of the house and turn the key in the back door, opening it wide into a small yard. The wind rushes in through the open space, bringing with it a handful of leaves and an old McDonald's wrapper. But the fresh air carries with it more than rubbish; there is also the smell of the sea. I recall that day I took the decision to leave, sitting with Joshua, staring at the waves. I realise now that neither in life nor death did I ever manage to protect him. I close the door again, turn the key in the lock.

'There's nobody here,' I tell Guy.

He sits down on the windowsill and folds his arms across his chest. 'I'm very sorry,' he says, his voice soft. 'But it doesn't look to me like anybody has been living here for a while now. I don't think we are going to find Andrew here.'

But if he isn't living here, where the hell is he?

I climb the stairs and Guy follows. I find some of my clothes in my old bedroom and a bottle of perfume on the dresser. I spray a little on my wrist. It's the scent of my old life, the old me. It's an unwelcome reminder of just how far removed I am from the life I used to live. I rub my wrist against my trouser leg to get rid of the smell. I search the cupboards but find nothing that might have once belonged to Andrew.

I move towards a second bedroom, brushing my fingers across the panel of the door where two ragged holes have been drilled into the wood. I see a name plate in my mind, something that used to hang here: *Joshua's Room* in carved rainbow lettering. Somebody has since taken it away. I can feel Guy behind me, willing me on as I push the door open.

An acidic sickness rises to my throat as I look around the room. I swallow over and over as I step inside, but the lump will not go down. Instead it chokes me as I gaze at the blue bed, the chipped paintwork, the mattress stripped of sheets. To the side of the bed I see a small cupboard, the same peeling blue paintwork. Nothing on the top. Limp curtains frame the window, the elephant pattern tired and dated. I look up at the only picture on the wall: alphabet building blocks spelling out his name: *JOSHUA*. I edge away from it, against the bed. A tear breaks free from my eye. I don't know if I'm crying for Joshua and the life he lost, or me and the life that was taken from me. It might very well be both.

Guy draws the curtains wide, pushes open the window as far as it will go. A cold draught whips through, snatches up the material. Over that I can hear the chug of a bus and the chatter of shoppers in the street below.

'This was his room,' I say. I pull open a drawer, find it empty. 'But his stuff is all gone.' Who has been here and taken his things? My parents? Andrew?

Guy remains by the window, his hands twitching at his sides. For a moment he appears unsure, as if he doesn't know whether to approach me. He brings one hand up to his head, rubs at his brow, and then – as if it's a last-minute decision, to try to do the right thing – he comes towards me and wraps his arms around me.

The feeling of his body against mine is so good, so strong and solid. I find comfort in the warmth of his touch and the rhythm of his chest as he breathes. Because here on the edge of my old life, I have never felt the loss of myself more keenly. The loss of my son. And at that moment Guy's touch and presence might be the only thing that keeps me from breaking. It feels like Andrew in the old mill all over again, the only thing capable of saving me from the pain of what my life has become.

'Maybe your parents cleared the house while you were in hospital.'

He brushes a tear from my cheek, and as I look up, his hand still on my skin, our eyes meet. For a second he stares at me, our faces only an inch apart. I can feel his hesitant fingers on my back. There's something in this moment, expectation and possibility. I freeze, unsure what I want. Even what I need.

Then his grip tightens against me, his instincts taking over. He pushes me back against the cupboard, his movements slow but certain. His hands move up into my hair and I can feel the weight of his body against mine. He kisses my lips, slowly at first, then more urgently. I feel his stubble graze against my skin, the sensation rippling through my body as he presses up against me.

It has been so long since somebody held me like this, craved me in this way. Even Andrew at the end didn't want me like this. At least I don't think so. I kiss him back, feel the closeness, the connection of skin against skin. I fumble at his clothes, kiss his neck with desire. His body fits together with mine as he hoists me up onto the chest of drawers. My scarred right leg is painful and hot, his actions almost forceful. But then as he pulls on my hair to tilt my head back I feel something return to me, a sensation I have felt before, the tingle on my scalp as a hand moves through my thick, unruly hair. I draw back abruptly. This man is not my husband.

'I can't do this,' I say, pulling away. 'It's not right.' I have an urge to stop, not to cheat. It surpasses my desire to be close to Guy. But is this even cheating? Am I still married? Does it count even if I am?

He steps away from me, straightens his clothes. 'I'm sorry, I shouldn't have brought you here. It's my fault.' He adjusts himself, uncomfortable, still aroused despite my resistance. 'It's not your fault, Chloe, it's just . . .' He pauses; looks towards the door. 'Shh,' he says, his voice no louder than a whisper, his finger to his lips. 'Did you hear that?'

At first I can't hear anything, at least nothing other than the people outside, the ever-present seagulls. We wait in silence for a moment longer, and then I hear knocking on the front door, followed by a voice. Somebody is calling my name.

Guy moves first, quick footsteps as he fiddles his shirt back into his trousers. I straighten my hair as best I can, check the damp dressing on my head is still in place. Then I follow him as he descends the first few steps. The voice calls out again.

'Chloe, is that you?' It's a man's voice. 'Chloe, have you come home?'

28

Fear and excitement swell as I consider who it might be. Andrew? Damien Treadstone? Thoughts of the graveyard come to mind, DS Gray's doubts and suspicions. But I have this gut instinct that the voice belongs neither to Andrew nor Treadstone. It is old, frail. It doesn't sound like the voice that came at me through the mist.

'Chloe,' it says again. 'Are you there?' More knocking. I motion for Guy to open the door.

Before us stands an old man, the weight of his hunched body balanced on a metal stick with four plastic feet. If it had been a wooden cane, all crooked and gnarled, he could almost be a caricature from a fairy tale. His hair is grey, swept back from his face in a deep comb-over. The wind has worked several wisps loose and they trouble at his mouth and eyes. In his other hand he's holding a red umbrella, a pattern of little birds flying across the surface. I remember him immediately.

'Cecil,' I say, but it sounds like a question. 'Cecil,' I say again, more confident this time. I step forward and my response is enough to relax Guy, who until that point has been standing at the door like a nightclub bouncer, blocking the man's path.

'It's good to see you, my dear,' he says as he steps past Guy, giving him a nudge with the end of his stick so that he moves out of the way. He glances towards the damaged lock and the fragments of wood but makes no comment as he moves towards me. 'I heard you up and down on the staircase. Recognised your voice.' He's in front of me now, reaching out with a frail hand. 'Your father told me about the accident. I'm so very sorry, Chloe.'

'Thank you,' I say, surprised, part of me wondering what exactly he knows. Does he think Andrew is dead? Has Andrew been here recently at all?

Cecil motions for me to move into the living room, and I step through, my mind racing. I hear footsteps following, the thud of the stick and the shuffle of cautious feet on the floor. Guy is trailing behind; by the time he arrives in the living room, Cecil is already sitting next to me on the edge of the tartan couch.

'It's been quiet here without you.' The old man brushes the rain from his shoulders as if it's dandruff. It splashes against the floor, glimmering on the polished wooden slats. I remember Andrew varnishing them right after we first moved in, a brief glimpse of a memory of good times. 'I've missed you being around. When will you be coming back?'

Unconsciously I bring my hand up to my hair. Cecil's gaze follows the movement, noticing the dressing on my head, my shrunken, suffering frame. I know I still look a mess, but it isn't that that bothers me. I'm more concerned that he will somehow realise that something has happened between me and Guy. I'm aware of the tingling of my skin, the red blush perhaps where his stubble grazed against my cheek.

'I'm not sure yet. My father thinks it best if I stay with them for a while.'

He nods. 'Well, that does sound sensible.' He takes a second glance at the dressing. 'He told me about the knock you took. With something like that you really don't want to rush things. When Alice slipped and broke her hip, she bumped her head and I couldn't make sense of her for days afterwards.'

Alice? His wife? I don't want to let on that I can't really remember her, so I carry on as if I am sure. 'That was a few years back, wasn't it?' I guess.

'Indeed it was.' He looks away, down towards his ring finger, on which he wears a dull and scratched band. It's loose, spinning as he touches it. Where is my wedding ring now? I wonder. 'Always thought I'd be the first to go, God bless her.' He closes his eyes a moment, lost in the memory. 'Not that we didn't have a long life together to be grateful for. Eighty-three was a grand age, and more than our dear Lord blessed upon your boys.'

My boys? The use of the plural gives rise to a degree of suspicion; I'm sure in that moment that my father has told Cecil that Andrew is dead. If that's the case, it would be impossible for him to have been back here since the crash.

'God rest their souls, I've been praying for them, Chloe, and for you too.' Cecil shakes his head, memories of loved ones brought simmering to the surface. He fiddles a small crucifix out from inside his jumper and gives it a light kiss. Then he opens his eyes from a place of quiet contemplation and turns to take a look at Guy. 'And who might you be?' he asks, his tone shifting, harsher and less friendly.

Guy appears anxious, fidgety. He nibbles on the edge of his index finger. 'I'm a friend of Chloe's, and one of her father's colleagues.' He smiles, but somehow it manages to seem forced and awkward. He leans against the wall, shifts his weight from one foot to the other. I assume after all the talk of my husband and child that he must be feeling guilty about what we almost did upstairs. I feel awful, and so stupid. I'm supposed to be here mourning my child, searching for my husband, and in a moment of desperation I ended up kissing the man who had offered to help.

It seems to take forever for Cecil to avert his gaze. But eventually he does, turning back to me. 'I think staying with your family is a good plan. Your father did tell me that that's where you were when he was here last week.' I exchange a glance with Guy, both of us realising that it must have been my father who cleared the house. Really, who else would it have been? Cecil brings a hand up to his head as if he's confused. 'I guess it could have been a couple of weeks ago now. With you not being out on your daily milk run, I've lost track of the days. I really have missed your afternoon visits.' He smiles at me, strokes the back of my hand.

A multitude of memories concerning my old routine are still missing. But now as I think about what Cecil said, I think I can recall dropping by his house every day, delivering him a pint of milk if he needed it.

'After getting home with Joshua, right?'

'Yes, that's right.'

It feels good to know I was connected to Cecil in this way, something kind and neighbourly, an effort to help somebody in need. Perhaps it was because he was old and infirm. Maybe because I knew he was lonely. But I don't really believe it was only for those reasons. Instead I am sure I used to go there because *I* was lonely. We had both lost our spouses, even if it was in different ways. I think I used to go there because he understood me.

'Is there anything else you can tell me about my old routine?' I ask. He waits for me to elaborate, his eyes narrowing a little, a deep crease forming between his eyes. 'It's just that I can't remember all that much, Cecil. Anything you can tell me would be a great help. Like things I used to do, places I used to go. Perhaps people I used to talk about.'

He rubs one of his arthritic hands against his chin. Guy sits down on the arm of a chair, crosses one leg over the other. 'To be honest with you, Chloe, you were quite a private person. You didn't seem to have many friends, but there was this one girl you talked to a lot. Her name was Sara, I think. You used to speak to her every day.'

'Really?'

'Yes. I think she worked with you.'

I can't remember anybody called Sara, but if she used to work with me, she should be easy to find. If she really was such a good friend, maybe she will know where I can find Andrew, how I was feeling before the crash.

I stand up purposefully. I need to uncover the truth of those days before the accident. Once I do that, I might be able to understand my life, find a way to move forward. 'Cecil, I hate to rush you off,' I say, holding out a hand to help him to his feet. 'But we really have to be going. My father is expecting me home.'

When I return to the lounge after seeing Cecil out, I find Guy still sitting on the arm of the chair. He looks out of place and uncomfortable. I notice that his shirt is still partly untucked at the waist.

'Chloe, about what happened. I should—' he begins, but I cut him off. I don't want to hear what he has to say.

'You don't need to apologise,' I say, a flush of embarrassment spreading up my neck and into my cheeks. What happened wasn't his fault. I stare out of the window, at the people, the noise; so many lives right there within reach. Not one of them is mine. 'You don't owe me anything, Guy.'

'But I—'

I don't mean to raise my voice, but I can't help it. I hope Cecil is already out of earshot. 'No, Guy. I should never have kissed you.'

He nods his head, one hand brushing against his forehead as he lets go of a long breath. 'Just listen for a moment. Let me at least say this.' He seems distressed and urgent as he moves towards me, almost close enough to touch me. 'I know that at the moment your life is complicated, and you have a lot on your mind. But I wouldn't have kissed you back if I didn't want it. I'm a grown man, I know my own mind.'

'Guy, I'm here to find my husband and instead we nearly end up . . .' I can't bring myself to say it.

'No, Chloe. Don't do that. Don't say it like it's shameful.' He reaches a hand out towards me before he seems to change his mind. 'You don't even know where your husband is.'

I stare out of the window, see a couple walking past hand

211

in hand, smiling at each other. Will I ever have that again? 'It *was* shameful, Guy, and it should never have happened. I got carried away. Can't we please leave it at that?'

He takes another long breath, and stares at the floor, perhaps searching for answers, perhaps just unable to look at me. He's so tall, broad-shouldered, but in that moment he appears small and shrivelled. 'Is that what you want? To just forget it happened? To be tied to a life that doesn't exist any more? Bound to a past that you can't even remember?'

Is it? I'm not sure. What I do know is that I have so many other things to think about right now, and the most important of all is finding my husband so I can start to understand what happened that night. I can't get distracted by talking about a kiss that was never meant to be.

'I can't move on unless I understand the past, Guy. I need to find out what led to my accident in the first place, and in order to do that, I have to find Andrew.'

'OK. So do you want me to take you back to your parents' house?'

'No. I want to call by my old work. Maybe this Sara woman is there. She might know where I can find Andrew.'

'I'll take you.'

'No, I'll find my own way there.' I can't ask for his help again, not after what just happened. 'You've already done enough.'

But he's shaking his head. 'Don't be silly. How are you going to get there? Let me help you. After your recent surgery, you shouldn't really be alone.'

It's difficult to admit, but he's right. Even if I was to go on my own, what next? What would I do and where would

I go after that? Back here? Back to my parents' house? Neither of those options feels good.

We cross the road together, climb into the car. We head towards the coast, towards the place where I used to seek solace. I feel his eyes upon me as we drive, but I keep my focus on the road ahead, taking in the sounds and sights of the shore. Trying to remember something of my life here. I stare out at the water, feel the chill of it against my skin. I feel an urge to get out of the car, walk down the beach and sink into the waves. The sea always could calm me, I know that now.

'All I want to do is help you, Chloe. Help you find what you're looking for. Right now, that is the most important thing.'

'Thank you,' I say.

As we pull away from the red lights he speaks once more.

'Because once you do, I know that everything will start to make sense.'

29

I'm not sure where exactly I used to work, but I remember the name of the charity: Fresh Starts. Guy knows it, says it isn't far from his house in Hove. All manner of thoughts are going round in my head. Will this trip to my old office reveal anything about my life before the accident? Will Sara be there? Will she be able to tell me anything more about Andrew, where I might be able to find him?

We drive along the open seafront, the angry waves crashing against the shingle. 'Do you remember this place?' Guy asks as we pass a large hotel. The red-brick facade is dull in the greyness of the weather despite its ostentatious design. It needs the benefit of sunlight to illuminate its grandeur. I peer through the window as we pass a glass portico under which a concierge shelters, his boots shiny, his coat heavy and wet. I look up for the sign, find it gracing the front of the building on one of the higher floors: Brighton Metropole.

'No,' I tell him as I sit back in my seat. 'Should I?'

He shrugs his shoulders before reaching to shift down the gears. 'Perhaps you would if you hadn't suffered the epidural haematoma.'

We pull up at the traffic lights and he reaches over, presses his fingers to my head. His touch feels heavy, the wound underneath still sore. The last time I looked under the dressing I found a thick scar, red and inflamed. I'm not looking forward to having the bandage removed. I turn away, glancing out to sea, where the skeletal remains of the West Pier peek through a misty sky.

'I saw the scans,' he says. 'It was an extensive bleed you suffered. No wonder you are still struggling now.'

'Yes, it was,' I say as he draws his hand from my head. The lights change to green and we pull back into the stream of traffic, away from the water's edge. I don't want to talk about the accident. 'But what about that hotel? Why should I remember it?'

'It was where the Roberta awards were held. The night you had that photograph taken with your family.' He laughs, looks away. I notice his cheeks flush pink. 'I didn't want to confuse you by telling you at first, but we actually spoke that night.'

'Really?'

'Yes, but it's a bit embarrassing.' He takes a breath, laughs again. He's shy, I realise. Embarrassed to tell me. 'I didn't know that you were Dr Daniels' daughter, and the first thing I said to you was a bit corny.'

Now it's my turn to laugh. 'Why, what did you say?'

'That you looked too beautiful to be standing alone.' I feel my face getting warm. 'Pathetic, right? But it's your hair that does it. You really stand out in a crowd.' I become instantly aware of it, the mass of red curls, the shaved section bisected by a scar and a dressing. 'And then who should turn up but your father to ask me if we had been properly introduced. Thank goodness your husband wasn't there. I would have looked an even bigger fool.'

We continue along the seafront, passing the statue of an angel holding an olive branch in one hand, an orb in the other. She stands for peace, something else I now know; I suddenly remember learning about it on a school trip. They told us that the orb was an emblem of eternity, of something never-ending, but after everything that's happened I view it through iconoclastic eyes, see it as nothing more than fantastical. I know now that nothing lasts forever.

'So what did I say?' I ask as we turn right onto a leafy street of stucco properties, grand and emotionless as suburbia overtakes the nearby wilds of the sea. Children walk with their mothers, primary-colour raincoats dazzling in the headlights of the cars. School must have finished for the day.

'To me or your dad?'

'To you.'

'That it was the worst chat-up line you'd ever heard. But you did laugh, so I didn't feel too bad about making a fool of myself. After your dad turned up, you told him that we were already acquainted, and you gave me a bit of a wink. I didn't hang around for long after that; found my way to my seat to lick my wounds.'

'I don't remember that at all.' I can't even remember the ceremony.

'I'm sure it'll come back to you at some point. We could go there together if you like, walk the corridors, sit in the bar. It's important you do these sorts of things, Chloe; visit the places from your past. That's why I was so keen to help you today. Exposure therapy. Your father isn't a big fan, but I believe in it. It'll help you recall the lost memories.'

'You think it would make a difference? To go there, I mean.'

'It might do.' And then, suddenly, all the joviality is gone. 'But when I say you should visit places you used to go, I also include in that the site of the accident. At some point you will have to face it, see if you can remember what happened there. It'll help you move forward.'

'I'm not ready for that.' Seeing the pictures with DS Gray was bad enough. The thought of having to visit the site where Joshua lost his life is terrifying.

'We could go together, on the way back, if you—'

'I said I'm not ready.'

I'm staring out of the window, my eyes following the line of the houses, yet I can sense him nodding along in agreement. 'OK, Chloe. Don't worry about it for now. Whenever you feel ready, I'll be here to help.' He waits for me to recover, for our eyes to meet, before he smiles. 'Here we are,' he says as he pulls up at a nearby kerb. He yanks on the handbrake, unclips his seat belt. 'This is the place we're looking for.'

I step from the car, walk towards the bonnet, the car engine still idling, warming the surrounding air. I see a row of shops nearby, catch the scent of mustard in the air, mixed with the smell of fresh meat. When I turn, I see the deli from which I used to buy my sandwiches, the place I used to come every day before going to the beach to swim, as I remembered in my dream. I dip under the awning and the man inside notices me. He smiles, waves, leaving me in no doubt that he knows me. I wave back. It feels so good to be recognised.

I look along the road at the shops: first a hairdressing salon, the window misted over with condensation. Next to that a linen shop where I suddenly remember I once bought a Christmas tablecloth. It sparks a memory of a dry turkey crown, mushy sprouts, and sticky toffee pudding for dessert. Happy memories of Andrew and Joshua. Yes, we had those times, I think. It wasn't all bad. Further along there's an independent bookshop, which glows softly in the encroaching dark, somebody in the window creating a display. And it's above the bookshop that I see a sign reading *Fresh Starts*, alongside a telephone number and website address.

I turn to speak to Guy, only to realise he isn't there. I look at the car, see he is still sitting in it. I open the passenger door and lean down. Gentle rain strikes the back of my neck. 'Aren't you going to come?'

He shakes his head. 'I don't need to, Chloe. These people are your friends. I think it would help for you to do this alone.'

A wave of nerves hits me, a fear of being alone, of wandering lost into my past. I look at the sign and then back at Guy. 'Maybe I should call ahead? There might not even be anybody there.'

'There are lights on, see?' He points up at the building, and I realise he is right. 'Just go and knock on the door,' he says. 'You do work there, right? They must be expecting you at some point.' He hands me an umbrella. 'I'm going to wait here. Take as long as you like.'

I shut the door and take a deep breath, stepping off the

kerb to cross the road. My heart is pounding, the anticipation of returning to a place where I might once have belonged.
I pop open the umbrella and the sound of the rain intensifies as I bring it over my head. I pass the bookshop and
then start up the external steps on the side of the building.

By the time I arrive at the top, my right leg is sore. I
shake the umbrella dry and turn to the door. And that's
when I realise that the light we could see is only an external
light, working on a sensor, no doubt disturbed by the wind
and flyaway leaves. A sign on the door has the working
hours written on it. The place is closed until tomorrow.

I return to the car, dodging the puddles, not bothering
with the umbrella. I find Guy dragging on a cigarette, and
the urge to smoke hits me again, just like it did in DS Gray's
poky little office.

'It's closed.' I slam the door shut and he tosses his half-
smoked cigarette out of the window. 'I'll have to come back
tomorrow.'

'OK. No problem.' For a while we sit there in silence,
neither of us sure what to suggest. It's Guy who speaks first.
'Where do you want me to take you now?'

And in that moment I really don't know. Here I am, away
from my father's grip and on the edge of my old life, but
still I have absolutely no idea what to do. There should be
a mental list of places I feel safe, of people to whom I could
turn. But there isn't. I don't feel as if I can return to my
parents' house, but where else can I go? I am homeless.
Lifeless.

'I don't know.'

'Well, you are absolutely drenched.' He takes the folded

umbrella from me and throws it onto the back seat. 'Why don't we go back to mine? It's only a few roads from here. You can have a shower and we can stick your clothes in the tumble dryer. We can even order a pizza if you like.'

Part of me is desperate to say yes. The idea of being free, being out on my own: I like that. It feels like life. But I'm not sure that going back to his house, after what happened earlier, is such a good idea. 'I'm not sure.'

'Oh come on. So we kissed. Big deal. We're both adults. We can share a pizza, can't we? Unless you like ham and pineapple?' He winks. 'Then you're on your own.'

I nod, knowing I have nowhere else to go. He starts the engine; pulls away into a steady stream of traffic.

'Once we get there, we'll call your parents, let them know you're with me. Your father will be all right with that, I'm sure. We'll say we met for a coffee, something simple. He knows I'll take good care of you, Chloe.'

30

He parks the car in one of the spaces outside a large Victorian building. It's tall and narrow, looks like it will have a lot of stairs. My leg hurts just thinking about it.

He pushes open the heavy door and checks his mailbox for post, pulling out a couple of letters, which he tucks under his arm. Inside it feels warm, cosy, and I can feel the blood rushing back into my extremities, my toes tingling, fingers waking. The walls are painted a toasty shade of yellow, like early-morning sunshine. I follow him as he walks towards the stairs, thinking how strange it is to be here, just witnessing normal things. Even the collection of his letters suggests a connection to the outside world that I don't really share, life continuing all around me. I feel so far removed that I can't help but wonder how I'll ever make it back to some degree of normality.

'You go first,' he says, stepping aside to let me pass. The hallway is wide, big enough for an art deco table along one wall with a huge mirror above it, but still our bodies are close as I move past. 'That way if you get stuck on the stairs with that dodgy leg of yours I can give you a nudge in the right direction.'

We take it slowly, stopping for a short break on the second landing. When we arrive on the third floor, he tells me to wait, edges past me to get to his front door. The space is narrower here, and this time as he moves past me his body brushes mine, the heat almost instant. He pushes open the door, and as he steps inside a woman comes out from one of the other flats. She's wearing sports gear, a rainproof jacket and a woolly hat with earbuds already in place. 'Hi,' she says, waving.

'Hi,' I reply, taken aback by her friendliness. I look to Guy, who's holding the door open. I see him smile at the woman but he doesn't say anything, offering a quick motion with his chin and a brief raising of his eyebrows to acknowledge her.

'Well, see you,' she hollers as she skips down the stairs two at a time. I lean over the banister to watch her. Jealousy rises in me, longing, the hope that one day I will achieve something as simple and easy as that: leaving my home, heading confidently out towards life. Guy is right. I need to work on facing up to things on my own.

He closes the door behind me as I move into a large open-plan living room. It's quiet inside, not a sound from the outside world. No heating pipes or household appliances rattling into action. No television or radio to give the impression we aren't alone.

'Why don't you take a seat,' he says, setting the mail down on a table. He pulls off his coat and tosses it across the back of a chair before pointing to the sofa along the far wall. After the stairs I find my leg is sore, my head woozy and light. I can feel even the smallest of my muscles trembling with the effort. 'I promise it's comfier than it looks.'

I sit as instructed on the modern replica of a mid-century-style sofa, cold black leather, shiny and uninviting. I can hear Guy moving about in the kitchen on the other side of the wall. I look around the room. The walls are white, interrupted only by the window and a large flat-screen TV. No paintings hang here like they do in my parents' home. A couple of shelves house a limited selection of books, a half-built model boat, and a picture of a man with two boys in a thin-edged silver frame. I stand up, take off my coat and place it alongside Guy's, then cross the room towards the photograph. The boys in the picture have dark hair. Is one of them Guy? I pick it up, gaze at their faces, both of them happy, kissed by the sun. The man behind them has wrinkles stretching deeply across his cheeks, much like Guy does now. I set it down quickly as I hear him arriving from the kitchen.

He's carrying two mugs and hands me one decorated with a picture of Brighton Pier. 'You don't need to stand on ceremony,' he says. 'Come on. Take a seat.'

I do as he asks, and watch him as he moves about the room. He sets his mug down on a glass table in front of the sofa and then fiddles with a thermostat on the wall. I listen as the radiators kick in. Next he crosses to a narrow table that runs along the wall underneath the window. The sky is so white outside that if it hadn't been for the frame I would barely have noticed the break in the surface of the walls. He presses a button on an answering machine before going over to lock the door. I listen as a woman's voice crackles through after the beep.

'*Hey, Guy, it's Julia. I was just wondering what time you wanted to meet this evening and—*'

He rushes back to the machine, presses at buttons until the recording stops. He scratches his head, covers his mouth with one hand. He takes a moment to compose himself, to find the right words. 'I'm sorry about that,' is all he manages to come up with.

'You really don't need to be.' I feel I have intruded, even though it was him who invited me here. I have heard something private that I shouldn't have. I perch on the edge of the sofa, willing it to swallow me up. 'I can leave soon,' I tell him, thoughts of his plans going around in my head. Of a woman called Julia. Of where I will go next. 'I can call a taxi if I'm putting you out.'

'No, no, don't be stupid,' he says, waving his hands at me. He sits down next to me on the sofa. The way he lies back makes it impossible for me to see him behind me. So I sit back too, although I hold myself stiffly. I can't relax here with him. 'I'll call her later and cancel.'

'You really don't need to do that. I've already taken up enough of your time.'

He laughs, quiet and warm, his legs spread wide across the couch. Then he speaks. 'Of all the things you've said today, that's the silliest.' Despite his efforts to appear relaxed, I can tell that he too feels somewhat uncomfortable about the message I heard, struggling to make eye contact with me. 'Really, it's no big deal. I'm not in the mood to see her anyway.'

The shift in atmosphere makes me feel out of place. Like I shouldn't be here. I'm the antithesis of this cool, sterile room, the white walls and monochromatic furniture. I feel torn and filthy, unkempt and patched up. I'm suddenly self-conscious about my appearance and the intrusion I have created in Guy's life. Who am I to make demands of his time, beg for his help to drive me about in search of a past I know so little about? I think back to my memories of who I was before the accident: a grown woman with a job, a husband. Marital problems. A car. A child who adored me, although I was unable to shield him from his father's problems. A habit of swimming in the sea. All of those things are gone. I never realised how loosely the elements of my life were held together until it all unravelled. One broken stitch and it came spiralling apart, leaving me with almost nothing recognisable to help me find my way forward.

'Well I'm sorry to ruin your evening, anyway.'

'Really, it's fine. You didn't ruin anything,' he says, but I notice a cherry blush creeping up his neck. 'In actual fact, and at the risk of sounding inconsiderate, I'm glad to cancel the plans I had with her. Now, why don't you finish your cup of tea and go take a shower. It will do you good to get out of those wet clothes. I'll find you something to wear. After that you can call your parents if you like, let them know where you are.'

He shows me to the spare room, hands me a fresh towel. I look about the room, the spotless bedside table, the bed with crease-free sheets. Everything is so neat and tidy it only serves to make me feel like even more of a mess.

'Here's some shower gel, shampoo.' They are feminine products and remind me of Julia from the message. Has she been here, in this shower, in his bed? Are these her things I'll be using now? 'Take as long as you like,' he says, leaving me alone in his bathroom.

I peel my clothes away like an old wet skin until I'm standing in my underwear. It's impossible to avoid looking at myself, a wide floor-length mirror completing one of the walls. I look down, gaze at my scarred leg, then up at the cuts on my face. I finger through my hair, the thing Guy said he noticed the first time he met me. And despite my earlier reservations about the mess, I realise something here with my whole self on display: I look better than I did when I first left the hospital. I have put on weight, have more colour in my skin. I'm damaged, sure, still healing, but I'm not broken beyond repair in the way I thought I was. The idea gives me hope that perhaps my life, just like my body, can also be rebuilt.

I stand under the water, let it wash over me, my eyes closed. But in that blackness I can't help but think of my parents: how they have lied to me, how they have manipulated me, how they have made my recovery so much harder. They have behaved in ways I can't even begin to explain or excuse. But I also think of moments of genuine tenderness: my father's reaction to the photo of me and Joshua on Facebook; the tender way my mother mopped my brow. Nothing about any of this makes sense.

I dry off and fold the towel into a neat square, then dress in an old tracksuit of Guy's that he left for me on the spare bed. It's soft, smells freshly laundered. Homely. When I return to the lounge I find him sitting on the settee, a laptop on his knees.

He looks up as I arrive in the doorway. 'You look better.' I washed my hair, and it has already started bouncing up, falling into the shape of my curls. 'Have a seat, I've got something to show you.' I sit alongside him, keeping a distance, and he turns the laptop so that I can see. 'I was interested in what you said about your father this morning. The drug, propanolol. It's a beta blocker, usually used to treat hypertension. But it does have some uses in psychiatry. Specifically in the treatment of post-traumatic stress disorders.'

He closes the laptop, twists in his seat. 'There was an interesting study to come out of MIT a few years back. The researchers realised that if you administered propanolol before the recollection of traumatic experiences, it was possible to diminish levels of ongoing stress associated with the index event. They found that people started to care less about their past, and stopped being debilitated by their trauma. The theory is called reconsolidation, the same thing your father mentioned to you. Sort of a reorganisation of your memories. By recalling the memory it becomes malleable. It's almost as if you are storing it for the first time, and hence it's amenable to change.'

'You think that's what he's doing to me?'

He shakes his head, appears indecisive. 'Chloe, it has been hypothesised that the same technique could be used not only to minimise stress, but also to remove memories that incapacitate a patient.'

'So you think he's trying to erase my husband from my mind? My son?'

He fidgets, clearly uncomfortable. 'I'm not sure. But I don't think you should have any more therapy sessions with him just yet. Not until we can establish what's going on. It's not right for a patient to be in the dark about their treatment like that.'

He orders a pizza, and before it arrives he pours himself a drink, kicks off his shoes. He puts on an old movie, something from the eighties about two teenage boys who manage to bring a mannequin to life. He laughs along with the terrible jokes, the pizza box between us smelling of grease and cheese. I end up with my legs curled up on the sofa, my belly full and plump. For a moment, just the briefest of seconds, I forget.

I wonder if it really is so bad of me to enjoy being around Guy like this. To want to be around him. Part of me feels guilty, as if somehow it's duplicitous to even think it; as if the joy I find in his company is a betrayal, disloyal to a man I can barely remember. Yet being here with him makes me feel whole. He makes me feel like more than just a victim, more than a woman lost. As if I'm a person with a life. Surely there's no better reason to spend time with somebody than that. Surely such a feeling shouldn't be something to feel guilty about.

After the movie finishes, I find my eyes drawn to the framed picture of the two boys on the shelf. I realise that apart from the model boat, it is the only personal item in the room. Guy mutes the television, and when I turn to look at him, I see he has caught me staring.

'Sorry, I don't mean to pry,' I say.

He stands up, walks to the shelf and picks the picture up. 'You're not prying.' He hands it to me and I study it hard, conscious of my greasy fingers as I gaze at the two small boys. Now that I'm looking close up, one of them is undoubtedly Guy, the dark eyes and curly hair the same as today. Even at that young age it is easy to see his bone structure, the pout to his lips, and the high line of his hair. The other boy looks the same, albeit with softer features.

'Your brother?' I ask, remembering his story about the younger brother who died.

'Yes. My father loved to sail.' He takes a sip of his drink. 'Kept a boat near Holly Hill beach, on the River Hamble. It was only a small thing,' he says, almost apologetic, as if he should be embarrassed for having a boat. 'He used to take it down the Solent, to the Needles and back. Do you know the northern coastline of the Isle of Wight?' I shake my head. 'Well it's beautiful. Towns nestled on the water, boats everywhere. Striking green cliffs that merge into brilliant white rocks. All the way down to the Old Battery lighthouse.'

The picture he creates is idyllic, potentially the beginnings of a happy memory. But I set the frame down on the sofa, knowing that there is something awful to come.

'He was a year younger than me, always excited to be on the water. Me, never so much, and I was a bit reckless, I suppose. Slapdash, my dad used to call me. Never did things quite the way I should.' His eyes blink in rapid motion. His discomfort causes a tight pain in my chest. 'The day we lost him, I hadn't tied the boom in properly. It swung out, knocked him overboard.' He looks down into his glass and brings it to his lips, draining it. 'We never found him.'

For a moment I can't say anything. The thought of a young boy's death. I look up, find Guy composed, his bottom lip nibbled between his teeth. 'I'm so sorry,' I stutter, knowing first hand just how empty a sentiment that is. How little it helps. But it is, in that moment, all I can find.

'It was never the same after that. They didn't want to blame me, but they couldn't forgive me either. As soon as I could, I left. I felt like I'd become his ghost, you know? No matter how many tears they cried, no matter how hard I tried to be perfect for them, none of us ever managed to raise the dead. Can you imagine, living in that house for another ten years after the accident, being blamed for my brother's death, even though I was only eight years old at the time?'

And the thing is, I don't think I can. Because even now, after everything that's happened, my family want me around, despite the problems they have and the complications that my accident has caused. I remember them at my bedside in the hospital, and even when I protested their presence, claimed I didn't know who they were, they stayed there with me, sometimes throughout the night. No matter what, I always felt wanted.

'It's pretty late and I've had a drink,' he says. I look at the clock, see that it's coming up to ten in the evening. I have been here for hours, but it hasn't felt like it. 'Why don't you just stay the night? The spare bed is already made up.'

'OK,' I say. I don't know where else he thought I might have been able to go.

I lie awake for over an hour, unable to relax in the unfamiliar surroundings. Eventually I get up, walk in the dark through to the lounge. I open one of the windows and listen to the distant hum of the waves breaking against the shore. Joshua's ashes somewhere out there in the cold. Andrew somewhere else, a potential suspect. It's hard to keep my mind focused. After a while, I close the window and move back through the lounge, along the corridor, until I find myself standing outside Guy's bedroom.

'Come in,' he says when he hears me knocking. He's sitting up on top of his bed, nursing a brandy. The sheets are crumpled and messy beneath him, and he has photographs strewn about across the surface. 'Everything all right?' he asks as he organises some of the pictures into a pile. 'Was there something you needed?'

'I can't sleep. Want some company?' He nods his head and I sit on the edge of the bed, my hands tucked beneath my legs. But I see him move aside, motion to the space alongside him. Part of me feels that I should stay where I am, but I came in here for the company and so I shuffle up the bed as he scoops yet more pictures away. It's hot in his bedroom, the air dry. 'What are you looking at?' I ask.

'Just old photographs. Sometimes I get them out, take a look. I suppose it's because we spoke about it earlier. Still searching for answers I guess, same as you are. Wondering whether it could have been different.' He smiles and gives a little shake of his head. 'If *I* could have been different.'

'Nothing is ever different, though, is it?' I say, remembering what Joshua said to me that day at the beach. Guy casts his eyes down to the bed, takes another brief look at the pictures of his brother. He hands me his brandy and I sip it, without question. I feel it go to my head, my eyes blurring.

'You're right. It's always the same. You can't change the past, unfortunately. Only yourself.'

'Can I ask you something?' He looks up, waits. 'If you could take a pill, have some sort of treatment to forget like my father is trying to give me, would you do it?'

He shuffles about, brings one leg up to his chest, wraps his arm around it. 'No, Chloe, I wouldn't. Life is not ours to manipulate. Life is given to us, a gift. We follow our path, meet people, experience pain and joy and all the things that make us who we are as part of that gift. It's like that expression, what is it?' He glances off into the distance as the wind whistles past the window. 'It's the journey that matters, not the destination. Something like that, anyway. Without our past, we are not ourselves. Without our memories, we cannot explain our choices. Why try to forget when instead you can use the past and everything you have ever learned in order to become something better. I'm stronger because of what's happened to me, including what happened with my brother. Yes, the mistake I made still hurts, but it's a lesson.'

Our conversation flows between his pain and mine, a dead brother, a lost son. 'I just wish something made sense to me. That I could remember something more solid than snippets of memory. That something would feel *real*.' I think of his kiss in the bedroom at my old house, how that moment offered me more comfort than anything else since I have woken up. Is that why I agreed to come back here, and why I wandered about in the dark until I found myself here on his bed? To feel something? Something real?

He takes the glass from me and sets it on the side. He edges towards me and I can feel his body close to mine. His heartbeat. The heat. His pulse. 'I'm real,' he whispers. And then he kisses my lips, his stubble soft against my skin. This time I don't stop him. I touch his face, his cheekbone, the curve of his shoulder, the muscles flexing in his arm as I run my hand across it. I press myself against him, savouring the taste of his kiss.

He lifts my arms up, his movements gentle, nothing like the urgency in the bedroom earlier on. That was a stolen moment, but this, now, is ours. He knows I'm not going to push him away. He doesn't have to rush. He slides the jumper over my head, exposing my skin, and traces his lips across my neck. He stops, stares at me. I don't look away. He runs his hands from my face to my shoulder, across my bare chest and down to my side. I shiver at his touch, his fingers light.

'Let me make it go away,' he says. 'Let me make it just me and you.' And I think in that moment: yes, I want that. What I crave most is to forget, to simply feel the moment I'm in. I close my eyes, and for a while, with his consuming weight on top of me, I am lost.

31

When I wake the next morning, it's still dark. I am naked under the sheet with Guy's arms wrapped around me. His breath is fluttering across the back of my neck. My head is sore, the pain behind my scar immense. The ease with which we lay together the night before seems lost to me now. I shouldn't be here like this, tucked against this stranger in his bed. But last night all I wanted was something new, something that might bring me peace, and the chance to feel the comfort of another person's touch. And for a while I found it.

I sense him stirring behind me. I use the opportunity to slip out from underneath his heavy arm. He fidgets for a moment, but doesn't wake, burying his face deep into the pillow. Rain strikes the window, and it feels like violent condemnation, passing judgement, screaming at me: *What did you do, Chloe? What did you do?*

What did I do?

What am I doing?

The sex comes back to me as flashes of memory. As guilt. As pleasure. As relief. I stand up, my feet on his family photographs, the cold hitting my body. My movements are awkward and stiff as I collect his old tracksuit from the floor. With no curtains at the window a weak grey light bathes everything silver, including my naked skin. I feel as if the whole world can see me as I creep from the room like I've done something wrong. Have I done something wrong? I just don't know any more.

I move to the bathroom, dress in his old clothes and splash my face with steaming hot water. I rummage in the cabinet for something that looks like pain relief, but all I find are sticking plasters, a spray for athlete's foot, and a half-used box of condoms. The realisation that we didn't use anything last night scares me. The idea of being pregnant is terrifying. How could I protect any child I bring into this life when I don't even know the truth about who I am?

I find my clothes creased in a pile in the tumble dryer; I slip them on and leave his old tracksuit in their place. I move into the living room and stand at the bare window, looking out to sea, watching the waves, endless in their efforts. The air outside is grey, full and heavy, a mist hanging over the horizon. I can just make out the outline of the seafront Ferris wheel, little more than a ghost appearing through the haze.

I glance down to see a light flickering on the answering machine beside me. Five messages in total. I don't even want to think about who they might be from. I make a cup of tea and find some paracetamol in one of the kitchen cupboards, then sit down at the table, the flat and me both silent. I think about leaving, even though I have no idea where I would go. Still, it's tempting to slink away, to avoid the shame of admitting that last night shouldn't have happened. What was I thinking?

But then I hear the handle of a door, footsteps coming down the corridor. Seconds later Guy is in the doorway, just his boxer shorts between us. His body looks so good, tanned and strong. I can still feel him on my skin, remember the way he touched me. The memory feels so good I have to look away.

'Good morning,' he says, ruffling a hand through his hair.

'Morning,' I say, my eyes cast down at the table. 'I'm sorry about last night.'

'Really?' He looks almost disappointed. He flicks the kettle back on, reaches for a mug. I watch his muscles rippling, the contraction across his stomach and the movement of his hip.

'I just . . . I guess I just feel like we shouldn't have done that.'

'Why not?' He sits down at the table with his mug of tea, prodding at the bag with a teaspoon. When I don't answer, he says, 'Listen, Chloe. You wanted it and I wanted it. There's no harm done, is there? Did I hurt you, force you into it?'

I shake my head. 'No, of course not.'

'Well then,' he says, as if that is that.

He splashes some milk into his tea and takes a sip. I take in his puffy eyes and messy night-time hair. For some reason I think of Julia, the girl he blew off last night so that he could be with me. Did he know what would happen when he made that decision? Did he expect it? Can he read me better than I can read myself?

'We agreed yesterday to put the kiss behind us and nothing has changed,' he adds.

It's a relief that he doesn't have any expectations of me, but strange to feel a twinge of disappointment too. But it's for the best, I know: I couldn't manage anybody else's feelings on top of my own right now.

'When I woke up and you weren't there, I wondered if you had done a runner,' he tells me. 'I'm glad you hadn't.'

Perhaps I should have left. But although I have nowhere else to go, it all comes down to one simple fact: I didn't want to leave. I felt something here with Guy last night. It was a genuine connection to another person, and no matter how loose or physical it was, it was more than I've had elsewhere. I stayed because I don't want to give that up just yet, for it to be over almost as soon as I found it.

He reaches over and his fingers brush against mine. At first I hold back. But as he persists, doesn't give up on my touch, I allow his fingers to weave around mine. And as we sit there holding hands, I realise that right now there's nowhere else I'd rather be.

'You should check in with your parents,' he says. 'Call them, let them know you're OK.' He stands up and grabs a couple of bowls, sets them on the table. He reaches into another cupboard and holds up a box of chocolate muesli. 'After we get some food inside us, I believe we have an office to visit, right?'

'Don't you have work to go to?' I look at the clock. It's coming up to 8 a.m.

'I'll call in sick.' He tips some cereal into his bowl, then he smiles, and his eyes meet mine. 'I'd rather be here with you.'

32

As I push open the door, I'm hit by the warmth of central heating. A woman wearing a red T-shirt sits at a desk just inside the door, tapping away on her computer. The atmosphere is damp, condensation blanketing the windows. I realise that I know her name, and that this desk functions as a reception for the office.

'Dawn?' I ask, and the woman looks up. It takes a moment for her to place me, find the features she knows on the sallow, drawn face masquerading as my own. But then she sees it, a flash of recognition as she stands up.

'Oh my God, Chloe.' She shuffles out from behind the desk, hurries into a position where she can get close to me. She seems to want to hug me, but backs off at the last minute when she sees the dressing on my head. It results in an awkward embrace, the type where nobody is sure about the rules. 'We heard about your accident. We didn't think . . . We heard that . . . Oh God, Chloe, I'm so sorry.'

The fuss Dawn is creating begins spilling out across the floor, bringing with it a flurry of others to see the woman who has returned from the brink of death. They hover around me, question after question about how I am feeling and whether my head is still sore. The name Damien Treadstone is passed about between them, each in turn incredulous over how anybody could leave the scene of an accident and then deny he was ever there. They exclaim how it's a miracle I survived. How they are just so very sorry. But despite my best efforts to answer, my focus is drawn to the building rather than the people.

Because as I gaze about the room at the posters on the wall, a mixture of info graphics and advertising campaigns warning against the dangers of drinking to excess, I realise that this place feels familiar. I know it, and more importantly I know myself in it: all the contracts I have approved, the late nights I've worked, the tireless hopes that somehow my work here will make somebody's life more bearable than mine. I look over at a desk near the corner, alongside which there's a small window. I know it has a view to a brick wall and lets in a draught, even in the summer. There's a young woman in a smart dress sitting at it now. She looks strong, her arms well shaped as if she visits the gym. She notices the attention but she doesn't get up, continues with her work. I don't know who she is.

'Come on through,' says one of the guys – George, I think his name is – and he leads me away from the throng of people, all slowly returning to their desks after the excitement of my arrival has died down. 'Janice is in the office. She'd love to see you. Go on,' he says as he edges me towards a door with a sign on it reading *Office Manager*. Underneath that somebody has stuck a piece of A4 paper with the words *Head Honcho* printed on it, around which everybody who works here has signed their name to officialise the document.

I see what looks to be my signature, bottom left. Not at all shaky like when I write now. *Chloe Jameson*, it reads, the person I used to be.

I take a deep breath and knock. 'Come in,' I hear, and I open the door. Janice rises to her feet, brings one hand to her mouth in shock. Her nails are well shaped and painted red. I feel her eyes taking me in, her stare settling on the dressing covering part of my head. I finger my hair into place and she beckons me through to sit in one of the low armchairs.

I recognise her, know instinctively that we share a past. I know her curvy body, the soft blond hair cut into a sharp bob. The chunky oversized necklace like sweets around her neck. She's my boss, has been for years.

'I can't believe it, Chloe.' She sits down opposite me, pulls her chair in close. She gazes away for a moment, lost in thought, before shaking her head as she looks back towards me. She makes one more assessment of my injuries, those still visible and those that are healing, things she must have read about in the paper. 'I tried calling, but nobody answered. I went to the house too, but there was nobody there.' She shrugs, defeated. 'I had no other way to reach you.' She sounds apologetic, distraught, as if in some way she has let me down.

'It doesn't matter, Janice. You did what you could.'

'Still, it wasn't enough, was it? I want you to know we were thinking of you. All of us. And Joshua, too. I don't even know what to say, Chloe. When I read the news . . .' She shakes her head again, her eyes filling with tears. She reaches across and takes my hand. People seem to do this a lot since I woke up after the crash. 'I'm just so very sorry.'

'Thanks. It means a lot.' And it really does. It was nice to experience their warm welcome when I walked through the door, a crowd of people pleased to see me. Because in my broken memories of this place, it seems to me that I was distracted when I was here, not really part of the team. But today I feel wanted and well liked. As if this is a place I once belonged. And if that's the case, I need to get back to work as soon as I can. It will help me rediscover myself. Find the person I used to be. 'So much has changed in the last few weeks. It's nice to be here, somewhere familiar.'

'I can only begin to imagine.' She lets go of my hand before sitting back in her chair. 'I don't even know where I would begin if I were in your shoes.' Her honesty is a relief: somebody acknowledging the mammoth climb ahead of me. 'Tell me. How's Andrew taking it?'

So she knows the truth, that Andrew is alive. 'I'm not sure,' I admit.

Her eyes narrow for a moment before her lips draw together. 'You don't know where he is, do you?'

'No,' I say as I shake my head.

'I take it he does know what happened?'

I realise that I don't actually know for sure. DS Gray told me that he had spoken to him, but, is he aware that our son is dead? Something close to disbelief washes over me as I realise that I never even considered this until now.

'Actually, I don't know that either,' I tell Janice. 'My father said he took money.' For a moment she appears confused. 'In order to leave me alone.'

She stands up, pours two glasses of water from a jug on the side. I look down, see my hands are shaking. She breathes a heavy sigh. 'What an absolute mess,' she says as she sits again. 'He was always letting you down, Chloe, but I do feel for him in this. We weren't exactly friends, you and I. You liked to keep yourself to yourself. Thought you could hide what was going on at home if you shut yourself away from the world.'

'What do you mean?'

'The drinking, Chloe. We all knew it was difficult for you.' She pauses. 'I suppose I should keep quiet. I have no right to speak this way about him. It's just that you gave that man so many chances, and all any of us wanted was to see some effort on his part. Goodness knows he had all the support in the world from you. How many times a day would I see you looking at your phone, waiting for a call or checking in on him?'

'Really?'

'Yes,' she says, and in that moment she almost seems irritated by him. 'And now that you really need him, he has gone AWOL. You have helped so many people with your work here, but the one man you really wanted to help would never let you. What an awful disease it is.'

'Yes, it is,' I say quietly, my sympathy for Andrew rising, even knowing that he took my father's money.

'I used to see you sometimes at lunchtime down on the beach. On your own. You were so lonely. I was so pleased for you when you decided to make a fresh start.'

'What do you mean, fresh start?'

'The fact that you left him. I was sure it was for the best

when you told me. Everybody did, I suppose. I didn't know anything about the money, though. The Chloe you were before the accident wouldn't have told me about that.'

I am beginning to realise that my life with Andrew was a disaster that everybody knew about. I suppose there was no way to hide it, his drinking tarnishing everything. And I suppose that now he isn't dead and is simply missing – potentially paid off if my father is in any way to be believed – I'm starting to feel a certain satisfaction that I did decide to leave. I found the strength and courage to demand something better for myself and Joshua. But what doesn't make sense is that according to DS Gray, I was supposed to be meeting Andrew on the night of the crash. If I was leaving him, trying to get away, why would I arrange to meet him first?

'There's a lot of the past I can't remember, Janice. I'm trying to piece things together, but to do that I have to find Andrew, find out what he knows.'

She nods. 'You just need to take it steady. One step at a time, Chloe.'

'I need to start moving forward too.' I'm beginning to feel the prospect of a future tantalisingly close. At least now I know where my home is, that I have a job, and a life outside of my parents' confinement. Only last night I found comfort in another man's arms. I can recreate something, can't I, try to move on and start a new life. Do I have any other choice? 'I'd love to come back to work soon, maybe on a phased return or something like that.'

Janice sips her water, then sets the glass down on a coaster in the shape of a seashell. She takes another look at the dressing on my head. 'What do you mean, come back?'

'Well, the doctor has to agree to it first, I know, but soon enough—'

She cuts me off, shaking one of her fingers. 'No, I don't mean that. When you say come back, do you mean to work here?'

'Of course. It feels good to be back. I want to get into a routine as soon as possible. Perhaps I could start with a couple of days a week, or a few hours a day.' Already in my head I'm planning my return to Brighton, my second escape.

She fiddles with an oversized earring in the shape of a fish. A moment of anxiety sits heavily between us. 'But Chloe,' she says eventually, staring at her desk, 'you don't work here any more.'

'What?' My mouth goes dry. 'What do you mean?'

Her voice is quiet, her words accompanied by shaky breaths. 'You handed in your resignation. You were due to leave, but about a week prior you had your accident.'

I can't believe it. 'But I loved my job. I would never have done that.'

She stands up, walks over to a filing cabinet covered in stickers. She rifles through and locates a letter, pulls it out with those perfect nails. It's dated August, and is signed by me, a request to terminate my contract. I stare down at the decision I had taken. 'You said that you were going to make a go of it elsewhere,' she says.

I let the paper fall to my lap. I look up at Janice, then back to the letter. 'But it doesn't make any sense. I don't remember planning to go anywhere.'

'I'm so sorry, Chloe, but I don't know what else to say. You were a very private person. You didn't tell us much about your life. But we knew through the charity about Andrew and his drinking. When you told me you were leaving, I figured it was to get away from him. I know you had been staying with your parents, but I don't know where you planned to go from there.'

'So when you said I'd decided to make a fresh start, you meant I was leaving everything, wiping the slate clean.' She nods, looking genuinely sorry for me. 'Surely I must have told somebody where I was planning to go.'

'Maybe, but you didn't tell me. You said it was better that way; that nobody could accidentally pass information on if they didn't know where you were. I'm sorry I don't know anything more, but that's how you wanted it.'

And then I remember what Cecil said, the idea of a good friend. Surely I would have confided in her if I was planning to leave. 'What about Sara? Maybe I told her something. Is she here? Can I talk to her?'

She shakes her head. 'I'm sorry, Chloe, but nobody called Sara works here.'

'But my old neighbour said that I used to talk to her every day. He thought maybe she was a work friend.'

She shuffles some papers into a pile, pauses. 'Well, you did occasionally mention a friend called Sara. You used to say that you were meeting her at lunchtime for a coffee.' For a moment she looks away, as if she's unsure about whatever it is running through her mind. 'I saw you once, down at the beach. You had told me that you were meeting her that day. But you were with a man.'

'What man?'

She takes the resignation letter from me before setting it

down on the cluttered desk. It's too hot in here. My armpits are damp, my cheeks on fire. What is she trying to tell me?

'All I know is that it wasn't Andrew. Not long after that, you told me you were leaving. I put two and two together, came up with five, I guess.'

She reaches forward, tries to take my hand again, but I pull it away. All this time I thought we were separated because of Andrew's drinking, and now I find out that it could have been my fault; that I left because I was seeing somebody else. Is that even possible?

'Don't feel bad, Chloe. After what you went through with Andrew, anybody would be able to understand it.' I stand up, turn towards the door. 'Chloe, wait,' she says, but I am already through it, desperate to get out. I can't be here.

She catches up with me just as I reach reception.

'I have to leave,' I tell her, pulling away from her desperate hands. I notice the others watching us. They are talking amongst themselves, but each and every one of them is looking my way. I have lived this moment before, I realise, the weight of their eyes upon me as I move. I am still the subject of office gossip. Which of them here saw me at the beach?

Janice hands me a leaflet for a rehab centre in a village just outside Brighton. 'Perhaps I shouldn't be telling you this, but I heard Andrew was staying here. He's on a detox programme, trying to work things through. Maybe he can help explain the things you can't remember.'

I return to the car and sit in silence. Guy is quiet, waits for me to speak.

'Well?' he asks eventually. 'How did it go?'

I fold the leaflet in my hands, crumple it up into a ball. What should I say? I am so ashamed, I don't want to tell him anything, especially not after what happened between us last night. What kind of person am I? All this time I have been pleading my case, trying to search for Andrew, and all along my father was right: I didn't love him. I had left, was hoping to start again away from here. With another man. How could I have done that to Andrew when I knew he needed help?

'Chloe, how did it go?' Guy asks again.

I turn to look at him. He is smiling, waiting for my answer, that grin that only yesterday offered me hope. I hear a lone gull cry out. 'She said I could start back whenever I want.'

'Oh, really?' He seems surprised. He rubs at his stubble-covered face, starts the engine. 'Well, that's great. Soon enough you'll be back to normal, eh? Get your life back on track.' He reaches over, pats me on the knee. I freeze, my whole body tight. His touch brings none of the comfort or excitement it did last night. I feel only shame now, over who I was. Who I still am.

I think of everything Janice told me. That I was seeing another man. That I had left my job. Only two days after that, I crashed my car in an accident that didn't make sense. How is this all connected?

The more I learn about my past, the less I know myself, the less I understand what happened. What I am beginning to realise is that in order to go forward, I have to go back as far as I can, to the place where all the lies began. And if I'm to do that, there's only one person who can help me now. The one person I vowed I would never need again.

33

I call my father and tell him I am on my way back. By the time I get home he is crazed, pacing the floorboards of the hallway, still in his clothes from the day before. My mother is trying desperately to calm herself down and looks in need of a drink. Jess is there too, appearing relieved to see me when the front door opens. I asked Guy to drop me off at the end of the driveway. I am too ashamed to let them see me with him.

'Where the bloody hell have you been?' My father doesn't give me a chance to answer. 'And what were you thinking, staying out all night? I kept calling, left messages. When I see Guy . . .' His breath is shaky, his cheeks ruddy and flushed. I was so angry with him yesterday, angry that he'd lied, over my assumption he'd cleared out my house. Only a couple of hours ago I was ready never to see him again, but now I think I might understand. Now, after what Janice told me, I need to give him a chance to explain.

'Thomas, please,' Mum says, arriving at my side. She takes my coat, hangs it over the banister. 'Give her a chance to breathe. She's not a prisoner, is she?' She walks me through to the living room and Jess sits down next to me on the settee. 'Do you want to tell us what happened, Chloe? We have been very worried.'

'I didn't want to come home last night,' I tell her. I look to my father, see his anger increasing, that same tight look that I saw the night he found me in the mill with Andrew. I feel small and weak, sitting here in his shadow as he paces about in front of me. But I push on, looking up at him, bracing myself for what's to come. 'I want to talk about what you've been doing to me. The reconsolidation therapy.'

He stops pacing, glances towards my mother. He scratches his head, checks the pocket of his jacket. He folds his arms across his chest, steps closer. 'What is it you want to know?'

His openness throws me. Thoughts fly around my brain. Possibilities. I snatch at one, run with it. 'Can it be used to change people's memories? To make them forget?'

'Yes.' Just like that, an answer. Just like that, he admits he has been manipulating and lying to me all along.

'And did you try to make me forget Andrew and Joshua?'

My mother yelps, brings a hand up to her head like she might pass out. My father scoffs, shakes his head. He is angry with me, irritated.

'How could you make such an absurd suggestion? Why would I want that? Why would I want you to forget your son?'

'For the same reason you didn't tell me about him when I first woke up.'

He is indignant. 'You think I was happy about that? That you couldn't remember your own child? My grandson? I might have been pleased that you couldn't remember that poor excuse of a husband, but to think I would try to erase them from your memory . . . Chloe, I've been trying my best to help you recall them. Both of them.'

Is he lying? How can I know? If he wanted me to remember then surely he could have taken me back to my house instead of trying to keep it a secret, could have given me access to their things. I look him in the eye. 'Was it you who took their things?'

He shakes his head, disgusted, as if I just keep making things worse. 'You've been to the house as well? First he keeps you overnight, then he takes you there.' He looks to my mother in the hope that she shares his outrage. She doesn't. She is bewildered. 'I'm going to kill Guy when I see him.' And then, as if what I have accused him of suddenly registers, he says. 'How could you think that of me, Chloe? I'm your father. I love you, for goodness' sake.'

'But I went to my house,' I say, shaking my head in disbelief. 'It was like you had tried to erase them. And the therapy sessions, they leave me so confused. I can't remember anything properly.' I'm losing some of my strength, I can feel it. My certainty is going up in smoke, the slow drift of embers from a fire.

He steps forwards, offers me his hand. I don't take it, don't want his skin against mine. 'Come with me, Chloe.'

We leave the drawing room, me two paces behind him until we reach the door to the cellar. Without a word he turns the key, opens the door and reaches for the light switch. Halfway down the steps, he stops, turns to face me, my mouth dry, my hands shaking. 'I thought you said you wanted their things. You don't look very sure about it to me.'

From where I am standing my father is cast in shade, his eyes two black pits without emotion. I don't want to be down here with him. But if he has their things, perhaps seeing them, holding them in my hands, will help me remember them better. Help me remember myself and explain the mess I have created. I watch every step I take as I follow him into the dark.

When we reach the bottom, he pulls another ceiling cord and a second hanging light above our heads sputters awake. I can just about make out the boundary walls as the light rocks back and forth, our shadows swelling and receding. Dust fills my throat and lungs with each breath. He turns and beckons me to follow, his pale face grey as a corpse.

Fear swells inside me, like a fever. I try to convince myself that it's just the cellar that scares me, silly childhood demons about what lurks down here in the underbelly of our house. But it's my father I'm frightened of, the rage I have seen spill from him, his expert manipulations and the fact that he knows so many things I do not. He has all the answers, but I don't even know the questions to ask. He can tell me who I am, but after what I have learned, I'm no longer sure I want to know.

In a small windowless chamber he crouches down, peels back a grey dust sheet. We cough and wheeze as a cloud of dirt encircles us like smog. Underneath there are four bulging black refuse sacks, each sealed at the top with a cross of brown packaging tape. I watch as he retrieves a Stanley knife from a cupboard and slices through the first cross, splitting it open with one silvery pass of the blade. Men's clothes spill out like autumn leaves from a weathered garden sack.

He stands back, holds out a hand. 'That's what you want, isn't it?'

I drop to my knees in front of the open bag and rifle through, lifting shirts and scarves and old T-shirts. A faint smell of mould drifts into the air, and I notice that some of the clothes have furry patches of green spreading across them. At one point I hear my mother arrive behind me, but my father shoos her away. Then, as I pull an old tartan shirt from the bag, a small white garment falls to the floor, closed at the bottom with three silvery buttons. A babygro. I hold it up to my nose, try to breathe in the scent. I get nothing. No memory comes back to me, no soft aroma of bathtime and cuddles, no tangible trace of an old life still lingering down here in the dark.

I feel my father's hand on my shoulder. With a degree of effort he sits down on the cold, damp floor.

'Leave me alone,' I tell him.

'I can't do that,' he says softly, shuffling closer. He's a different person from moments ago, a complete shift in personality. Where is the anger, the irritation, the certainty that he knows best? He reaches for my hand but I move it away. I don't want his comfort. I'm not even sure I deserve it.

'Why, Dad? Why did you keep their things from me?'

When I look up, he is blinking anxiously. He isn't sure of himself any more, and I realise he is about to cry. It all comes back in that moment. I remember the day I stood in the hallway and told my parents I was pregnant. How my father wept over Joshua's conception, how he saw my life failing before it had even got started. He thought Andrew was a loser, and believed that the little thing growing in my womb, no bigger than my fingernail at the time, was going to tie me to him forever. How wrong he was; how fickle life is, I think as we sit here now, crying over my son's death.

'I'm sorry,' he says finally. He reaches into his pocket and produces my wedding ring. He holds it out for me to take. I turn it over in my fingers, unsure what to do with it. 'I found it under the footstool.' Then he looks at the bags. 'It wasn't like I threw their things away, Chloe. I brought them here to be kept safe.'

But what does it even matter any more? These clothes are just things, belongings. The ring, despite the engraving of our names on the inside surface, is just a ring. There are no memories locked inside. I can never get Joshua back, and it sounds as though what I had with Andrew was ruined before the crash even happened. Regardless, I slip the ring back in place on my left hand.

'I left him, Dad. I left him and took his son. Now Andrew's in rehab, Joshua's dead, and I can never undo what I've done.'

He moves towards me and holds me tight. 'This isn't your fault, Chloe. You could never have known what was going to happen. It was just a terrible accident.'

I draw back. 'That's not what you said in the beginning, though, is it? You told me I was to blame.'

'I was wrong. It was just an—'

'No, you were right. I understand now.' I remember all the times I left Andrew crying; the times I ran away leaving him begging for my forgiveness. I used to scoop Joshua up, take him from the house. In Andrew's darkest moments I took the precious thing we had created away from him. What kind of person must I have been to leave when he needed me most? Even though I had to protect Joshua, how could I have abandoned the man I loved, letting him sink further into the darkness of his addiction? 'You knew I was having an affair, didn't you?' I say. 'You tried to cover it up by not telling me what had happened.'

My father edges away, puts his hands in his pockets and then pulls them out again. It takes him a moment to answer. 'No, Chloe, that can't be true. You loved Andrew. I was wrong to tell you that you didn't.'

'Then why did I leave him?'

'Because of his drinking, of course.' He is using the voice he thinks will make me believe him. The voice that suggests he knows best. 'You would never have done something like that, Chloe. How could you—'

'Yes she would.'

We both look up to see Jess standing at the foot of the stairs.

'She would, Dad, and you know it.'

He takes a step towards her. 'Jessica, get back up those stairs,' he says. There's a hint of familiar anger in his voice, and a slither of fear returns to me. I see Jess gripping the handrail, desperately trying to be strong. 'That's quite enough from you.'

But she's shaking her head. 'No, Dad. She has to know. This isn't working. She has to know the truth.'

'Jessica, I'm warning—'

'Chloe, you *were* having an affair,' she blurts out. She comes forward, moving into the light. She looks older in that moment, as the light shines down on her face, shadows forming beneath her eyes and in the hollows of her cheeks. She has been drained by this too, just like the rest of us. 'You came here two weeks before the accident, told us that you were leaving Andrew. That you'd met somebody else,' she continues. 'But then you talked to Andrew again and he promised you it would be different this time. You told me you weren't sure, that you were having doubts about leaving with this other man. Dad was devastated, thought your second chance was slipping through your fingers.'

I glance over at my father, whose head is hanging in shame. He looks defeated. He knows it's too late now, that there's no turning back from the truth. I look back at Jess, see the tendons in her neck strained and tight.

'On the night of the crash, you announced that you were going back to Andrew. You'd changed your mind, you said. You'd given up your job and the three of you were going to move away. Dad tried to stop you, and you argued. You left angry. Then you had the accident, and when you woke up, you couldn't remember anything about what had happened. Couldn't remember them, or us. But you kept dreaming about that night. About the crash. Dad was only trying to help you, Chloe.'

I look over at him, leaning against the wall by the stairs. 'Trying to help?'

He wipes his eyes on a handkerchief. He looks so small and broken, all his efforts in vain. 'You felt so guilty about the affair, Chloe. Before you left here that night, you told me you were going to tell this other man once and for all that it was over.' He shakes his head, unable to believe where we have found ourselves. 'I didn't agree, wanted you to leave Andrew. But you told me you wished you'd never started the relationship, wished that you could turn back the clock. I knew I could help you do that, if it was what you really wanted. I've been trying to help you forget about the accident because I believed it was the only way you might forget Damien.'

'Damien?'

'Yes, Chloe,' he says, looking away. 'He was the man you were seeing.'

For a moment I remain silent. I try to place a memory of him, a memory of us. But I can't. How is it that I can't remember anything about what must have been such a significant part of my life? 'Are you sure?'

'Ask yourself this: why else would he have been there on that night?'

So there's the truth. Is this why Damien is now trying to convince everyone that he wasn't there at the crash? Is this why he has no verifiable alibi? Does it explain why I thought he seemed familiar? Because we were having an affair and I was going to tell him it was over between us?

I walk towards the stairs, dumbstruck at what my father has told me. Jessica speaks but I don't hear what she says. When my father steps in my path I put up no resistance. I wait for him to relent. He does, let's me pass.

'Chloe?' he asks. I stop, turn to face him. 'What now?' I say nothing and walk away.

I have to find Andrew, face up to what I did. Because

through my actions alone, my decision to have an affair, I am responsible for everything that has happened. I know now that my father was right all along: I am to blame for the death of my son.

I don't know what you thought would happen. What did you expect when we left together that night? It was you who started it, kissing me like that. It was you who led me away from the crowd, told me I had more important things to do. You, Chloe. You wanted me to do you.

Yeah, that's what you told me. That's what you whispered, letting your tongue brush against my ear. You wanted me to do you. To fuck you. Who would have turned that down? For God's sake, just look at you. You are beautiful. So wonderful. Your skin, your eyes, the curve of your lips. Your fingers, and the way I learned they could touch me. You became so much more to me than a one-night stand. I knew from the moment I touched you that that was it for me. No, that's a lie. Nothing but the truth from here on in. I knew from the moment I saw you.

Andrew sounded like a waste of space, somebody who was dragging you down, making your life hell. You deserved so much more. Joshua deserved more. I knew I could give it to you. I tried to play it cool, but it was hard. So hard to smile, to watch you walk away like I didn't care, as if we had all the time in the world to get it right. But which world, Chloe? It was as if we were living in two separate dimensions. You with him, then you with me. Which life did you want? I was sure I knew. I was so damn sure. I still am. I know you still want me.

So just be brave that little bit longer, Chloe. Try to hold it together. I've taken care of it all. I've made it so damn easy for you, just like you made it for me on that first night we were together. Just like I'm going to make the rest of your life. All you have to do is say yes.

34

I let them call me a taxi, and when she offers, I take twenty pounds from my mother to pay for it. They ask me where I'm going, but I won't tell them. I don't want them to know where he is or what I'm doing. I want this for myself, a moment between a husband and a wife. I want to say sorry, to try to put things right, and to get back what I've lost from my memory. The things my father took. I want more than anything to protect Andrew when it seems that recently I might well have been doing anything but.

Light shines from the windows of New Hope rehab centre in the small village of Westmeston. I can smell woodsmoke, and as I step from the car, I see a man walking his dog, his hood pulled low, shoulders hunched against the cold.

'You going to be all right?' the taxi driver asks.

'I'll be fine,' I say as I peer through the window, hand over the money, the soft sounds of the radio jazz barely audible.

The car pulls away and I'm left standing all alone in an unfamiliar village. I told the driver I'd be fine, but I don't know whether that's true. I'm getting ready to face a man I have betrayed, a man I hardly even remember.

I stand there for a while, looking up at the building. New Hope is a sprawling place that looks as if it might once have been a farm. It reminds me of the old mill in that its function is no longer clear to see. To my left there is a new extension, while on the far side of the grounds I spot the ruinous remains of a barn, broken walls and holes in the roof that might on a clear night let moonlight shine through. Old machinery fills the space.

I take a deep breath and walk up the pockmarked driveway edged with overgrown winter roses. There's a scent that takes me back to that night. Roses, I think. something to do with the crash. But the memory leaves as quickly as it came to me, and I push on towards the building. Beyond it I can make out a distant outline of trees, picked out by the weak lunar light sneaking through a momentary break in the clouds. It's just a chink in the armour of a deep night sky, a heavy expanse of black stretching endlessly ahead.

Apart from the presence of a small sign mounted on the external wall, the building resembles a slightly unloved house, a large but tired family home. The paintwork around the door is peeling and the grass is overgrown. There are patches of moss swamping the paving slabs and the lower segments of wall. But from inside I can hear noise and commotion, laughter and cheer. Music playing, an old George Michael song just ending. Another starting up in its place, perhaps the Pogues. Christmas music, I think, relieved to even have such a memory.

I knock on the door and wait. At the last minute I can feel the dressing on my head come loose, flapping about in the breeze. I don't even need it any more, the wound long since healed. Up until now I just couldn't bear to look at it so left it in place. I pull it off, slip it in my pocket, exposing the scar to the elements. After a moment I hear footsteps, soft on the other side, a voice in the tail end of conversation. I take a quick glance at my reflection in the glass and ponder what a mess I look, but it's too late to worry now. It doesn't matter. I hear the door handle, and seconds later heat hits me as a tall woman with long hair and a soft fringe opens the door.

She looks me up and down and I fiddle with my wedding ring, more uncertain of myself than ever before. She pulls the door shut behind her so the wind can't get in. 'Can I help you?'

'My name's Chloe. I was hoping to speak to Andrew. Andrew Jameson. I'm his wife.' I swallow hard, aware of the pale skin and red scar cutting my left temple. It feels so cold and new.

'Chloe,' she says with understanding, her eyes kind. She moves aside, beckons me forward. 'You had better come in.'

She opens the door wide and I step onto the plush red carpet of the hallway. A long table holds books, a floral arrangement, and a selection of mismatched knick-knacks. A large mirror hangs above, and I know if I see myself in this unforgiving light, I will look even worse than usual. I'm not ready to see the scar. The Christmas music continues, voices singing along, laughter in the background. The heat is almost unbearable.

'You'd better sign in first,' she says, pointing to a book on the table. I notice a box alongside it full of Christmas raffle tickets. 'Then have a seat. I'll go and let Andrew know that you're here.'

I pick up the pen, my hand poised above the page. I take a deep breath, press the nib down, and write my name. Chloe Jameson. The peculiarity of something so instinctive surprises me, a signature I haven't tested in weeks. Chloe Jameson: am I still her? My handwriting is neater than a few days ago, forward-sloping and elegant in a modern way. I sit down in a chair and wait.

People pass by, women and men. They seem well put together, nice clothes and kind faces, a few who are wearing tabard uniforms. A stocky cleaner with sweaty hair and a red face wanders through carrying a mop and bucket, followed by a man in a black polo shirt with a foldaway ladder under his arm. They both smile at me, almost as if they have been expecting my arrival.

'Is somebody seeing to you?' the man with the ladder asks, breaking his stride when he gets close. He's old, approaching retirement, his skin weathered and lined. When he smiles, his wrinkles deepen, forming a near-continuous crease across his cheeks, around his eyes and over his brow.

'Yes, thanks,' I say, and he gives me a satisfied nod, heading down a couple of steps where the light seems brighter and kinder. It's as if he doesn't even notice my injuries. I watch as he walks away, his casual and cheerful manner, and feel jealous of his easy life. His arrival in what I assume to be the kitchen is met with the clatter of pots and pans and laugher resonating through the corridor. It brings a smile to my face, reminds me of the cheery woman in Guy's apartment building who was heading out for a run. Will I ever be able to find something simple like this again?

But then I realise that a man is standing in front of me,

sense his presence like a shiver across skin. I look up, see the bright blond hair and familiar grey eyes. Is it really him? For a moment I hesitate, until I hear him say my name.

'Chloe.'

I stand, unable to breathe. Part of me wants to run, and I can't help but look to the door, in instant fear of his judgement. But when I find the courage to look back, it isn't anger I see on his face, but regret. He's almost smiling at me in fact.

'How did you know I was here?'

I take a breath. I glance at his body, slimmer than I remember, his face older. But it's still him, the man I once knew so well. I can feel it, the knowledge that I know him inside and out, even if I can't remember how. 'Janice told me she thought you might be here, and I wanted to see you.' It seems in that moment like such a stupid thing to say. Yet he shrugs his shoulders, holds his palms out wide.

'Well, here I am.'

I nod, but don't know where to look. He takes a step towards me and I can feel my anxiety increasing. The closer he comes, the worse it gets: so many questions to be asked and apologies that need to be offered. So many things I have to say and I wouldn't even know where to begin. My breath becomes laboured and my hands are shaking. The words fight for a place on my lips: *sorry, forgive me, I wish* . . . But as he narrows the distance between us, only one word comes out.

'Joshua . . .' As I say his name, my voice breaks, the tears flowing freely down my cheeks. The only thing that stops me from falling is Andrew. I feel his arms reach for me, hold me close. And standing there in this alien hallway, I feel more at home than I have done in weeks. He holds me as I sob, says nothing, my wet cheek pressed against his shoulder. I know his touch, the way our bodies fit together. He is routine, simple. He is what we crave, and then tire of, and then lament once we lose it. The relief of that realisation is consuming and terrifying all at once.

'Andrew, I'm so sorry,' I tell him. 'I don't know what to say, or where to start.' My words jumble as I reach up to wipe my eyes.

He's shaking his head, still holding me close. 'Let's not do this here.' His voice is cracking too, a tear that could rip apart at any moment. He looks away, up the stairs. 'We're not supposed to have people in our rooms, but we can talk in private up there. I think we need that, don't we?'

He heads towards the narrow staircase. His fingers find mine, guiding me along behind him. He feels like the past. And in that moment I experience that connection for which I've been searching since the moment I woke up: something real, with a history, without lies or untruths. That's what home is, I think, knowing yourself alongside another person, not being able to explain why but being sure that you're supposed to be together. It's knowing there are problems but still being able to see the emptiness of life if that person didn't exist. In that moment it is just Andrew, and me. *It's us, isn't it?* Just like he asked me a thousand times when he was in pain. And it is us, but I wonder now just how much of us is left.

35

He opens the door to his room and we step inside. It's smaller than I anticipated, long and narrow, with a single bed pressed up against the far wall. A hessian runner covers the length of the floor, and a farmhouse wardrobe consumes most of the rest of the space. Pictures hang on the walls: boats, old Brighton, and a large black-and-white photograph of the Undercliff Walk at Saltdean, the name written in neat black lettering underneath. I recognise it as a place we have been together. It conjures an image of hot summer days lounging in the old Lido, the coastal breeze cooling our sunburnt skin. Ice creams in a café overlooking the water as the waves roll into shore and the sun dips below the horizon. Days when we felt the invincibility of youth, when we thought we knew everything and yet knew so little. Did he hang that picture there because it reminds him of us?

He sits down on the edge of the bed and leans his head down into his hands, his elbows propped on his knees. His face is tired in comparison to the pictures I've seen of him at my parents' house, hollow and aged, his features older and less refined. He looks worn out. The same way I feel.

But he has cut his hair since the last time I saw him, the line of it square and neat around his neck. He looks better than I remember or expect. I don't suppose he can say the same about me.

'That looks painful,' he says as he points to the scar on my head. I am standing just inside the room, next to the door, as if I am ready to escape.

I reach up, trace my fingers along the raised red line of scar tissue. 'It's sore, but I'm OK.' I sit down on the edge of the bed, leaving a space between us.

'Your voice sounds funny, too,' he says as he stands up. At first I think perhaps his movement stems from a desire to not be near me. But as I watch he opens a drawer, pulls out a pack of cigarettes. I take in his movements, the way he licks his lips, rubs at his eye, the way he seems more settled once there's something in his hands. A distraction from my presence. When he catches me staring, I look away, only to see that on the bedside table he has placed a framed picture of the three of us, wrapped up together and sitting on Brighton beach. Me, Andrew, and Joshua. It must have been winter, the sky cloudy, my wild hair ravaged by the wind. Looking at it makes my eyes sting, and I have to look away. Still, the very fact that it's there gives me some hope to carry on.

'It's because of the accident. They had to drain a bleed from my brain,' I explain.

He nods, draws on his cigarette long and hard. 'I know, Chloe. I was there at the hospital.'

'You were there?' Can that possibly be true?

'Of course I was. As soon as I heard about the accident,

I rushed to your side. You are my wife.' But as he says the word, his throat catches; either sadness or anger. Anger, I think, which hurts so much. 'Anyway, you're alive, so it means you got off lightly.' He sits down next to me again, closer this time. I can't argue. I suppose I did get off lightly, in comparison.

He holds the packet of cigarettes out, offers me one. I take it, even though I'm not sure if I smoke or not. But I remember that craving I've had a number of times before today, and as I hold the thing between my fingers, the motion feels natural. He snaps his finger over the wheel of a lighter and holds the flame close for me. Smoke floods my lungs as I draw on the cigarette. For a moment we are silent.

'I'm so sorry, Andrew.'

'Sorry for what?'

'Everything.' I wish I could offer him something more than an empty apology. But I have nothing else left. Nothing that matters, anyway.

He presses his fingers deep into his tired, sunken eyes. 'Don't, Chloe. I know you didn't really get off lightly. You nearly died and you lost your son. You could never have known it would end up like this.' He turns to me, and for the first time since I arrived he really looks at me. We're so close I can see the different colours in his eyes, streaks of brown and yellow fanning out like the sun's rays from around the pupil, the dark blue outline of his iris. Beautiful, I think. 'I just never imagined, not even when they told me how serious it was, that when you finally woke up you wouldn't remember me.'

The thought that he was there during those early days

comes as a surprising comfort. 'What I don't understand is why I don't remember you being at the hospital.'

He shakes his head a little. 'Because I wasn't there when you woke up. I'd gone home to get a change of clothes. Your mother told you that I'd be back soon. "Andrew won't be long," she said. But you just stared at her and asked, "Who's Andrew?" You knew nothing, couldn't remember a thing. Your dad thought it would be confusing if I came in when you couldn't remember me. So I stayed away, waiting for them to tell me when it was safe to visit. When it was appropriate.' A moment of anger passes over him, his eyes cold. 'Of course it never was. That was no great surprise. He always wanted you to get rid of me. When you couldn't remember me, I guess he took his chance.'

'But why didn't you come and see me anyway? Why didn't you just ignore him?'

'Because I believed him at first. I thought I was doing the right thing, giving you time.'

'He told me he paid you off. That he gave you a blank cheque to leave me alone.'

He shakes his head. I notice his jaw setting tight. 'The man is just unbelievable. Look, there's no denying that I was a mess, Chloe. We had our problems and you left me. But when I heard about the crash, I was at your side. I sat with you for hours, begging you to wake up, making promises about what I would do if you did. That's why I'm here. I promised you that if you woke up, I'd go into rehab, get my act together. I stayed away like your father asked because I thought it was the best thing for you.' A sad smile passes his lips. 'Sounds a bit stupid now, doesn't it? But he was being so reasonable with me and he kept me up to date with how you were, so I believed him. Plus he helped me a great deal with Joshua's funeral. Most supportive of me he's ever been.' He wipes away a tear. 'It was my idea to scatter the ashes from the pier. I thought you would like that.'

'So you were there.'

'Of course I was there. I'm sorry that we held it without you, but we thought . . .'

'You don't have to say it. I understand.'

'What I can't stop thinking about is that Joshua was alone when he died. How much pain he must have been in. How scared he must have felt.'

And I know in that instant that this is something I can give him. Will the knowledge that I was there, and that our son died in my arms, ease his pain? 'He wasn't alone, Andrew. I was with him.'

He shakes his head, draws smoke into his lungs. Some of the easiness between us is lost. 'No you weren't. You were found in the driver's seat. Joshua was outside the car, on the ground. DS Gray told me what happened.' He closes his eyes. 'He showed me pictures.'

'That's true, but DS Gray told me other details too. Things that don't make sense. I can't remember exactly what happened, or explain how, but I know I was with Joshua when he died.' I stand up. I can't sit next to him as I tell him what I know of that night. I can feel the tension in his limbs, an urge to flee from the details. He doesn't want to hear this any more than I want to say it. But both of us know we have no choice. 'Something else happened that night, Andrew. I've spoken to the police. There are a lot of inconsistencies.'

'Nothing about it makes sense. Where were you going? We were supposed to be meeting by the pier.'

'That's what DS Gray told me.'

He looks confused. 'Don't you remember that either?'

I shake my head, lean against the door. I feel a new fluidity in my movements. It's Andrew that makes the difference. He makes me fit in my skin, helps remind me who I am. 'I have only the vaguest memories of that day. I don't remember why I didn't come.' It's on my lips, the possibility that I went to meet somebody else, but my courage fails me. 'But I remember that at some point that night I was in the woods, running towards Joshua.' When I look up, Andrew is staring at me, hanging on my every word. I take a breath, steel myself. 'He was on the ground, and I knelt at his side and held him. The police found his blood on my dress. I didn't leave him alone. I was with him when he died.'

He brings his knees up to his chest, stares out of the window. Perhaps towards Brighton, the memory of a life we once shared in that little house. A house that is no longer our home. 'So how did you end up back in the car?'

I shake my head, even though he isn't looking at me. I have to carry on. 'I don't know. But the police think there was a second car involved, and that the driver of that car might have put me there.'

'For a while they thought it might be me. Thank Christ I was standing like a mug at the pier waiting for you. They got me on CCTV. And then in a bar after that.' He begins to circle the room, takes one last drag on his cigarette before

271

stubbing it out. He opens the window to let in some fresh air. 'So tell me. Were you with *him*?'

My world bottoms out and my stomach somersaults. I have been dancing around the subject, trying to find the strength to tell him what I must, and all along he has known. 'You knew?'

'I found out on the day of the crash. He called me, told me you were going to be leaving with him. I didn't believe it at first. Only half an hour before that we had spoken on the phone, agreed to meet. You wanted us to go somewhere new, make a fresh start. And then I pick up the phone and this motherfucker tells me that you won't be coming back to me; that instead you are leaving with him. I didn't know what to believe, Chloe. I tried calling you, but all I got was your voicemail. I called your parents. Your dad told me that you had left the house upset and not to call again, as if you being upset was my fault.'

'He didn't want us to get back together because of your drinking,' I say.

'Chloe, I hadn't had a drink in weeks, not since you walked out that night with Joshua.' He nibbles on his lip, rubs at his eyes with his palms. 'I thought we were doing OK, that we were working on things. When you left me, I knew it was my last chance. You said that was it, but I kept telling you I'd change, that we could make it work. Eventually you agreed. Like I said, I thought we were going to meet at the pier, try again somewhere else. I'd booked us a hotel in Eastbourne for a few nights, somewhere to stay until we decided what we were going to do.'

I can feel his gaze upon me but I can't bring myself to

look up. How much we both hurt each other. Hurt Joshua.
All those memories that have been coming back to me of
my loneliness and his drinking; they didn't tell the whole
story. I start to cry.

'Don't blame yourself, Chloe. It was me who ruined us,
not you. I did all I could to push you away.'

I take a tissue from a box on the side, wipe my eyes. My
head is throbbing, my insides churning. 'Was it Damien
Treadstone who called you?'

'You don't remember who he was?' I shake my head. 'I'm
not sure. But when I read the reports about the accident
and that Damien Treadstone's car was found at the scene,
I assumed it was him. The police tried to trace the phone
records, but he called me from a payphone. That's why
nobody can corroborate his alibi, Chloe, because really he
was with you and he doesn't want to admit it. He's married
with a kid. Now that he's lost you he wants to hang on to
his life, whereas ours has gone up in smoke.'

I stub my cigarette out in a small ceramic dish and lean
against the wall. How can he be so kind, excuse me of any
blame? 'It was you in the graveyard, wasn't it? You were
trying to reach me.'

'I just wanted to see you. Your father kept telling me to
wait, but I'd lost everything. Lost you both.' He shakes his
head. 'I was desperate. I had taken the decision to stay away,
to let you get well, but then I started to doubt what your
father was telling me.'

'Why?'

'Because he's a liar, Chloe. He had no intention of ever
telling you about me. I worked that out a while back. But

you seemed so frightened when I tried to approach that I took the decision to finish my programme here first, get the house in some sort of order and then come and find you, tell you the truth. Your parents have got quite a hold on you.'

I'm so angry, with my father and myself. He never had any intention of helping me remember; even today, just an hour or so ago, he was still lying to me about what he was trying to do. Telling me he was helping me forget the man I had an affair with.

Andrew motions for me to sit down next to him, then takes my hands in his. 'Don't blame yourself. You could never have predicted how this would end up. Neither of us could have.'

We sit together for a while, share another cigarette. He tells me some stories about when we were young, about Joshua's birth, and the good holidays we had. He also tells me about the bad times, some of which I remember, many of which I don't. I tell him that I remember taking Joshua down to the beach to get away from him. That I'm sorry I always left when it got hard. But he doesn't agree, his head shaking.

'You used to take him to the beach because it was a place we all loved. You said it made you feel close to me even when I wasn't there.' He reaches across and picks up the family picture. 'See. We were always at the beach. You said the sound of the water reminded you of the river at the bottom of your parents' garden, the mill and the times we used to spend there together.' He reaches up, strokes my face and uses his thumb to wipe under my eyes. 'Maybe it's hard to remember it all, Chloe, but there was a time when you and I had everything. If only we had realised it then, eh?'

I leave not long after that. I sign out and we hug at the doorway. 'So what now?' he asks.

'What do you mean?'

'Where do you go from here? Will you be all right?' I look out into the dark night. The taxi I called is already waiting outside, its engine ticking over. Andrew has given me the money to pay for it.

'All I know is that I have to understand what happened. I have to know what part I played in all of this, and why I took Joshua with me that evening.' He nods along. 'What about you? Will you be OK?'

He leans against the door frame, tucking his hands up into his armpits. 'I need some time, Chloe. After I lost you both, I went off the rails a bit. I need to focus on getting myself right. But it's weeks since I drank. I'm doing OK. After that, who knows? All I know at the moment is that I'm glad you came and found me.'

As I walk to the car, I know what I have to do. I must find Damien Treadstone. Were we having an affair? I'm not sure, but I realise that I have to face up to whatever it is I did. Safety is no longer a person or a place, a makeshift bed in an old mill in the arms of a boy too young to know better. It's not in the arms of a strange lover either. This time I will find safety, or at least some form of it, in the truth.

It didn't have to be like this, Chloe. We could have done this with a smile on our faces, with your hand in mine. We could have made plans, told your parents, watched the joy spread across your father's face when you finally told him you'd left your waste-of-space husband.

Instead, you've made it hard. I didn't want that. I wanted you to be honest. I wanted you to walk away with your head held high. One little act of bravery that would lead to a lifetime together. Why couldn't you do that? Why couldn't you meet me that night and prove to the world how much you wanted me? Why couldn't you prove it to me? Why, why, why, Chloe?

You made me question us. You made me question you, and what kind of commitment you could make. I wasn't just something to use for a while then throw away. Didn't you realise that? I wasn't yours to fuck in the back seat of my car or under the pier when you needed a change and then pretend I didn't exist when it was time to go back to your life. He's got problems, you told me. I can't leave him, you said. Not yet. Not now. Well then, when, Chloe? Because here's the thing. I don't fucking care about him! What I care about is us!

So no, I'm sorry, but I won't let you hurt me like this. You don't get that right. You are the only thing I have ever begged for. Don't you see how special that makes you? But that's not who I am, Chloe. I'm not a beggar.

You have made me pathetic. But there is a difference between us that you don't seem to appreciate: you deserve this. Yeah, that's right. You deserve it. You deserve everything that's gone wrong for you because you are weak. Too weak to claim what you want. What's rightfully yours. So in all this mess that you helped create, I want you to hurt. I want to see your tears. I want you to question everything you think you used to know. And then finally you'll hurt just as much as I do now.

But once everything is done, Chloe, I promise I'll be the one to make it all better again.

36

The taxi drives me away from New Hope rehab centre through narrow thread-like lanes. The animals in the surrounding farms have been shut up for the night. The houses lining the roads are concealed by thick hedges, red berries and ivy tangled up with thickets of holly. The glowing windows look warm and inviting. Protected. Safe.

We pull up at a junction and I see an old-fashioned road sign, black and white with small peeling letters: Ditchling. We are heading onto Ditchling Road, where I crashed. I didn't realise that it is so close to where Andrew is staying. Will I recognise the place? Will being there help me remember the painful memories of that night?

We are going at speed and it's difficult to see, only freckles of light sneaking through the trees. My eyes trawl the hedgerows for signs of damage. The winding road is slick with rain, glimmering and shiny in the glare of the headlights. We continue on, revving and slowing as the twists and turns close in. Then we slow almost to a stop as the road curves into a sharp one-eighty-degree chicane. I see the land fall away from the kerb as we approach, and there, flickering in the wind, is what remains of a white-and-blue police ticker tape.

Beyond it the trees are broken, snapped both left and right. I turn back, stare from the rear window as we pass, the area behind me bathed in a light as red as blood. I know without doubt that this is the place where I crashed.

'You heard about it too, then?' the taxi driver asks. 'Terrible shame, wasn't it?'

'You mean the crash that happened here?' I ask as I pull the seat belt tight across me.

'Yeah, it's been all over the news, that poor little boy losing his life. People are demanding crash barriers, but you know what the council's like.' He touches his thumb to his fingers and makes the sign for money. 'Not enough of this, is there?'

When we pull up in Brighton, I get out of the car and hand over the notes that Andrew has given me. Ahead of me, underneath the two triangular peaked roofs of the ornate Victorian shelter, is the train station.

If I had enough money, I would purchase a ticket to Maidstone to go looking for Damien Treadstone. But I don't, so instead I plan to bring him to me. I see a phone box and start to cross the road towards it, jumping back in shock when I hear a horn blaring, a car skidding past only inches away. And as the wheels race by, forcing me out of the road, I think of the night of the accident. Memories seem to slot into place. I see myself in a park, sitting on a bench. Then running, almost getting hit by a car. Where was I? What was I doing there? Was I meeting Damien Treadstone? I check both ways for traffic, take a breath, run towards the station. I reach the phone box, pull the door open and step inside.

A putrid smell rises from the sticky floor underfoot. I pick up the handset, hold it to my ear, listening for the sound of the dialling tone. I punch in the number for the operator and wait.

I give the woman Damien's details, as much as I know at least, hoping that there aren't any other Damien Treadstones in the directory. Will she be able to find him with just a name and town? I don't have any money left, so I tell her I want to reverse the charges. I wait on the line, wondering whether he will accept the call. A moment later it sounds as if the line cuts out, but then I hear a click, followed by a voice.

'Chloe?' he asks. It's a shock as he speaks, the soft tone gentle in pitch. 'Chloe Daniels?'

'Yes,' I say, my fingers fiddling with the flex of the handset. Is this the voice of the man who killed my son? Who ran me off the road? The man with whom I was having an affair? What should I ask him first? There is so much I can't put into words. 'You're Damien Treadstone, right?'

'Yes.' His voice is shaky. 'You shouldn't have called.'

'I need to talk about that night. About what happened.'

'We shouldn't. They said not to contact you.' His breathing is deep. 'What we are doing now could destroy my case. But when the operator said it was you, I had to. I just had to.' And then, after a moment of silence, he says, 'Chloe, would you agree to meet me? You're right that we have to talk about what happened that night. And if there's any part of you that cares about what happens to me, before you take me to court, there is something you have to know.'

37

He won't talk any more on the phone, but even though it's late, he agrees to meet me tonight. In fact, it sounds as if he is desperate to see me, which stirs a degree of fear. I tell him I'm at Brighton train station, and suggest we meet there. But he refuses, saying that it's too busy, too visible: he can't be seen talking to me, or captured on CCTV. As we make the arrangements, I realise that part of his desperation is a lack of trust. He doesn't want to meet me, but feels he must. He doesn't trust me, just as I don't trust him. No matter what has happened between us before, the last few weeks have changed everything. So he suggests somewhere outdoors, somewhere that benefits from the cover of darkness.

'I'll meet you in Preston Park, Chloe. I know you know where that is.'

As soon as he says the name of that park, I realise it is the place I know from my dreams. My memory of meeting somebody now suddenly enriched by so many other details. I see myself with Joshua, there to ride his bike and visit the playground. Stopping at the café, the small building that resembles a Tudor boathouse, for ice cream with flakes and chocolate sauce. I see myself alone, sitting on a bench, waiting for a man. Time after time, waiting for a man.

It takes me just over fifteen minutes to get to the entrance of Preston Park. A gentle mist clings to the ground. My feet are freezing, my toes numb. Still I walk on, determined. I see the rotunda café ahead, flanked by the skeletons of two trees stripped bare by the winter. The entrance to the rose garden opens up before me. I walk the paths, through the fragrant winter blooms, past a pond brimming from the recent rains. I have been here before. The smell of the roses. The smell of freshly cut grass. And I know now that it's the same place I went that night, the place I went when I should have been meeting Andrew.

As I reach the other end of the garden, the park opens out before me. An expanse of dark green lawn stretches ahead, but I know that in the summer the wild-flower meadow will once again bloom full and fragrant. I know that kids will fill the nearby playground, and the sound of tennis balls being knocked back and forth will ring out all week long. Laughter and fun will fill this place.

I see a path to the left and another to the right. I take the right-hand fork, following Damien's instructions, walking until I see a bench partially shaded by evergreen bushes. A leafless sycamore tree stands tall beside it, and I think of Joshua, how we used to come here, collect the little seed pods and spin them through the air. *Look, a helicopter, Mummy.* Kicking leaves in autumn, making swords of broken branches in winter. I hear my mother's voice: *You'll have someone's eye out with that*, advice we hear as children, and then pass on as adults. I have sat on this bench many times before. I was sitting here that night, not long before the crash that took Joshua from me.

The wooden slats of the bench are rotten in places, scratched with obscenities. I notice the glow of a cigarette in a nearby copse of trees. A man dressed in a long trench coat lingers on the other side of the park, near the road I know is called The Ride. Is one of them Damien, hanging back, observing me? I realise how isolated and vulnerable I am, here in the dark, waiting for a man I might or might not know.

Moments later, I hear footsteps behind me. I turn, watch a shadowy figure as it approaches. I sit still, frozen, unable to move, breathe or run. Because as the gap between us narrows, I realise that the face I see before me is a face I recognise. It's Damien Treadstone. Right there, only a short distance away. And I know that he was here in this park on the night of the crash.

38

His pace slows as he steps under the semi-shelter of the naked tree. He peels back his hood. 'I wasn't sure you'd be here,' he says 'To be honest, I wasn't even sure if it was really you on the phone.' He's shaking his head. 'This totally breaches my conditions of bail.'

I take a few shallow breaths. 'I had to talk to you. I need you to tell me what happened that night, and why you were chasing me in your car.'

He nibbles on his lip. I can see his fists twisting and turning in his pockets, his anger like a bolt of lightning in search of ground. He pushes his hands deeper, takes a step closer. 'I can't believe you're still accusing me. I thought that if you wanted to talk, maybe you had finally come to your senses.'

His words give me the strength to push on. How can he still deny it? I remember him being here. I remember seeing him that night. I stand up, close the gap between us. 'It doesn't matter what you say. I know you were there.' I feel myself getting angry, my voice becoming tight and shrill. I look over to the distant trees. No light from a cigarette shines now, no man on the other side of the park. We're alone. How easy it would be for him to hit me, kill me, do anything to me in the dark silence of the park. Nobody would know. Nobody would hear me. 'You ran me off the road.'

'I didn't run anybody off the road.'

'But your car was there. You don't have an alibi.' I try to imagine that I know him, to recall a time we might have been here together. Did we share a kiss behind one of these trees, or make love in a car in the nearby woods? I stop for a second: is that a memory? Making love in a car, pushed up against the glass with the door handle pressing in my back? I know it is. But when I look up at Damien's face, though it seems familiar, I don't know how it *feels*. Not his touch. Surely there would be something about him that made sense to me if we had been together like that?

'Damien, I need to ask you something.' I try to swallow, find my throat dry, no moisture on my lips. 'Are you lying to me because we were having an affair?'

'What?' He steps past me, sits down on the bench. I realise there is a look of utter bewilderment on his face. He rests his head in his palms. At last he turns, his eyes meeting mine. 'How many more things are you going to accuse me of?'

'But we must have been,' I persist, despite my reservations. 'Why else would I have been meeting you here?'

'For a start, Chloe, you weren't meeting me here. And I can assure you we most certainly were *not* having an affair.' He regards me with disgust, as if the very idea of it makes him sick. 'I had no idea who you were until my lawyer got hold of some photos of the crash and the victims. You didn't even get your picture in the paper thanks to victim confidentiality. Not like me.' I see his fists clenching before he stretches his fingers out, straight as knives. 'Everybody knows who I am now, thinks they know what I've done. Do you know how people look at me? Like I'm a killer.'

His anger stirs something inside me. How dare he worry what people think of him when the death of my son should be on his conscience? 'They look at you like that because you killed my son,' I spit.

'No I didn't. Aren't you listening to me, Chloe? I wasn't there at the time of the accident.'

'But your car was there with the keys in it. You had mud on your trousers. Paint from your car was found on mine. You *had* to have been there.' The taste of sick swells and recedes. 'If I'm so wrong, tell me what you think happened.'

'I can't. I can't tell you because I don't know. I wish I did, but I have absolutely no idea what happened to you or your child.'

Although he is full of rage, I don't fear him in that moment. And I think it's because he seems so genuinely bewildered. If he was lying to me, surely he'd offer me another version of events. Surely he would have a story prepared. His uncertainty makes me want to hear him out. I realise that he seems more desperate than anything else, hopeful that I might believe him. In that instant, I think that just maybe I do.

'I don't understand, Damien.'

He wipes his eyes, sits back on the bench. 'Neither do I, but I promise you, Chloe, I have no idea what happened that night. That's why I called you as a witness. I hoped that when you saw me in court you would realise that it wasn't me driving the other car. I assumed you wouldn't want to see an innocent man go to prison for such a horrible crime.' He pulls a tissue from his pocket, blows his nose. 'I have a son too. Jonathon. I would do anything for him. But now I realise you don't have a clue what happened either, so I'm fucked.'

He breaks down, hangs his head in his hands. I see a couple on the other side of the park, their eyes on us. My sympathy for him suddenly outweighs my anger. He is as broken as I am. I reach out, rest my hand on his shoulder. After a moment he straightens up, composes himself.

'Why would you think we were having an affair, Chloe? We don't even know each other.'

I feel so ashamed to tell him, but I have no other choice. I can feel myself getting hot, flushed, guilt oozing out of me. But if I can admit it to Andrew, I can admit it to this man. 'I was having an affair with somebody. I came here to this park to meet him, I think. When you suggested meeting here, I assumed it was connected. When you gave an alibi that nobody could corroborate, I thought you were trying to protect yourself.'

'I gave the only alibi that I could, Chloe. You're right about me wanting to protect myself, even right that I'm guilty, but not in the way you think. We were both in this park on the night of the accident but we weren't together. My car was stolen.' He points across to the road. 'I was parked just over there, on The Ride. I shouldn't have been here, but I'd been working in Brighton that day.' He takes a deep breath, stands up. For a second I think he's about to leave. 'Ah, fuck it. I might as well tell you. Being honest is my only hope now. I was here to meet somebody. A man.'

'What man?'

'I don't know, Chloe. Anybody. Casual sex. People come to this park for that. I couldn't tell the truth about being here because I'm married with a kid and I was out here looking for sex.' He wipes his eyes on his sleeve. 'After my car was taken I wasn't thinking straight and ended up going for a drink in town with the man I met here. When they arrested me a few hours later I was drunk and I panicked, so I lied about where I'd been.'

'Why didn't you call the police when you realised your car was gone?'

'A mistake,' he says, hanging his head. 'If I had I wouldn't be in this mess. But I called you as a witness in the hope that your inability to confirm my presence that night might be enough to get me off. My lawyer is pushing me to tell the truth, but I'm trying to protect my wife and son. If she finds out she'll take my son away from me. So when you called me tonight I suggested we meet here thinking that maybe it would jog your memory as to what you were really doing here. That you would remember who was really in the second car and make things easier for me. I was walking away along The Ride, towards those bushes.' He points across the grass. 'Somebody called out to me but I didn't want to be seen here, so I started to run. The person who called out was you.'

'Me?'

'Yes. I must've dropped my car keys. I heard you shouting, saw you waving at me. I thought you were somebody I knew and I didn't want to be seen, so I hurried away, headed into the bushes. About five minutes later, I heard a woman screaming. I came out to see if somebody needed help, and I saw a car racing away up The Ride. It was a black sedan. A Volkswagen.'

'That's my car.'

'I looked down the road and the lights of my car were on. I reached into my pocket for my keys, only to find they weren't there. Then my car came screeching past, chasing after the Volkswagen.'

'Well who was driving it? If you saw who was driving it, then we can go to the police together, explain things.'

'You've literally got no idea, have you?' I shake my head. He seems to feel sorry for me. 'It was you, Chloe. You were driving my car.'

39

I walk away from Damien Treadstone, my head down, my hair swept left and right as the wind picks it up like flames. I find it hard to comprehend everything he has told me, to understand how his truth fits with mine. What we both think we know are two separate pieces of a puzzle. The edges don't align; it is an abstract painting that makes no sense. Part of me wants to think he is lying, that this is nothing more than a ruse to exploit my amnesia. But I don't believe that. He never tried to contact me between that night and now. He was relying on me going to court, relying on my inability to identify him. He trusts his account of that night. Because he is telling the truth.

I wander without purpose, confused, until I arrive at the seafront. I sit in one of the Victorian shelters with the glow of an ornate street lamp above me and gaze out to the ocean, the vast blackness of it. The lights of the Palace Pier shine through the mist, the dome lit up. The waves charge towards the shore like a squadron of cavalry, crash-landing across the shingle beach. I can feel the spray of the water on my face, a fine mist. I see the ghost of the West Pier and, as I turn, the Brighton Metropole behind me. I've been here before, I know it. Seen this same view. Further up the road a couple laugh as they share a bag of fish and chips.

I wrap my arms around my body and consider what Damien Treadstone told me. I believe his version of events. He is adamant that he wasn't involved in the accident. It makes more sense than anything else I've heard. At least now I know why I can remember running through the trees to reach the clearing where Joshua died. It makes sense why I was found with cuts all over my face, and why my injuries seemed inconsistent with the findings from the crash site: I wasn't driving my car. But why would somebody else be driving it with Joshua in it? And how did I end up in it before I was found by the police? Although I can't explain everything, I now know I was in Preston Park prior to the crash. I need to talk to the police.

I find my way to my house, my old home, and with a rock from the beach I break a pane of glass in the door to let myself in. It is dark, cold without the electricity or heating, filled with that scent of a house left empty. The vulnerability of being alone smothers me. I move into the kitchen, stand there for a moment just looking. Trying to make sense of the things I have remembered. But I can't. Instead I look through the drawers. Although most of them are empty, in one drawer I find an old kitchen knife. I take it out, run my finger along the edge of the blade. I take it with me, sit down on the couch and pull the phone towards me. I find DS Gray's number in my pocket and punch it into the handset.

When he picks up, I tell him what I know: that I was in Preston Park on the night of the crash; that I believe I stole

Damien Treadstone's car because somebody else had stolen mine with my son inside. For a moment there's silence, and I wonder whether he is going to believe me. But then, just as I am about to prompt him, he speaks.

'I'll struggle to get any CCTV from that area overnight, but I'll do my best. If you remember anything else, be sure to let me know. And Chloe, there's something else I should tell you before you go.' He pauses. 'Andrew's alibi checks out.'

Of course it does.

I hang up the phone. In some ways I'm relieved to know I wasn't driving the car that crashed with Joshua in it, but at the same time I can remember DS Gray telling me there was paint transfer between the vehicles, indicating that the two cars touched. I might still be responsible for causing the crash, which in some way is even worse. I look down at the knife, wonder how well it might cut.

I take off the coat which belongs to my mother, the one she forced across my shoulders before I left my parents' house. I curl up on the sofa, hugging my legs in close with a dusty throw from the settee pulled over me to get warm. I think of Andrew alone in that tiny room, trying to fix himself even though he has lost the people most precious to him in the world. I am comforted by the idea that we were going to try again, by the thought that even now he is prepared to forgive me, that he understands we both messed up. Somehow it makes my mistakes easier to bear.

What I also know is that going to Preston Park has triggered certain memories, helped push my story further on. I knew as soon as I walked through the rose garden that

I had been there that night. Now I know I must visit the scene of the crash, understand that night once and for all. I pick up the phone and dial Guy's number.

'Hello?'

'Hi, Guy, it's Chloe.'

'Hey, it's good to hear from you. I've missed you.'

He sounds coy, adolescent. We haven't spoken since he dropped me at my parents' house earlier, but surely that's not enough time to miss me? The night we shared hangs over us, but he doesn't seem bothered by it like I am. Should I be ashamed that we had sex? That's certainly how I feel. But he is the only person who can help me now.

I explain what happened: the meeting with Damien, the certainty that somebody else was at the scene of the crash. I even admit that I think I was having an affair, because it now seems pointless not to. Andrew knows, and he has, in some small way, forgiven me. He doesn't blame me like I blame myself. That somehow makes it easier.

'Will you take me to the crash site?' I ask. 'I think you were right about facing up to things. Going there might help me remember the final pieces of the puzzle.'

'Are you sure you're ready?'

'I don't have a choice. I have to try to remember, and you're the only person who can help me with this.'

'OK. Let's say nine in the morning. Do you want me to pick you up from your parents' house?'

'No. I want to go now.'

'Isn't it a bit late to go today? It's nearly nine p.m.'

'I have to do this now. I've already told the police about what I've remembered. I can't wait.'

The flippancy leaves his voice. 'The police? What did you call them for?'

'Because I'm convinced that Damien Treadstone is telling the truth, Guy. Somebody else took my car with Joshua in it. The police are already looking for CCTV from Preston Park now that Damien has admitted where he really was, and if they find what they're looking for, we'll know who took my car, killed my son and left me for dead. But what if they can't find anything? I have to go there, Guy, and maybe then I'll remember who it was.'

I listen as he takes a breath. For a moment I worry that he is going to say no. 'OK, Chloe. When you put it like that . . . I'm on my way.'

I hang up the phone, pull the small throw from the back of the sofa and position it over my legs. It's freezing cold in this house, the life gone. I dial one more number and hope my sister will answer. She does.

'Chloe?'

'Yes, it's me.'

She lets out a long breath. 'Chloe, where are you? You've been gone for hours.' I can hear her footsteps pacing back and forth in the hallway, my mother in the background trying to take the phone from her. My father? Where is he now? 'Just tell us where you are so that we can come and get you. It's not safe for you to be alone for too long.' It's sometimes easy to forget that I'm only a few weeks past brain surgery, despite the reminder every time I look in the mirror.

'It's not necessary, Jess. I'm with Guy.' What is one more little lie? 'I've already spoken to the police. I know now where I was that night. I have to go and see the scene of the crash for myself.'

'Chloe, why don't you just wait for the police to do their job?'

'I can't do that. I'll call you later, Jess, OK?'

And with that I hang up the phone. When it begins to ring, I pull the cable from the wall and the house goes silent. Guy will be here soon and then I can try to put this right. I close my eyes, let my head rest back, awash in the knowledge of everything I've remembered. It's only minutes before sleep takes me.

40

My breathing was fast as I set down the phone, my hands shaking. I could see my father in the rear-view mirror, waving at me to come back. I could still hear his words ringing in my head: *Don't go back to him, Chloe. Don't leave like this.* I looked to the passenger seat and Joshua glanced up at me. 'Are we still going to meet Daddy?'

I flashed him a warm smile, nodded my head. 'Of course we are.' We were on the cusp of a new start, one last chance to get things right. Andrew had agreed to leave tonight, to leave everything behind. But now it was all under threat. 'It's just that Mummy forgot she has to do something first. Before we meet Daddy we have to go somewhere. But it's a surprise, OK, so I need you to keep it a secret. Can you do that?' His smile widened, worry disappearing from his face. The guilt of the lie cut through me.

He gave his seat belt a tug, checked it was tight like he always did, and set himself facing front. I couldn't have felt worse, having to take him along with me, but I had to do this now. I had to end it before it went any further. Before he told Andrew like he had threatened to. It was so hot I felt sick, sweat in my armpits damp and sticky. Beads of it forming on my face.

'Who was that on the phone?' Joshua asked.

'Nobody, Josh. It was nothing.'

'But Mummy,' he said, his voice quiet and soft, 'you look upset.'

'That's just because I had a silly argument with Grandpa. It's nothing, Josh, I promise.'

I drove for twenty minutes, through the countryside, heading towards Brighton. I opened the window, but the air was so heavy I found no relief. I pulled up at the entrance to Preston Park, manoeuvred the car into the usual spot on The Ride, concealed from the road. I turned off the engine, listened as it settled to silence. Took a deep breath.

I saw another car parking behind me. Was it him? But seconds later a man I didn't recognise got out. He slammed the door, pulled up his collar and walked away from the car, looking over his shoulder, paying no attention to me.

Was I really doing this with Joshua here alongside me? Leaving him in the car while I went to talk to *him*? To demand he stop threatening to tell Andrew about our affair?

'Mummy, are you OK?'

I tried to smile, reached over and kissed him on the cheek. 'Of course. I'm fine. Just excited about seeing Daddy soon, that's all.' The smile that spread across Joshua's face was huge, the gap between his teeth where one had fallen out gaping and wide. And the saddest thing was that it was the truth: I *was* excited. How had I fucked this up so much? How was it that I was here in Preston Park demanding an end to the affair that threatened our future? How had he got Andrew's telephone number? 'I really need you to behave, OK, Joshua? I need you to stay here and look after the car.'

His smile disappeared. 'On my own? Can't I come with you?' He clicked his belt open, edged forward. 'I could help with the surprise.'

I shook my head. I could drive away now. I didn't have to do this, did I? I could end things tomorrow once I was far away from here, or the next day, or not at all. I could just disappear. He wouldn't go through with the threat and tell Andrew, would he? What would be the point if he did? It would ruin everything. But what if he was past that? What if all he wanted was revenge? No, I had to tell him now that it was over. If I did it face to face, I felt sure I could make him understand.

'I'm afraid not, Josh. You need to stay here. But I'm going to lock you in, OK? Don't open the door to anybody.'

I stepped from the car, clicked the button, and flashed Joshua a wink. My face felt flushed and damp. Heat and nerves. Josh was already settling in with *Harry Potter and the Chamber of Secrets*, his new obsession, magic and wizards. He wanted to be a wizard when he grew up, said he wanted to be able to change the world to make it anything he wanted it to be. I loved the idea that he hadn't lost faith in life being good, but hated the fact that he thought only magic would achieve it. I checked the locks, and then headed up the road.

The scent from the rose garden was heady, with waves of heat rising from the ground. Just up ahead, the man who had parked behind me was striding along, arms swinging.

I watched as he cut through to the left, next to the café. He was heading in the same direction I was.

I stepped up my pace, wanting to get it over and done with. I hadn't seen him in days. I'd been ignoring his text messages so I knew he was going to be angry. I had tried to end it once before, but he had worn me down with his promises of a better future. Together, he always told me, we could be a family, easy and simple, without any of the problems that had driven me to him in the first place. I would always fall for that, the idea of something better, something stable for Joshua. Something normal. But now Andrew was offering the same thing. He had promised to go to rehab once we settled into a new life, told me he would do anything to make things work. This time there was something different in his voice that made me believe he might just do it. Not just for me, but for all of us, so we didn't lose what we had. Our family. I had to try one last time, for Joshua's sake.

I suddenly noticed a set of keys on the path in front of me. I bent down, picked them up: a silver key chain in the shape of a D. Did they belong to the man walking ahead of me?

'Hey!' I called. I saw him glance over his shoulder. I waved the keys back and forth, hoped he could see what I was holding. 'Wait up!'

But instead of stopping, he began to hurry on even faster. It was strange, because he looked like he had heard me. As I picked up the pace in an effort to reach him, he sped up again. Seconds later, he disappeared into the bushes.

'You dropped your keys!' I shouted, but it was futile. I

decided I would leave them on his car, by the wipers, hoping that he found them before anybody else did.

I looked back to my own car, saw Joshua's blond head just visible through the side window. I could smell roses, freshly cut grass, hear the distant chugging from the engine of a ride-on lawn mower. Soon enough the seasons would change, things would be different. It was time for change. That was what we needed. At least that was what I hoped.

I shoved the keys into the pocket of my dress along with my own as I passed the café and took the right-hand fork, heading towards the bench, the place we had met so many times before over the course of the last three months.

He was late. It must have been ten minutes before I saw him walking towards me. He was obscured by shrubbery but it was unmistakably him. I noticed his car parked just out of view of the road like it always was, away from mine, safe from suspicion. He smiled as he approached, his large frame casting a shadow as he narrowed the distance. Still I felt a weakness for his touch, a need for his body to be close to mine, even now when I was determined to tell him it was over.

I took a breath.

I had to do this.

I had to do it now.

I had no other choice.

41

I wake with a start to the sound of a fist drumming against the door. When I pull it open, Guy is standing there. He steps forwards, stops abruptly.

'Oh Christ,' he says. 'What are you doing with that?' He reaches down, takes the knife from my hand, sets it down on the side.

'I was here alone,' I say.

He stares at the blade for a moment, then takes me into his arms. His grip is strong and powerful, his stubble rough against my cheek. 'I'm here now. I got stuck behind an accident and tried calling, but the line was dead.' He looks down at the phone, notices the cable unplugged from the wall. 'I thought something had happened to you.'

'I fell asleep. I pulled it out so my parents couldn't call me back. I knew they wouldn't leave me alone to do this.'

'Well, grab your coat. It's cold out tonight and it's started raining again.' He looks down at my trainers. 'You could do with a pair of wellies where we're going.'

'Should we wait a while, do you think?' I peer out of the window. The rain is battering the glass, streams of it rushing down in abstract waves. The street lights blink behind it.

'No,' he says. 'You were right in the first place. We need to do this now.' He reaches past me, grabs the coat from the sofa. 'But wear this, otherwise you'll freeze.'

We run to the car pressed up against each other as he tries to use his coat to shelter us both from the rain. I get into the passenger seat, and he rushes around the front to the driver's door. He struggles out of his wet coat, then starts the engine and pulls out into the road.

'I can't believe the weather,' he says as we drive through the city. But I can. I am thankful for it. It's just like that night.

'At least it will help me remember, don't you think?'

He smiles, running a hand through his wet hair. 'Well if this doesn't, nothing will.'

We speed through Brighton, past the gothic steeples of St Peter's church and onto Ditchling Road, the Victorian villas decreasing in numbers until the green plains of a golf course come into view on our right. Little white flags hang limp and drenched. The tail end of the city dwindles until eventually we leave it behind. And as the rain strikes the windows, the wipers swinging back and forth, I'm able to picture myself in Damien Treadstone's car. On this road. I was speeding, frantic, doing well above the speed limit. I know that I was alone in that car, closely following a set of red lights ahead, tears streaming down my face. It was my car in front, stolen with Joshua inside. I look across at Guy, reach to place my hand onto the steering wheel.

'Chloe, what is it? Are you OK?' he asks. He touches my knee. A shiver rises up my back, my mouth suddenly dry.

'Yeah,' I tell him, but I know that I sound less than sure. I feel less than sure as well.

'Did you remember something?' I nod as we slow for a corner, the wind buffeting the car. The force is so strong that Guy has to hold the wheel with both hands. He takes my hand, peels it away. 'Don't be scared. You're safe now. Everything is going to be OK.'

'No it's not. Damien Treadstone was telling the truth, Guy. Being here, I'm starting to remember more about what happened.'

'Well that's good.' He is gripping the wheel tighter, his knuckles white. 'Then tonight will tell us everything we need to know.'

'I hope so,' I say, staring out of the window.

He presses his foot to the accelerator. The land rises and falls, opens out wide to softly undulating countryside. Soon we are above the houses, the road long and curvy as we descend another hill. It seems to go on forever. After a while it begins to narrow, the trees rising higher as the road becomes curved and dangerous. A risk, an accident waiting to happen. I see the spot ahead where the tape flickers in the breeze.

'Just over there.' Guy pulls up on the verge, following my instruction. Seconds later he cuts the engine.

I step from the car. I see faint skid marks on the tarmac. The scar on my head throbs, the pain of that night suddenly as fresh as if it has just happened. Guy rests his hand on my shoulder and I take a deep breath. I am about to revisit the site where my son lost his life. I have no idea how to face that. I close my eyes, see my dreams before me: the damage to a tree just at the edge of the road. I open them again and spot an area of flattened undergrowth. The more I look, the more certain I become.

'That's where I pulled up,' I tell him, pointing. 'I skidded, crashed Damien Treadstone's car into it. But I was fine. I got out and ran down that way.' The realisation gives me strength, the knowledge that the truth is close.

I push my way past brambles and bare branches, slipping on the same slimy ground as I remember from that night, only just managing to hang on and stop myself from sliding down the perilous slope. Guy follows behind me, calling out instructions to be careful. Up ahead I see the tree with the missing bark, a strong old oak against which my car came to a halt. I see the clearing where Joshua lay, the place where I fell to my knees and cradled him in my arms as he died.

'What can you remember?' Guy asks at my side.

I point to the tree. 'My car was crashed there.' I move towards the clearing, my breath catching as my throat tightens. It feels in that second as if every moment I ever lived with Joshua passes before my eyes: his birth, his first day of school. Our afternoons together on the beach. Night-time snuggles and bad dreams. First steps, first words. Last words. 'This is where I found him,' I whisper.

I sink to my knees, the ground so soft it almost swallows me up. It is as if I am back there on that terrible night, rain pummelling me, the wet earth soaking into my trousers. I see Joshua's body lying there before me. I remember how he spoke, just one last word before his life slipped away.

Mummy.

'He was here,' I say as I press my hands to the soft wet leaves. 'This is where I found him. This is where he died, Guy.' I remember the sound of my engine ticking over, the steam rising from the crushed bonnet. I remember the feeling of his warm body as I pulled him close, limp and weak as I hugged him against me. I whispered to him, promised him that everything would be all right, pledges I couldn't keep. I told him that Mummy and Daddy loved him so much. I knew he was going to die.

'Do you remember yet?' I hear Guy ask.

I feel one of his hands rest against my shoulder and I bring my left hand up to his. His fingertips brush across mine, heavy and comforting and protective. But then he stops, his touch moving across to my wedding ring. He holds it, his grip firm.

'You weren't wearing this before.'

I twist my body to look up at him. I stare at his face, into his eyes, the rain blurring my vision. His fingers are still touching the ring, his jaw set tight, teeth showing. The pressure on my hand begins to hurt.

Then before I can move, he brings his right hand up in the air, drives it towards my head. I try to duck away as I see the sharp-edged rock coming towards me, but he makes contact, strikes me hard. I fall face down on the spot where Joshua died. I feel hands grip my body, haul me across the ground, dragging me through the wet leaves, catching on rocks and twigs and tree roots. I grapple for something to hold, find nothing. It's only seconds before my sight begins to dim.

'I remember, Guy,' I manage to say. I try to stay awake and fight. The pain in my head intensifies. And then my eyes glaze over, flicker closed, and I am gone.

As I stepped out from behind the cover of the trees and began to walk down the path, you stood up, your face a mixture of anger and relief. I expected you'd be angry with me. But I was angry at you too, Chloe. I could feel it in the way my fingers clenched and stretched, that urgency I had to make you pay for just how far you'd taken this. Just how close to the line. But I shoved my hands in my pockets, tried to push the feelings down. I didn't want you to see that ugly side of me. Not yet.

It was only when I threatened you that you gave in, wasn't it? Is that what your daddy taught you? But still, you were so pleased to see me that night. I could see it on your face, the relief of my presence; feel it in the way you were slipping back inside me, swelling against my skin. That's what it's supposed to be like, Chloe. Nothing like drowning. It's supposed to feel like that when you're in love. If it doesn't consume you, it's not worth the effort.

And then after all the waiting to get you back, you were there, only an arm's length between us. I could barely believe you came. You opened your mouth to speak, but I knew I had to get in first. Because before you said anything,

I wanted you to know that it's always been you. I never cared that you were married. I didn't care that you were supposed to be his. I needed you to know that you were mine and always would be, just like I was yours. Am yours, Chloe. It's only you I want. Just you and me, for ever and ever, until death do us part.

42

Friday 1 September 2017, 7.45 p.m.

'So you came. I wasn't sure you would.'

He looked tense, his shoulders tight, hands in his pockets. There was a part of me that felt for him. I understood his anger, pitied his desperation. But I had to end this now if I was to save my marriage. This lust, this craving had to end. He had given me a way out, offered me an escape. I had to sacrifice this part of me in order to save something that meant so much more.

'Of course I came. You told me you were going to tell Andrew about us. I can't let you do that.'

He laughed, but it sounded bitter and twisted. My fear began to grow. I looked back towards the car. I could still make out Joshua's blond hair, his feet up on the dashboard, his head buried in his book.

'Somewhere you'd rather be?' Guy asked as he moved towards me. He gripped my arm and I felt his fingers needle into my skin. 'You think you can just tell me it's over and that's it?' He made a metallic clicking noise with his tongue against the roof of his mouth. He began to pull me, forcing me to start walking. 'Let's go. We have a lot to talk about.'

He marched me forward, my footsteps barely able to keep up. I could hear his breathing, his urgency. He was as desperate as I was scared. We stopped at a small clearing, almost surrounded by trees. I could no longer see the car. He shoved me up against one of them, the bark scratching my left shoulder. I felt the fresh rush of stinging blood. He circled the ground ahead of me, his hands on his hips.

'That hurt,' I said, touching my fingertips to my wounded shoulder. 'I came here to talk to you, not get pushed around.'

But he wasn't listening. 'Three days, Chloe. Do you remember what a phone is? When you get messages, you are supposed to reply.'

'What is wrong with you, Guy? I told you already, it's over. You expect me to answer you when you keep demanding to meet? When you tell me you're going to come to my parents' house, or Joshua's school? I've told you already, I can't see you any more.' I stepped forward, stopped when he moved into my path. 'Get out of my way. I only came here to tell you to stop calling me. We are finished. You have to understand that.'

He took three fast paces towards me and I felt his hands make contact with my arms. The motor of the lawnmower was getting closer. If I shouted, would somebody hear me?

'You don't get to play with my feelings, Chloe. I can't switch off how I feel. Just because you say it's over doesn't mean I can move on, forget you exist. I love you.'

I shook my head. I didn't want to hear it. 'You can't love me,' I said. 'I'm not yours to love.'

His grip intensified and he pushed me back against the same tree, then pressed himself up against me. He tried to kiss me, but I turned away from his lips. He moved down, found my neck, held me tight. I couldn't breathe as his hands roamed across my body, hitched up my dress. I remembered what it felt like to want him, the wave of desire and lust from that very first night when we should have been watching my father's presentation at the Roberta awards. Instead we went to the beach, where we fucked underneath the pier as we listened to footsteps treading the boards above. It was dangerous, exciting. It was an escape, and in that brief, intoxicating moment I became somebody else. In that moment I wasn't the wife of an alcoholic. I wasn't a mother scared for her son. And now here he was, up against me, his hands moving, wanting to get inside my body. But this time it felt so different.

'I don't want this, Guy. I don't want you.' I pushed him away, watched as he staggered back, surprised by my strength. I began to run. I had to get away. I heard his footsteps on the ground behind me as I felt the first drops of a summer downpour, my silk dress blushing black as it became wet. He reached out, made contact with my hand. Despite the slippery grip, he managed to pull me backwards. I turned to him, brought my free hand up, slapped him hard across the face.

'Stop it, Chloe,' he said, shaking me. He tried to pull me back towards the clearing. 'I love you. Doesn't that mean anything to you any more? You used to tell me you loved me too. Where have those feelings gone?' I had said it, yes, but had I really meant it? I wasn't sure. Was it love or just infatuation? The idea of a new life? 'Please, Chloe,' he said as he began to cry. 'I need you.'

I had lain in his bed with his skin against mine, the soft touch of his hand running along the length of my body, and shivered when he whispered those words. I had needed him then too. I had fallen for him in those private moments, his touch, his presence, his stability. He was prepared to give me everything I wanted. Wasn't that what I desired from a man? Wasn't that the woman I wanted to be?

'I can't do it, Guy. I can't leave him. I can't do it to Joshua.'

'You deserve something better than *him*. So does Joshua. I have begged you for a chance to be his father. Why don't you understand how good it could be? I can be there for you both. I can be what you need. I promise I will love your son like I love—'

'Don't say it.' I couldn't listen. I couldn't let him break me. 'I can't do it to Andrew.'

I watched his face contort. 'Don't you say his name. Not to me.'

'But he's my husband, Guy.'

'I don't care. *I'm* the man you love.'

He inched towards me. I felt him close, pressed up against me. But then I felt his grip tighten and it began to hurt. He couldn't let me go. Not now, not then. Not ever.

'It doesn't matter how we feel, Guy. Andrew can never find out about us. It would destroy him.'

For a second we were both still as he gripped my face, stared right into my eyes. And then he spoke. 'But he already knows. I told him half an hour ago.'

I pulled back and he let me go. I reached down into my pocket, found my mobile. It was on silent because of Guy's constant messaging. I had seven missed calls, all in the last thirty minutes. All from Andrew.

'He's been calling you, right? You see, you might as well come with me.' I saw his desperation, saw him drowning. He was praying I might offer him a future together. 'I did it so we never have to be apart. So we can be free.'

I knew then that I had nothing left for him. I shouldn't have come here. I would get in the car, go to meet Andrew, and we would leave together. That was what I had to do. I could explain this. I couldn't let my mistake be the thing that destroyed him, pushed him back to the drink. Everything about Guy was a mistake. For me and Andrew. For me and Joshua. I could still put this right. That was what I wanted, wasn't it?

I turned and ran towards the café, nearing the rose garden. I could see my car just up ahead. I slid my hand into my pocket in search of my keys, but the set I pulled out was unfamiliar. I looked down, realised they were the keys I had picked up from the path. I dropped them and reached back into my pocket, but as I pulled out my own set, I felt Guy's weight against me, tackling me to the ground. I glanced up and saw Joshua at the car window, staring as I struggled to get away. And then for a second he stopped, saw Joshua too, his little hands pressed up against the glass. I felt Guy's hand grappling against mine, reaching for my keys.

'No!' I shouted, but he slapped me hard across my cheek and tore the keys from my grasp, and then he was on his feet, running towards the car. Towards my son. 'Don't you take him!' I screamed. I waved frantically. 'Josh! Get out of the car.' I saw his door begin to open, felt a wave of relief. But then Guy pulled him back inside, slamming the door shut, and before I could reach them, he had started the engine, was pulling out.

The wipers were flipping back and forth as he tore up the road towards me. Gravel and wet earth spewed from beneath the wheels. I could see Joshua's face pressed up against the window. I couldn't hear him, but I knew that he was screaming. His mouth was open wide, his eyes narrow and tight. Tears were streaming down his face. He had never met Guy. He had no idea who was taking him.

I stood defiantly in the path of the car, sure that Guy would stop. But as he got closer and closer, I realised he had no intention of avoiding me. I fell back, the wing of the car just clipping my leg as he flew past, then scrambled to my knees and watched helplessly as he sped away, the back wheels swinging left and right.

For a second I didn't know what to do. I stood there looking for help, some way to undo what I had done. And then I remembered the other keys, the bunch I had thrown to the ground. I snatched them up, ran to the car that had parked behind mine. As I pulled away, I saw a man rushing towards me, his hands flailing in the air. He was shouting, screaming at me to stop, to get out of his car. I would have hit him as I accelerated, but he jumped out of the way just in time.

I raced up the road as fast as the car would go. I saw my car turning right out of the park gates. I didn't stop as I reached the junction; only just missed a pedestrian on the

313

crossing. All I could see before me was the red rear lights of my car, a blur in the distance. The wipers batted back and forth. All I could imagine was Joshua screaming my name. *Mummy. Mummy. Mummy.*

The car turned onto Ditchling Road, and I followed. I could see it slipping all over the place. At one point I got too close and felt a collision. And then as the rain intensified and the road became narrower, I saw it skid, crash through the undergrowth and disappear down the embankment. I slammed on the brakes, sliding to a halt against a tree. I forced the door open and ran as fast as I could.

'Joshua!' I shouted. But all I could hear was the rain drumming against the canopy of trees.

I scrambled down the embankment, falling in the under-growth, cutting my leg open on a branch. I yelped in pain as I pulled myself on, grappling to get to my feet. And then I saw it. My car. Wrecked. My child. Lying on the ground. I ran forward, sank to my knees, pulled him close.

'Joshua, it's OK. Mummy's here now.'

'Mummy,' he said. I panicked, unsure what to do. I scooped him up, scared to touch him but knowing it was the only thing I had left. I held him close to my chest and watched as his breathing grew faster, then slower. I stroked the rain away from his eyes, tried to shelter him so that he didn't get wet. 'Mummy,' he said again. Seconds later, he took his last breath. And I felt my world crumble. Every dream I'd ever had shattered. I held his floppy body close, screamed into the wild night air. I could feel him leaving me, a physical pain. How could it be that I would never see him again, hear his sweet voice, kiss his warm skin?

Everything I cared about was gone, fallen apart. I had led us here, to this moment when all time stopped. There was nothing left for me after this.

I laid him gently down on the ground, positioned his arms carefully at his sides. Then I reached for the nearest fallen tree branch, something large, something heavy, something with which I could protect myself. Something that could hurt Guy. I wanted to tear him apart, feel the rip of his skin, the breaking of his bones.

I heard shuffling in the undergrowth, footsteps staggering through wet leaves. I turned, and there he was, edging towards me, barely a scratch on him. I charged forward, ready to strike. But he blocked me with his left arm and struck me with his right, and I fell to the ground, out cold.

When I lost my son, I lost my past and my future too. Guy might have given me back myself when I couldn't remember who I was, but he had also taken everything I held dear.

43

I can hear his footsteps as he paces the ground, feel the rain as it falls, heavy and cold. My head is in agony, a lump already forming when I reach up to touch it. How long have I been out? My sight is blurred, but I can see Guy up ahead, hear him talking, mumbling to himself. I attempt to sit up, push myself to safety, but my arms are weak. I hear footsteps. It's him, striding towards me.

'No, Chloe, be careful. Don't move.'

I try to edge away from him, but he scoops me up in his arms, holds me close.

'Get away from me,' I tell him, my words slurred and incoherent. I have no energy to fight.

'I can't understand you.' He lies me down, tucks his body close. He kisses me, his lips cold and wet against mine. 'I never could understand you, Chloe. All I wanted was for you to be with me, for us to be a family. You should have stayed with me. I never wanted to hurt you. Not then. Not now.' He squeezes me tight.

I don't know how long we stay there, lying in a nest of wet leaves, his arms wrapped around me. I can feel his weight, his breath, the warmth of his touch. I drift for a while, in and out like I did in the hospital, uncertain whether I am awake or asleep. Am I bleeding again? Is my brain swelling? I try to wriggle out of his grasp, but as soon as I move, he reaches for me again.

'Get away from me,' I say, pushing at him with limp arms.

'We can forget all this, Chloe. Put it behind us. We have both made mistakes, right?'

'You killed my son,' I shout, edging away from him. 'You took him from me.'

'You think I killed him?' He looks as if he might cry, one hand on his chest, his palm flat against his heart. 'How could you say that after I told you what happened with my brother? It was an accident. You hit the car, forced me off the road.'

I shake my head. Pain tears through me, throbbing hot and cold all at once. 'You took him. It's your fault he's dead.'

'You wouldn't listen, Chloe. You forgot how perfect we could be.' He gets to his feet and looks down at me huddled in the dirt. 'I think even now you can't remember how good we were together. How many times will it take for you to fall for me before you understand what we have? Your father keeps telling me to be patient, to give him time, but how long am I supposed to wait?'

'My father?'

'He's helping you, Chloe. He's helping *us*. Soon you'll have forgotten your old life, and we can build a new one together. It'll be so good, I promise. Only yesterday you woke in my arms in my flat. How many nights did we dream of that? Don't tell me it didn't feel good. I know it did.

That's why I can't understand why you're wearing that.' He snatches at my hand, pulls at my finger in a desperate attempt to remove my wedding ring.

I struggle against him, try to fight. Thoughts of my father's lies overwhelm me. 'Whatever we have between us now is not real, Guy. I didn't know what you'd done.'

He stands like a jack-in-the-box, dropping my hand. 'I didn't do anything,' he shouts. He begins pacing back and forth, his feet heavy in the wet ground. Talking to himself. 'It wasn't my fault. You hit the car. You ran me off the road.'

'You kidnapped my son.' I haul myself backwards, desperate to get away. The effort feels monumental. I listen out for the sound of a car on the road above, but I hear nothing. Nobody will find me here. I feel around on the ground, searching for something to arm myself with. A rock, a branch. Anything.

'It's not too late. You can still tell the police that Damien Treadstone ran you off the road. That would be it, over. Finished. Your father told me that's what you would do, and I don't understand what's changed.' I shake my head. He takes two quick steps, one foot either side of my body. 'But if you're not going to do that, you leave me with little choice.'

I see him raise his fist, bring it down towards me. In a desperate burst of energy I kick up with my legs, one foot striking him in the groin. He buckles and I use the chance to crawl away, hauling myself across the ground. I can feel his hands grappling for my foot and I urge myself forward, my fingertips struggling to find a grip. I scream as he drags me back, pulls himself on top of me. It's hard to breathe as he grips my throat.

'Stop shouting, Chloe,' he says. 'Nobody can hear you.'

My hearing begins to fuzz over, his lips moving soundlessly. And in that moment, as my vision fades, I know that this is the place where I will die. I try to focus on his face, my eyes full of rain.

'When will you understand that I won't let you go?' he says. 'I can't, Chloe. I love you so much.' The pressure of his grip grows, his fingers locked around my neck. I try to breathe. I can't. I can't see. This is it. He's going to kill me.

'I'm sorry,' I say, as loudly as I can, though it comes out as little more than a whisper. But my apology isn't for him. It is for Joshua, for the fact that he was lost because of my mistake. It is for Andrew because I ruined our last chance to make things work. It is also for me, to beg for absolution in my last moments.

'I'm sorry too, Chloe,' he says.

At that moment I see blurred movement behind him, and the pressure of his touch eases as he senses something coming towards us. I watch as his eyes widen, as his body collapses away from mine. A deck of cards, down. And in his place I see Andrew standing there, a huge tree branch gripped in one hand. With the other, he reaches down and scoops me up, and I cling to him as we make for the embankment. We reach out for anything we can find to hold onto, hauling ourselves forward up the uncertain slope. But before we reach the road, we hear movement behind us, and I turn to see Guy back up on his feet.

'Andrew, faster,' I shout, but it is Guy who picks up his

pace. He lunges forwards, grabs hold of my leg. Despite Andrew's efforts to hold me tight, I slip back down the embankment. Guy grapples for my arms, but this time his movements are slower, less precise. I manage to slip from his grasp and pull myself forward on the strong root of a sturdy tree. I cling on tight with one hand, search for a weapon with the other. Still Guy's hands grip my leg. And then finally my fingers brush against the sharp surface of a rock, and my hand slips around it. As Guy pulls me back towards him, I let go of the tree root.

I don't give him a chance to take hold of me. I channel all my strength into the rock, striking him again and again, the spray of blood warm against my cheeks. He slips to the ground, lifeless, just as Andrew reaches my side.

He helps me up and we stand there for a moment, staring at Guy's body, prone, face down. 'I think I killed him,' I say, dazed. Andrew doesn't react; instead, he picks me up and carries me up the embankment, not stopping until we reach the edge of the road.

There he sets me down and cradles me close. His fingers move to check my head, oozing blood. I can barely see the trees on the other side of the road, but I can hear them, disturbed by rain and strong wind. I hear the wail of a police siren approaching. I keep my eyes on the embankment, waiting for movement through the leaves, waiting for Guy to appear. What will we do if he does? Andrew holds me tight as we both gasp for breath.

'Are you OK?' he asks.

'I don't know,' I reply. I look at my husband, here, now, saving me. 'How did you know I'd be here?'

'The police got the CCTV footage, found evidence of Guy taking your car on the night of the crash. They went to his house to look for him, but he'd already left. They called your parents and Jess told them you were with him, and where you were going. She called me because she knew I was closer than the police. She found the New Hope flyer in your coat pocket.'

Thank God he came. I gaze down the dark road towards the sound of the sirens getting closer. 'They'll be here soon.' I look back to Andrew. 'What if I've killed him?' I ask, certain after that many strikes he must be dead.

He shakes his head. 'Then it's over,' he says.

The first police car pulls up along the side of the road. I see DS Gray heading towards us. DC Barclay runs just behind. She pulls a torch from her belt and flicks it on, veers off towards the trees.

'Is he down there?' DS Gray asks, and I nod in reply. He calls to DC Barclay. 'Cath, be careful.'

I watch the torch beam as it bleeds into the thickness of the woods, disappearing as DC Barclay descends the slope, and I think about everything I've lost. Precious things that can never be replaced. But that is also how I know that Andrew is still mine.

Because after everything that's happened, he is still here, still holding on. Despite all those years, all those times I thought he was lost, I realise, as he holds me in his arms, that he must have been here all along.

44

My mother knocks on the door a little after eight, sets a
steaming cup of tea on my bedside table alongside the picture
of me with Andrew and Joshua.

'We should be looking to leave at about nine,' she says.
I sit up, push the sheets away from me. The air is cool but
comfortable. 'Anything you want for breakfast?'

'Just some toast,' I say as I reach for my tea.

I tie my hair into a pigtail and slip on a pair of jeans,
pulling a light cardigan over the top. I stare in the mirror
at the scar across my head. All that's visible is an inch-long
discolouration that extends from underneath my hairline.
The rest of it is covered by new growth, and can only be
seen if you part my hair in the right place.

After breakfast, we climb into the car. I sit in the front
seat next to my mother. In the boot is one small suitcase,
the last of my possessions to be taken from my old room
here. I look up at the house, almost unable to believe that
I won't be coming back.

'It'll be strange once you've gone,' I hear my mother say,
her voice quiet, apologetic.

'I know,' I say as I reach over and touch her hand. 'But you'll get used to it.'

She laughs a little, but there's no humour in it. 'I'm not so sure about that. It's a big house to be in on your own.' She sighs heavily. 'Maybe I should sell it.'

'Where would you go?'

'Oh, I don't know. Maybe Brighton,' she says, a small smile hovering on her lips. 'A nice little house near the sea.' I can appreciate that kind of dream. 'I could move closer to you.'

I smile. 'I would like that.'

I chose to come back here after that night in the woods. The doctors wouldn't let me return to my house alone. Andrew wasn't anywhere near ready to leave rehab or be responsible for me, and I had nowhere else. But I refused to return to the place where my father was living. So my mother told him to leave.

'Are we all set?' she asks as she starts the engine. 'Ready to go?'

I look back at the house one last time, the winter sun bright in the windows. There is a light, almost transparent mist floating above the lawn. 'Ready if you are,' I say.

I still struggle to believe that my father was helping Guy resurrect the brief relationship we'd shared, that he lied about my husband and the death of my child. He's been back to the house just once since I returned here, in order to collect some things. He lingered in his study until he caught me briefly in the hall. He wanted to apologise, he said, for everything he'd done. He told me he couldn't bring himself to verbalise the lies one by one. But I think even now he is most upset by the fact that he got it wrong, that he trusted Guy when he told him he had nothing to do with the accident. That he believed Guy loved me and wanted us to create a life together.

My father had known about the two of us for weeks before the accident; he admitted that he had seen us together. He thought Guy was my second chance. I suppose we both got it wrong, misjudged the person Guy really was. Still, my father's meaningless apology and feigned remorse failed to move me. He still calls the house sometimes, talks to my mother on the phone. But we are finished. I want nothing more to do with him, and I think my mother feels the same. I've heard her late at night talking on the phone with Peter. Once I even heard her laughing. I tell myself to keep believing that she too can move forward after this.

At the hospital, Dr Gleeson asks me a whole list of questions before he tells me I am doing just fine. After that, we drive along the coast road, the same journey we took on the day I was first discharged. But that is where the similarity with that journey ends. Now I see everything through different eyes. Back then I thought there was no hope of remembering who I was. Who I am. But now I know that hope resides in the darkest of places. You just have to be prepared to search in the shadows, because alongside them you will always find the light.

My mother stops the car in the lay-by outside the entrance to the Palace Pier, just as we agreed. The lights are bright and glaring, the hum of the music audible over the song of the rolling waves. She pulls on the handbrake, turns to face me.

'Don't forget this,' she says, handing me a rolled-up towel. The gulls call out overhead, circling in excitement in the weak sunlight. I listen to the distant sounds coming from the amusement arcade halfway along the pier. 'I'll take your bag and drop it off like you asked me to. I'll put the key back through the letter box.'

'No,' I say as I step from the car to the sound of breaking waves, the push of the wind strong against my skin. 'Hang onto it. You never know when I might need a spare.'

For a moment she looks as if she might cry, that briefest moment of trust stirring something unexpected in her. 'Chloe, please tell him again how sorry I am. For everything I was a part of.' And then she drives away, and I wonder when I'm going to see her again.

Sunshine comes and goes as fluffy grey clouds pass above me. I follow the steps down until I reach the beach, where I see Andrew waiting next to the kiosk selling fish and chips in cones. He is exactly where he said he would be. I look at my watch. I am early.

For a moment I just stand there, staring. His cheeks are pink from the wind, his lips chapped from the cold. It's Andrew who speaks first. 'Are you sure you want to do this today?'

'Dr Gleeson gave me the all-clear.' I look around the beach. There are only a few people here, braving the elements, sipping on drinks in the nearby café. It's a beautiful day, though, the sky bright. Eight weeks have passed since that night when I learned the truth, and since then, I have grown stronger. I need this moment for myself. 'And he did say that I am supposed to get back to normal life.'

We walk together in silence towards the water, the pebbles shifting and crunching under our feet. Today we have the whole stretch to ourselves. I hand Andrew the towel and pull my jumper over my head, exposing the plain black swimsuit underneath. I slip my feet from my trainers and step out of my trousers. I shiver as my bare feet touch the soft curves of the pebbles underfoot.

'Joshua would have loved this,' I tell him, and Andrew simply nods his head. This is our place, I think, the place we came to as a family. I reach down, arrange some of the stones into a little pile. 'So I know where to swim back to.' Then I notice a small dead flower that has been washed up on the beach. I pick it up and place it by the rock pile. It feels like he's here with me. Will it ever hurt less than this?

Andrew steps forwards, kisses me on the cheek. 'I'll be waiting for you when you get back.'

I walk down to the water's edge, let the cold bite my ankles. Once I'm out of sight, I look down at the tiny swelling of my stomach, not yet large enough to be noticeable to others. As I gaze out to sea, I smooth my hand over the growing bump. I don't know what Andrew will say when I tell him about this baby. About Guy's baby. I know he wants us to try again, but perhaps this is too much for us to get through. Either way, I know I have been blessed. Guy may have taken my child from me, but he has given me another. I will love this one no less than I loved Joshua.

I take a step forward and the water swirls up around my knees. A few steps more and it's up to my thighs. I stop, turn back. Andrew is still there, sitting on the beach, his cold hands tucked inside his armpits. He motions for me to get going. I turn, look out to sea. Whatever happens between us, I know things will be all right. I will make sure of that now.

Because I knew what had happened on the night of the accident even before Guy attacked me in the clearing where Joshua died. It came back to me while I was sitting in the bus shelter, looking out to sea after leaving the meeting with Damien Treadstone. It was the sight of the hotel behind me that did it, the place where the Roberta awards were held. The couple walking arm in arm. I suddenly remembered leading Guy away, luring him under the pier. What a thrill he was that night. And it all flooded back then: the park, the abduction, the accident. The affair. The fact that he had killed my son. And in that moment I wanted to hurt him so much, make him pay for what he had done. What he was doing.

When I picked up that knife in the kitchen, I wanted to kill him. But just the sight of him and I lost my nerve. Those few moments made me realise I couldn't use a weapon anyway, otherwise his death wouldn't look like self-defence. But I felt sure that if I could get him to the site of the accident, I could find a way to hurt him. I considered trying to crash the car as we drove through the city, even taking hold of the wheel. But I wasn't prepared to die for him. It was a risk that nearly backfired when he got the upper hand, overpowered me. But I got there in the end, drove that rock straight at him. He got what he deserved.

The police completed their investigation, but nobody questioned our version of events. He fell in the fight, banged his head when I pushed him away. I might have hit him once, but it was all just a blur. *I'm sorry, I can't remember.* But they didn't question it when I told them how Guy forced me into the car, threatened to kill me, especially once they saw the bruises he left on my skin in the struggle. They assumed he had decided to hurt me because I'd told him the police were involved and that we knew where the second car had been stolen from. They figured he was trying to cover up his mistakes, which I suppose wasn't all that far from the truth anyway.

Even though he's dead, there are still times I think I see him, following me, watching me. Just like he used to do while we were together, spying on me while I was down at the beach with Joshua. What a dangerous game I played. Even now, as I look up to the pier, the water chilling against my waist, I think for a second that I can see him there, hanging over the rails, watching me as I wade further and further from shore. But then I blink and he is gone. Will the memory of him trail me like a shadow for the rest of my life? Will this child inside me remind me of what I did? Remind me of how much I used to want him? Need him? Hate him? Maybe. I just don't know.

I look back once more at Andrew. I picture Joshua at his side, imagine him sitting on the beach alongside his father. If only I could go back, undo the things I've done. But I can't. The past is lost. You can never get it back. Now it's about the future, finding a new life. A new me, a mother again. I turn, look towards the horizon. And as I close my eyes and take a deep breath, I let myself slip silently beneath the waves.

Acknowledgements

Book two was always going to be tough, writing under contract for the first time in my life. It proved to be tougher than I anticipated, and a vast number of people are responsible for helping me over the finish line. In no particular order, these are my most sincere thanks.

To all those at Headline, both past and present. Emily Griffin, Kate Stephenson, and Toby Jones, three wonderful editors who all played their part. Sara Adams, thank you for the consistency and support, including your input when it came to the title, and the reminder that my acknowledgements were due prior to printing. Thank you also to Millie Seaward, Jo Liddiard, and the rest of the team who have helped make this book the very best it can be.

To everybody at the Madeleine Milburn Literary, TV, and Film Agency for your constant belief and editorial support. I am so lucky to have so many great minds and such expertise in my corner.

To my family, as always, those near and far, thank you for the constant encouragement and photographs of supermarket bookshelves. I am indebted and incredibly lucky. To Theo and Themis, you are growing into such wonderful people, and I'm thankful to have you in my life. You make me so proud to be a small part of it. Stasinos, my best friend, my lover, my husband, and now my child's father. You mean more to me today than you ever have before. Tap tap, more than yesterday, less than tomorrow.

And to Lelia. You were nothing more than a dream when I began writing this book, and by the time my edits came back my constant companion nestled into my chest, sleeping across one arm. You were the thing I dared to dream of and yet never truly believed would happen. This book, and everything since the day you came into my life, is for you.